Colton's SALVATION

A DEMENTED SONS MC NOVEL

To Debbie
Great meeting you at Sweet
Corn Days! Happy Reading! "

Kristine Allen

KRISTINE ALLEN

Warning: This book contains offensive language, violence and sexual situations. Mature audiences only, 18+ years of age.

Dedication

To my mom, who gave me my voracious appetite for books and
to my dad who always has unfailing belief in me
(but I still don't want you to read this)…

Chapter ONE

Stephanie

April 2013

I WAS SO CLOSE. NEARLY FOUR YEARS OF LATE NIGHTS, NO SLEEP, AND running myself into the ground trying to keep up my scholarship and working a side job so I would be able to eat. I'm told that is a little important—eating. Who knew? Even though there were times I wasn't sure I even ate. I was trying to study, but my roommate and best friend through all four years of hell, Becca, would not leave me alone about this year-end party. What was it about "I have finals coming up" that she could not seem to comprehend? I was stressed, I looked like total crap on a stick, I knew I had so much to study over the next few weeks that my head might actually explode, and yet she kept yapping on and on about this stupid party that I just didn't have time for.

"Come on! I don't think you have done a single thing for yourself in the last four years, Steph. When was the last time you let go and just had fun?" she pestered. "This is the biggest get-together of the year. We're almost graduates! It's Friday night, and you have tomorrow and Sunday to study. Please? Please just go with me. I heard Brent might be there, and I need you to be my wingman. You know I can barely say three coherent words around him—I need you for support."

Guilt.

Of course, she would lay on guilt.

And when had I *ever* been a good wingman for her? Although, she was correct in saying I hadn't done anything fun in forever. I could count on one hand the number of times we had gone out since we became roommates during our freshman year. I honestly didn't know why she was still friends with me. We were nearly polar opposites. She was the bubbly, cheerful, passionate one; I was the studious, quiet, focused one. The only thing I had been passionate about was my cooking.

Quite the ironic state of affairs, if you thought about it.

I was a soon-to-be chef and restaurant owner—God willing—who had survived through college on mac and cheese, cheerios, and ham sandwiches. It was disgusting, really. I absolutely loved to cook, which was why I was at Iowa State pursuing my degree in Culinary Science. I was sure that I would be the next Emeril or Bobby Flay... maybe Rachel Ray. Lordy, maybe I watched too much Food Network in High School. Why couldn't I have gone for teaching, accounting, or something "normal" as many of my friends did? But of course not. I had sworn to my grandmother, years ago, I would go to school to do something I enjoyed. With my minor in business management, I had dreams of owning my own restaurant someday—a restaurant where I was a world-renowned chef, of course. People would come from all over the world to sample my culinary masterpieces… Hey, if you're going to dream, it should be big, right?

"Are you even listening to me?" Becca whined.

Um, no.

Typical of me to get lost in my own little "food world." Sighing, I pulled the end of my pen from between my teeth where I had been nervously holding it as I *tried* to study.

"Becca, I can't. I just can't. I have to get a nearly perfect score on this Professional Communications test and the final if I want to maintain my GPA. You know Professor Higgins hates me because I was late to her class the first day. She has made my life miserable all semester because of that!"

She looked at me with a deadpan expression. "Seriously, Steph? You have gotten a solid A in every class since freshman year. I think you will be fine if you don't finish this class with perfect grades. Besides, after we graduate, it will probably be forever before I see you!" Then she pouted.

Yeah, that did it.

I knew she was right.

She was heading back home to Council Bluffs, and I was headed to the "Big City" somewhere to follow my dreams. I blew a clump of my long bangs out of my eyes and buried my face in my hands with my elbows resting on the table.

"Okay. Fine," I said, "but I'm not staying all night and I'm *not* drinking!"

Oh, the best laid plans…

Chapter TWO

Colton

WHY THE HELL HAD I AGREED TO GO TO A STUPID COLLEGE party?

I would have rather headed to a small bar to have a few beers and just chill.

Shit. Mason may be my battle buddy, but he sure knew how to fuck up my plans.

I figured heading home with him while on block leave would be a good distraction from our pending deployment, but I did *not* plan on hanging with a bunch of college pukes. Over eight years and five deployments in the Army as a Ranger Sniper, and I was on a totally different level than these kids. Making it through Airborne training then Ranger training, and Sniper School was hellacious training in itself, and I'd probably seen more shit in six months of a single deployment than they would see their entire lives.

Shit they couldn't imagine seeing.

I leaned back against the old barn, slowly drinking my beer, and watched Mason as he attempted to put the moves on a cute blonde over by the bonfire. She was a hot little thing and seemed to be falling hook, line, and sinker for his smile and flirting. Typical.

Looked like someone was getting lucky tonight, and it sure as hell wasn't me.

If you asked me, he put too much effort in that shit. Either the bitch wanted to get laid, or not. I preferred chicks who knew what the score was and didn't need sweet words and roses. Truthfully, tonight I just wanted to enjoy a cold beer and relax, which was exactly why I wanted to hit a small bar, not some crappy college frat party at a farm in the middle of Nowheresville, Iowa.

Fuck me.

As I tipped up my beer, I enjoyed the cold, slightly bitter, brew as it washed across my tongue and down my throat. Sitting in the cool grass, with the old wood of the barn pressed to my back, I continued to quietly scan the area as I rested my arms on my knees, the bottle dangling loosely from my hand.

Some habits die hard.

I took a deep breath, letting it out slow, trying to maintain my cool with the crowd milling around and the loud music and laughter coming from the barn. The early April night air was cool on my skin. I could feel the bass resonating through the wood of the barn to my spine, causing my heart to beat in tempo with the music. Everything felt a little too loud, a little too hectic.

Yeah, definitely not my scene.

Looking around the crowd once again and scanning over the people dancing on the makeshift dance floor under the trees strung with those Christmas-y looking white lights, I noticed a fiery redhead dancing with her arms in the air as a blonde football-star type held her waist from the back and ground against her ass. Fireball, as I dubbed her, seemed to be eating it up as she threw a coy, seductive smile over her shoulder to him. She was hot as hell, and I was surprised Mason hadn't gone for her since he loved redheads so much. When she danced to the side a little, I noticed her friend. She was dancing with another blonde dipshit football-star type behind her.

What? Did they mass produce these guys here, or what? Jesus.

Her friend was smiling and laughing until jock-face got touchy-feely and let his fingers do the walking up her waist to her tits. They were nice ones, but fuck if it wasn't almost obscene the way the sequins sparkled between his fingers as he cupped his hands with splayed fingers over them.

Damn asshole.

She obviously wasn't cool with that, because she grabbed his wrists, trying to bring his hands back down. That's when I saw him scowl and jerk her close as he said something in her ear. She didn't seem to like what he had to say because her smile completely vanished and she looked troubled as he began to back them slowly away from her friend. He grabbed her arm, dragging her over to a picnic table away from the rest of the party.

Of course, that happened to bring them within my earshot, but the darkness along the side of the barn concealed me from view so they didn't seem to notice me sitting there in the obscure shadows. I could hear him telling her she shouldn't be such a tease as he pushed her to sit on the end of the table. When he forced his body between her legs and ran his hand up her thigh, I felt my heart race and started to get a little pissed.

No, highly pissed and I didn't know why.

Hell, I didn't even know this chick, and I was sure she was entirely too young for the likes of me, but my momma raised me to be a gentleman as best she could before she died. I tried my best to remember that. When I heard her tell him to stop and plead with him to go back to the dance floor to join their friends, fire built inside me. When he tried to lean into her, forcing her to lie back toward the top of the table, she started to struggle. I found myself slowly rising to my feet and gripping my beer bottle by the neck to make a better weapon.

What the fuck?

Motherfucker didn't know what "no" meant, obviously. I knew I was making a big mistake getting involved, but something in her body language and the tone of her voice begged me to be the fucking hero. I knew better than this shit. I wasn't a hothead. In my line of work, that didn't fly and would end your career, and possibly even your life, quickly. As I walked the short distance toward them I thought to myself "Fucking John Wayne to the fuckin' rescue."

Shit.

Chapter THREE

Stephanie

DAMMIT, I KNEW I SHOULD HAVE STAYED HOME. I HAD BROKEN every damn rule I set for the night. Frickin' drinking every shot Becca handed me and dancing with Brent's asshole friend just so she could dance with Brent. At first I was having fun and it felt good to let loose for once and enjoy the attention of one of the gorgeous guys who always seemed to flock around Becca with her gorgeous auburn curls and beautiful model-like body. Let's face it, I usually didn't take the time to dress up and guys rarely looked twice when I was in my usual attire of T-shirts, hoodies, and sweats, topped with a messy bun.

Yep, that was my signature look. Vagrant extraordinaire.

Tonight I had let Becca pick out one of her cute little outfits with a flared, short skirt that felt waaaaay too short, and a tight, black, low-cut tee with "Harley" spelled out in sequins and cut-outs on the sides. I swore the girls were gonna pop out of Becca's loaned push-up bra if I breathed too deep. I was no member of the itty bitty titty committee to begin with. Not to mention, every little breeze made it feel like I wasn't wearing anything. A couple times I had to check to be sure my ass wasn't flashing everyone.

When Rick got a little too comfortable and his hands started roaming, the night went downhill fast. I knew I was beyond tipsy and my coordination was off, or I would have never let him drag my butt out in the dark.

Damn, damn, damn.... I tried to convince him to go back over by Becca and everyone else without causing a scene, but perhaps he was too drunk to register that I wasn't as into him as he was wanting to be "in" to me. He was starting to scare me, and I struggled to get away from him before the panic that was clawing up my throat took over.

Crap.

That's when I saw a hand land on Rick's shoulder as he was jerked around to face the guy behind him. I nervously brushed my skirt back down and slid off the table to stand up and sneak away while Rick was distracted.

"I think the young lady was pretty clear when she said stop." The voice seemed to be deceptively calm. As I sidled away and around Rick, my vision zeroed in on what had to have been the most stunning man I had ever laid my eyes on. He looked to be at least 6'3" with short-cropped, jet-black hair and what, even in the dark shadows of the barn, were the most vivid blue eyes in existence. Thick lashes framed those gorgeous baby blues, which upon closer inspection were flecked with darker blue, and one of his dark eyebrows raised in question. I felt frozen in place as my eyes swept down his body... and what a body it was.

Oh. My. Gawd...!

I saw firmly sculpted muscles outlined perfectly through his tight black T-shirt. Dark tattoos peeked from under the edge of the sleeves on both arms, making me wonder what kind of artwork the gods bestowed on him, because surely this man was not human. There was no way he was one of the guys from the college, as he had a maturity and worldliness about him—something that was lacking in every male here tonight. And he was just too beautiful for words.

Be still my ever-loving heart.

His worn-looking jeans hung low on his hips, and that butt, sweet baby Jesus, it should be a sin for a guy to have a butt that nice. Aw hell, what the heck was wrong with me? I needed to quit drooling over Mr. Sex-in-a-box and get back to Becca.

Ugh!

"Hey, man, this doesn't concern you. Me and my girl, here, were just trying to spend a little alone time together. Back the fuck off!" I heard Rick mouth off, causing me to stop in my tracks and spin back to the two of them. *Oh hell no.*

"Rick, I'm *not* your 'girl,' and I do *not* want to have any 'alone time' with you!" I said, as I felt my fists clench and my eyes flash. "I told you I wanted to go back to Becca, but you were too drunk for that to sink into your thick skull!" What an ass.

I saw Rick's face screw up in anger as he took a step toward me. "You fucking bitch! Maybe you shouldn't be such a dick tease!" My mouth fell open in shock. That's when Mr. Sexy—dang who *was* this guy?—dropped his beer bottle, grabbed him by the front of his shirt, and spun him around, slamming him against the side of the barn.

"Watch your fucking mouth, you piece of shit. Didn't your momma teach you not to talk to ladies like that?" He spoke in a deadly calm manner as he brought his face within centimeters of Rick's. He said something to Rick in such a low tone I couldn't make out what was said, but I saw fear in Rick's eyes before he covered it with an expression of false bravado. He jerked away from Mr. Sexy, straightened his shirt, then gave me a hate-filled look before he stomped off muttering, "Shit, you can have the dumb, stuck-up bitch, asshole. She doesn't put out, anyway."

I went to thank Mr. Sexy and stumbled over the uneven ground in Becca's stupid heels. Being more than tipsy, I couldn't seem to get my balance and started to fall. Just as I saw the ground coming up to hit my face, he grabbed me under my arms, pulling me up against him with my face buried in his abdomen.

Shit. Shit! *Shit!* How embarrassing.

Now I looked like a klutzy, dumbass, little girl who couldn't handle herself, or her alcohol. Great. Just freakin' fantastic. Way to make an impression, Steph! And Lordy, I may have broken my nose on his rock-hard abs. Heaven help me.

I looked up to see two deep, sexy dimples appear in his cheeks as he let out a quiet laugh.

Dimples? Seriously? I was a sucker for dimples. Great. Just great.

"Ummm, while I'm not complaining about your position, right now, I think this is what you were trying to avoid with jock-face, kiddo."

"Kiddo? Really? For your information, I'm almost twenty-two, and I'll be graduating from Iowa State in a couple of weeks. Wow, you must be, what? At least eighty, right?" I said, voice laced with a heavy dose of sarcasm and a smirk on my face.

Way to sound mature. God, alcohol made me stupid.

His grin widened, exposing straight white teeth. Man, did this guy have *any* flaws? I was beginning to feel a little self-conscious.

"Sweetheart," he drawled, "you have no idea how much older than you I am. I may be twenty-six in years, but I guarantee I'm older than any of these boys here in life experience." He stood me up and made sure I was steady before he let go of me. If I was any judge of the expression that flickered briefly on his face, he looked reluctant to release me. Mmmmm, interesting.

He started to walk away, and my heart sank before he looked over his shoulder at me. "I'm going to grab a new beer since jock-face made me drop mine. I would offer to get you one, but I kinda think you maybe need to hydrate a little with some water, unless you wanna feel like dragon dump tomorrow." I caught his smirk as he sauntered off toward the water troughs full of ice and beverages. I watched his amazing butt as he walked away, thinking I should be ashamed of where my thoughts were drifting, but I wasn't.

He returned with a beer, which was already frosting over after being pulled out of the ice, and it dripped water in the grass as he walked. A bottle of water was in his other hand, which he held out to me. He gestured over to the shadowed side of the barn. "Care to pull up a spot of grass and join me?" he asked. "I don't bite. Unless you want me to," he added with a wink.

"Ummm, yeah, okay." I mean, the guy did just save me from a potentially unpleasant encounter with "jock-face" Rick. And there was something about him that just put me at ease. As I took the bottle from him, the water from the surface slid across his fingers and ran down my hand to my wrist before dropping to the ground. Call me crazy, but I felt like that tiny stream held an electric current in it that connected us for that split second. My eyes lifted to his and we stared into each other's eyes for what seemed like hours, though I knew it was only seconds.

He cleared his throat, looked down, and moved over to sit by the barn. As we sat on the ground, I kicked off my shoes and tucked my legs off to the side to prevent my skirt from flipping up and flashing him. I couldn't help but think maybe the night was beginning to redeem itself.

Colton

I watched her take the cap off the bottle of water and tip it to her lips. As a small drop of water appear at the corner of her mouth, I couldn't stop myself from reaching a finger over and catching it before it dropped from her full lips. You have no idea how tempted I was to catch it with the tip of my tongue, but I gave myself a mental shake. She slowly lowered the bottle with her eyes wide and her lips remaining partially open as she watched me bring the drop to my mouth and lick it from my fingertip.

Oh, yes, little girl, there are things I could do to you with this mouth that would leave you breathless, indeed.

I have no idea what I was thinking when she leaned closer to me and I reached out to tuck a loose strand of her long, dark blonde bangs behind her ear. It was like I couldn't control the movements of my own body. Me, who was the epitome of self-control at my job.

What the fuck?

She looked so young and innocent, but I couldn't help taking in every detail of her. Her multi-colored, blonde hair, evident of her love for the sun. Her eyes were a soft cornflower blue, with a darker blue ring around the edge of her irises. They sparkled as they caught the light from the distant bonfire and strung lights. She had a classic beauty in her high cheekbones, softly arched brows, heart-shaped face, and full lips, which were screaming at me to kiss her. She had toned legs that seemed to go on for days, ending in the cutest feet with toes painted neon pink.

And for the record, I'm not big on a chick's feet. At all.

When the fuck did I start waxing all this poetic bullshit? Damn. Fucking Midwest girls. Holy shit this girl was smoking, though. They didn't grow them like this back in Tennessee, not that I'd been home in six years to know. What the fuck reason did I have to go back there anyway?

I looked up and saw that she had been watching me check her out. Not that I cared, but I did just save her from jock-face-gropey-hands, so I supposed I should at least *try* not to look like the horny dick I was. I saw her run her little pink tongue along the top of her bottle of water before she took another drink of the cold liquid. Her eyes never left mine as I stared at her and watched her throat move with each swallow. Yeah, that made my dick stand at attention. Maybe I needed to pour some of that shit down my pants to calm it down.

Well hell.

What was it about this girl that had my mind going all kinds of places it shouldn't? Looking into her eyes shouldn't have me wondering what she would be like as a military wife. There was no way a wife would ever fit in my career plans, and hell, I hadn't known this chick fifteen minutes. Fuck. Never had I thought about a wife in any way, shape, or form. Wherever my mind was going, I seriously wanted to fuck the sass right off of little miss college girl. Then take her back with me in my duffle bag and do it again, and again, and again.

Damn, I must be going crazy... My last reverse SRP must have lied—I was totally losing my shit.

"Sooooooooo... I'm guessing you don't go to school here," she said as she drew circles in the condensation of the water bottle with the tip of her index finger. I watched as the droplets trailed down the side of the bottle, then met her gaze. She looked up at me with a questioning expression, waiting for me to answer, and soft wisps of hair fell across her left eye. I reached over to brush it behind her ear, again, and felt the warmth of her breath as I drew my hand past her mouth, running a fingertip along her sexy-as-fuck bottom lip. I felt like the biggest pervert alive at that moment because I could totally see those plump lips wrapped around my cock as those blue eyes looked up at me under a half-lidded glance. She was just a kid, really.

Damn.

"Uh, no. My buddy and I are in the Army stationed down at Ft. Benning in Georgia. He's from some small town here and a bunch of the guys he went to high school with are here. They invited him down for this last big hurrah before they graduate. He just brought me along for the ride. We're heading back to post soon. Our leave is almost up." I didn't want to get into the fact that I was deploying to Afghanistan, again, because I just didn't want to think about that shit right now. I wanted to pretend that, for just that night, I was a normal twenty-six-year-old guy who met a hot blonde at a party.

I leaned back against the barn and stretched my legs out in front of me as I absently pulled blades of grass, running the silky-feeling stems between my fingers. She shivered and I noticed goose bumps break out across her arms. I reached over and pulled her close to my side, placing my arm around her as I ran my hand rapidly up and down her arm, trying to warm her up.

"Hope you don't mind?" I asked as an afterthought, and she shook her head as I watched her take her bottom lip between her teeth. I groaned to myself at seeing that sexy-as-fuck expression, and for just a moment, it felt like we were alone in the world. Of its own volition, my body leaned down to brush my lips against hers. Not even close enough to what I wanted to do. I ran my tongue along that bottom lip of hers, savoring whatever sweet-tasting lip gloss she had on and desperately wanting to see if the rest of her tasted as sweet. God help me, I felt myself losing control.

Calm down, Alcott. Fuck.

Taking a deep breath, I forced myself to pull back and put some space between us. We both ignored the brief awkwardness that followed the kiss and made companionable small talk. Time seemed to slip away from us. She was amazingly easy to talk to, and I felt myself relaxing and even laughing here and there. We didn't talk personal details. Hell, we didn't even exchange names. It was as if deep down we knew this was just for tonight. We mostly people-watched the drunk coeds stumble, drink, and grope each other. We shared a laugh when a guy who obviously thought he was in, got smacked on the face and the girl stormed off.

Fucking hilarious.

Our eyes met, sharing the humor. That's when everything seemed to stand still again. She took in a soft, excited breath and reached her hand up to my shoulder, allowing it to slowly slide up my neck until she was running her fingers across the short-cropped hair at the back of my head. I heard the rasp of the short hairs against her fingers and took a deep breath, inhaling her rich, exotic-smelling perfume. As if in slow motion, we leaned closer until our lips connected. The tip of her tongue tentatively hooked under my top lip, pulling me into her allure, leaving my senses completely intoxicated by her.

Our tongues, lips, and teeth dueled in a crazy battle for power before I pulled away, breath harshly entering and exiting my body. I rested my forehead against hers as my heart continued to race. "Baby girl, I'm trying really hard to keep myself in check, but there is only so much self-control I can tap into if we keep this up. I need to let you know before things go too far. Fair warning and all that shit."

She answered by tipping her head slightly, nipping my top lip before soothing it with her tongue, then whispered, "What if I don't want you to?" against my lips.

Yeah, all the invitation I needed.

Our kiss deepened and rapidly became a desperate, intense melding of lips, tongues, and bodies. It was like we couldn't get close enough to each other as she grabbed both sides of my face with her delicate hands and kissed me like the world was ending tomorrow. Maybe it was. Maybe this was just a frantic need to feel alive and connected as I pushed all thoughts of what my future held to the back of my mind.

God, what was it with this girl? She had me burning like an inferno for her, like I'd never burned for any other girl.

We laid back on the cool green grass and my leg slipped between hers as her skirt rode up and she pressed her core to my thigh, grinding in small circles. My hands fisted in her hair as we broke off the kiss, leaving us both panting. I knew she could feel how hard I was since my cock was pressed into her hip. I needed to get a fucking grip or I was going to come in my fucking jeans like some inexperienced teenage boy.

"We can't do this here where anyone could come walking up on us," I whispered with a groan. "You're so much better than that, baby girl. If we're doing this, we need to go somewhere more private." I needed her to understand where this was headed. She deserved better than a quick fuck in the grass at a party with drunk-ass idiots laughing and dance music reverberating through the night air.

"We can go back to my apartment if you want. I can tell Becca I'm tired and you're giving me a ride back. Let me just talk to her and make sure she'll be all right and she has a safe ride home, okay?"

"All right, I'll go let my buddy know we're taking off. He has his bike, so he has his own ride back. Do you have a car here or will you be okay with riding on my bike? Shit, never mind. You can't ride in those heels and that skirt," I said, feeling frustrated. I ran a nervous hand through the longer hair at the top of my head.

"Funny enough, I have jeans in Becca's car, but I only have running shoes. Will that be okay?" she asked in a breathless whisper.

"Yeah, better than those heels anyway. Meet me back here?"

"Yes," she said, "the sooner the better." She reached up and kissed me quickly on the lips before scooping up the sexy as fuck heels and running across the grass toward the doorway of the barn. Light, laughter, and music continued to spill out of the large, open sliding doors and people sat on hay bales drinking and talking. I watched her long, sexy legs for a few seconds as she ran. When she reached the door, I turned to find Mason to tell him I was taking off and I'd hook back up with him tomorrow.

Chapter FOUR

Stephanie

A S I RAN BAREFOOT ACROSS THE COOL SPRINGY GRASS, I FELT MY heart race with excitement. Me, straight-laced, studious, Steph was going to bring home a complete stranger—an absolutely sexy beast of a stranger.

Lordy, I must be out of my tree, but nothing has ever felt so right.

It was like we were meant to meet that night… like the fates had aligned the stars just right so we would meet at this party—one it turned out neither of us had initially wanted to attend. Okay, that sounded a little cliché, but whatever. I was *not* passing the chance up.

Oh heck no!

I found Becca sitting in Brent's lap on a bale of hay in the barn. She was laughing as her head was tipped back with riotous red curls trailing down her back and him placing soft kisses on the side of her neck. Oh yeah, looked like she really needed a "wingman." Sheesh.

Well, maybe to get creepy Rick out of the picture. Thanks for that, Bec. I mentally rolled my eyes. Luckily, he was nowhere to be seen by then.

I tried not to interrupt in a creepy, awkward way, but how does one do that really, when their friend is practically screwing someone on a hay bale?

Becca looked up at me and did her best to pull herself together before asking me if everything was okay. My excuse was, I was tired and a friend was giving me a ride home. She tried to tell me she would leave with me and take me home, but I could see the disappointment in her eyes at the thought of leaving Brent. With a smile, I assured her all was well and I would see her tomorrow. We hugged and I whispered for her to be careful and call me if she needed me. She promised she would, and I asked her if I could borrow her keys to get my bag from her car. I ran to the car, grabbed my bag, rushed her keys back to her, and gave her a kiss on the cheek and a quick hug. Her perfectly shaped eyebrow raised as she looked at me, and I prayed my blush didn't give me away as I hurried away, waving.

Trying to catch my breath, I arrived at the side of the barn to see him casually resting on the picnic table, legs crossed at the ankle and those amazing arms crossed at his chest. He was watching me with hooded eyes and a slight smirk on his lips.

"I wasn't sure you would come back," he said, eyes smoldering as they took in my breathlessness and the rise and fall of my breasts.

A smile hovered on my mouth. "Just had to grab my stuff and make sure Becca was okay." Stepping into the shadows, I pulled my jeans up my legs lifting my skirt as I pulled them over my ass. I may be preparing to jump his bones ASAP, but I wasn't about to give some wandering partygoer a show. Then I unzipped the skirt and slid it down over my jeans, stepping out of it and shoving it in my string bag with the heels, cinching it up and slinging it over my shoulders.

There were no socks in my bag, so I slipped my running shoes on barefoot—gross—but it wasn't forever. "Okay. Ready when you are!"

He took my hand and we walked through the parked cars to a couple of bikes that were under a large oak tree. There sat a sleek, metallic black Harley Fatboy decked out in shiny chrome.

Score one for the Harley shirt Becca loaned me. Yes! Sexy freakin' bike for a sexy guy.

"Hey, Colton!" A cute guy with light brown hair and laughing eyes came running up.

Jesus, they would run in pairs. Yummy.

He tossed a single key on a keychain to my Mr. Sexy, who now had a name. "In case you need to get in before I get there. I know where the spare is kept, so I'll be good." He gave me a grin and winked at Colton, then turned and jogged back to a cute, short, platinum blonde with full lips and pale blue eyes. Damn, he had a nice ass too. Of course, I may have been a little partial, but I thought Colton's was better.

Bad girl! Ugh!

"You ever ridden before?" he asked with a questioning look, pulling my gaze back to him.

With a coy smile, I told him, "I used to ride with my brother. It's been a while since I've ridden, but I think I can handle it." God, I sucked at being 'cute.'

On the upside, he didn't seem to be bothered by my ridiculously silly sex-kitten attempt, and he wrapped his arms around me, pulling me close. He smiled before gently nipping the shell of my ear and down the side of my neck. His hands slid to cup my butt, squeezing my butt cheeks and giving me a little pull into his hard shaft.

"Then let's go for a ride, baby girl," he said as he wiggled his eyebrows in a comical waggle and smiled, causing those dimples to flash. Dang, those sexy dimples had me hooked. I reached around and squeezed his butt like he did mine, but I knew my butt was not nearly *that* rock hard!

Seriously great ass. Be still my heart!

He shoved my bag in one of his saddlebags then handed me a helmet he had hanging from the handlebars. So I placed it over my head, crushing my curls, and he adjusted the chin strap to make it fit the best he could. I gave him what I knew was a huge grin as he tapped my nose with his finger and gave me another swift kiss before swinging his leg over the bike and firing it up. As soon as the bike roared to life and began to rumble, I felt myself get turned on. Holy shit, could anything *more* about him turn me on? He lifted it upright and flipped the kickstand up, then motioned for me to climb on. There was no sissy rest, just a little seat in the back, so, after I climbed on, I wrapped my arms around his waist and slid my hips close. I could feel those sexy-as-shit abs against my fingers, and I pressed my ample breasts into his back. He looked over his shoulder, raised an eyebrow, smiled, and said, "Hang on, baby, you're in for the ride of your life."

Lordy, I hope so, was all I could think.

Colton

Jesus, having those tits against my back, her hands running along my abs, and her pussy pushed up tight against my ass the whole way almost did me in.

This girl may just be the death of me.

We arrived at her apartment, which was actually the lower level of an old four-square style house. It wasn't huge, but it had a nice porch out front, and as she closed the door, I took in the visible area and noticed they had made the little apartment homey. I slid my arms around her waist and brushed her hair away from her neck with my face. I could still smell whatever shampoo she used mixed with her perfume as I ran my nose and lips up her neck to her jawline. I nipped her jaw then spun her around to face the wall, placing her hands flat on the wall as my hands slid down her arms and around to cup her tits. Sweet Mary, mother of God, her tits spilled over my hands—not huge, but definitely more than a handful. I rolled her nipples with my fingers through her bra and pinched them before reaching down for the hem of her shirt, raising it up over her lithe body and arms before tossing it on the nearest chair. My hands slid down her body, starting at her wrists, to her hips, and back up over her hands.

"You sure you want this? Last chance…." She whimpered and reached over, nipping my forearm. I took that as a yes. Thank God, because I may have died from blue balls if she changed her mind. I then reached around to her flat, smooth belly and unbuttoned her jeans, sliding the zipper down before slipping my fingers into her jeans and the tops of her panties.

Our breathing was harsh and rapid as I slid my fingers farther down, expecting to encounter soft curls, but fuck me, the girl shaved *everything*… sexy as fuck. I groaned as I reached the slick wetness.

"Fuck, baby, you're wet for me. Tell me what you want me to do to you." She moaned a sexy, little, low sound and I said, "No. Say it. Tell me what you want."

"You." She said, "I want you."

"You want me to fuck you with my fingers or my cock. You gotta say the words, baby." Damn, she was hot and I was ready to bend her ass over right here and fuck her long and hard, but shit, as fucking horny as I was, it may not last long… this time.

"Oh God, everything… I want it all," she moaned.

I groaned into her neck then shimmied her jeans down her legs and helped her step out of each leg, kicking them to the side. Then I went back to the waist of her panties and dropped to my knees behind her. I hooked my fingers in the sides of her sexy underwear, and as I exposed the globes of her ass, I licked, sucked, and kissed them both. Spreading her legs with my knees, I pushed my face into her pussy from behind, running my tongue from front to back before burying it deep into her wet slit.

She was so wet it was running down my chin as I lapped and circled her pussy, nipping gently at her pussy lips. When I reached around to circle and pinch her clit, she rubbed herself on my face and hand, her breath coming faster and shorter with little breathy moans slipping from her open mouth. I knew she was close to reaching the big "O," so I slowed down and softly kissed her wet pussy lips. God, this girl was responsive. I fucking loved it.

When I stopped and stood up, pressing my face into her hair, she cried out in frustration. I kissed her shoulder. "Not here, baby. Where's your room?"

She led me to her room, tossing hot looks over her shoulder as we headed down a short hall that ended with what looked like it must be the bathroom, and then she took the door to the left. As soon as we entered the room, she shut the door with her foot and pushed me the few steps to the bed. I grabbed her waist as the backs of my knees hit the bed and we tumbled onto the bed in a tangle of limbs, frantically kissing, nipping, and licking each other's necks, lips, chins—anywhere we could reach. I'd never felt so out of control in my life. This girl was off the charts fuckin' hot.

I flipped her to her back and kissed her deep, our tongues teasing and tangling. I left her mouth and trailed down her body, licking and sucking at her tits and drawing her nipples into my mouth, running my teeth along them gently as I let go. She reached up to unbutton my jeans and I knelt, grabbing the back of my shirt, pulling it over my head, and tossing it to the floor. After she had my jeans undone, she reached in and stroked my cock with slow firm thrusts. I had to grab her hand to stop her before I embarrassed myself and shot my load all over her soft, tanned belly. I slid my jeans down, my cock springing out. I thought I had died and gone to heaven when she leaned up and licked the drop of precum off the head of my cock.

Jesus.

I nipped and licked down the curve of her cleavage to her belly button. Fucking pierced. Jesus, she was sexy as hell. I rubbed my face along her firm, flat stomach, leaving faint redness behind from the light stubble of my beard.

Yeah, fuck the Army, I sure as shit wasn't shaving every day if I was on damn leave.

When I reached her shaved mound, I buried my face in that pussy like a starving man. I took her clit between my teeth and flicked it with my tongue, looking up at her and meeting those gorgeous eyes as they glazed over with desire. Her full lips were swollen and pink. As I licked her pussy in a long, slow sweep, she ran her tongue across her lips. With that, I just about flipped my shit. She was gonna come, and then I was going to bury my cock in that dripping wet pussy. I couldn't wait anymore.

"Come for me, baby." I continued to lick and suck on her pussy while I slipped a finger in her soaking core and stroked her G-spot. She moaned and thrashed as she tightened her thighs around my head. I knew she was close, so I slid a second finger in her—Jesus she was tight—and kept fucking her with my tongue and fingers until I heard her cry out in ecstasy. Her body tensed as her walls contracted and pulsed around my fingers. I didn't think it was possible, but she got even wetter as her cum gushed over my fingers and tongue and she screamed.

Yeah, baby, scream for me.

Fuck, she was ready, and I needed to be balls deep in that tight, sopping wet pussy or I may just fucking quit breathing. I slid up her body until the head of my cock skimmed along her wetness, and I kissed her, making her taste herself on my lips and tongue. Then, I pulled away, resting my forehead on hers and holding most of my weight on my forearms.

She looked up at me panting, with her own juices glistening on her lips from our kiss, and said the words I'd been waiting for…

"Fuck me, Colton. Jesus, please, fuck me now."

I slipped the tip of my cock in and out a couple of times before I looked her in the eye and slid into what felt like heaven.

Chapter FIVE

Stephanie

HAD ONLY BEEN WITH TWO GUYS MY WHOLE LIFE. ONE WAS A bumbling loss of my virginity in the back seat of a car to my first serious boyfriend, who moved away a month later. The other was a guy I dated for a few months my freshman year. Then he decided the brunette who sat next to us in algebra was better than me and shit-canned me. So my experience was definitely limited in the sex department, but holy hell… Colton was a sex *god*.

I was convinced.

As soon as we entered my apartment, it was like we sponta-neously combusted. I couldn't touch him or get close enough. If his body could have literally absorbed mine, I would have been happy. I had never felt so connected to someone on such a deep level. It was as if our bodies *knew* each other. He made me feel like my body was shattering into a million fragments and then falling back together. His body was rock hard *everywhere*, if you know what I mean, and abso-fucking-lutely gorgeous. Those tats I saw peeking out of his shirt sleeves were dark and light abstract designs that stretched up to his shoulders and wrapped around to the back of his arms. His eyes were an ice blue and those lashes.... *Lordy, why were guys always blessed with eyelashes like that? It just wasn't fair!*

When I first unbuttoned his jeans, freeing his cock from its confines, I almost swallowed my tongue. I was sure there was no way in hell he was going to fit. He was like silk-encased steel, and I could barely wrap my hand around him.

He teased me for a few seconds, gliding just the tip of his massive cock into my entrance. When he slid all the way in, there was a slight burn as I stretched to accommodate him. He held still in me with his chin dropped to his chest and his eyes tightly closed, breathing deep but ragged. He held his weight up on his arms, and I noticed his muscles were tense and quivering. He lifted his head and looked me in the eye as he pulled nearly all the way out.

"This one is going to be hard and fast. I can't hold back. I'll make it up to you, I promise," he whispered as he slammed his cock back in me. I raised my knees and wrapped my legs around his waist, allowing him better access to enter me deeper. Reaching up, I ran my hands along the defined muscles of his back, feeling every contour and ridge as I trailed my fingertips down to his tight ass as it tightened further with each thrust. The rhythm was frantic, but with each drive of his cock into my wet pussy, I felt a tingling as he massaged my G-spot over and over until I couldn't hold back.

"Oh my God, oh my God!" I wailed on repeat like a crazy banshee, arching my back as I felt my inner muscles pulse and squeeze his cock. My body exploded as I saw flashes of light behind my closed eyelids, my muscles all tensed up, and I felt myself quivering head to toe.

"Jesus, baby, you're so fucking tight. Oh shit, baby. Yessssss!" he growled out. I felt his cock swell even more before a roar burst from him as he came. He continued to stroke in and out slowly a few more times before he collapsed to his elbows and his hands framed my face as he kissed me gently, then rolled over to his back, pulling me with him and tucking me to his side. I felt our combined fluids run down the side of my thigh and instinctively clenched my thighs around his leg. He kissed the top of my head and let out a deep sigh.

"That was absolutely amazing," I said with a breathless voice. As he lightly stroked my back up and down with his hand, he chuckled softly and kissed my forehead.

"Yeah, that was definitely pretty incredible, babe. Sorry, it was so quick. I'm not usually like that, but you're fucking amazing."

I smiled shyly at him. What a time to be bashful. Damn, I just screwed him like a porn star. Part of me wanted to crawl into a hole and hide. What the hell had come over me? Shit. Evidently, I was a closet wanton. As I laughed, he looked at me with a questioning gaze. I giggled again and told him I was just thinking crazy things. He smiled, giving me those sexy dimples as he reached over and tucked my stupid long bangs back behind my ear again. Why did I even let the hair dresser tell me they were a good idea? Ugh. They were a pain in the ass.

I leaned and reached over the side of the bed, feeling for my phone before I remembered it was in the back pocket of my jeans in the living room. I saw his in his jeans and grabbed it, opening the camera and snuggling back into him. I held it above us, capturing our smiling faces on the screen. He took it from me, looking at the picture showing a grinning couple with total "just fucked" expressions; flushed cheeks, long dark blonde hair curling around his shoulder and laying up against his dark head of sweat-spiked hair. He smiled, then dropped his phone back to the floor as he kissed me again.

I felt his cock jump a little against my leg, and I quickly opened my eyes and looked at him. He smirked, shrugged, and said, "What?

You do crazy things to me. And I told you I would make it up to you, remember?"

I slid over him and raised up to guide his cock in me once more. He grabbed on tightly to my hips but let me set the pace as I rode him slow and sensually at first, and then faster as I felt another orgasm building. When it hit me, I felt on the edge of just falling apart—like molecules-scattered-across-the-room falling apart. I pulsed and tingled, gripping his cock hard with every spasm, making me throw my head back and moan. We were like two halves, and there was no telling where one started and the other stopped. I felt his hands glide up and cup my breasts, tweaking my nipples and massaging me. He slid his palms featherlight up and down my side before he slipped one hand down and his thumb circled my clit as he leaned up to suckle a nipple. As soon as his lips wrapped around my other nipple, I exploded again.

Jesus.

He gripped my hips, pounding up into me until I felt his hot cum fill me again, and I collapsed on his chest. Our mingled sweat made our chests glide across each other before I rested my head on his shoulder, panting like I'd just ran a marathon.

Holy cow. Wow. Just *wow.*

We went two more rounds before the sun lightened the sky and we collapsed, worn out and totally exhausted. I didn't think twice in one night was possible for a guy, let alone four.

Sweet heavens.

My eyelids grew heavy and I just couldn't keep them open. The last conscious thought I had was how a girl could definitely get used to this kind of treatment. Then I felt his firm lips whispering across my swollen, soft lips as I gave a sleepy smile and snuggled deeper into his warm body.

Colton

I hated to leave her, but I needed to track down Mason. I hadn't slept more than a few minutes here and there all fucking night, but we needed to hit the road if we planned on making it back in time. Top would have our fucking asses if we were AWOL. No way in hell was I getting my ass in a sling. He better not have disappeared with some fucking ho, or I was gonna have to kick his ass. I sent him a text telling him he better meet me at his cousin's place within the hour, if he wasn't there already.

As I dressed and gathered my phone and keys, I looked at the rumpled bed where my beautiful angel lay sleeping. God, she really did look like an angel with her golden hair and sun-kissed skin against the pale-blue sheets. Her hair was a crazy mess all around her head and across the pillow, but she was a beautiful sight. Her lashes lay soft against her cheeks, and her sexy-as-fuck lips were still kiss swollen and slightly parted. Shit, I wished I had time to wake her for one last round as I felt my cock twitch in my pants. I readjusted it and leaned over to kiss her softly on her head. I didn't want to wake her because I knew I wore her clean out. Poor girl.

Damn, I really didn't want to go, and I knew I was standing there staring at her like some crazy-ass stalker, but I need to pop smoke. Seeing a notebook and textbook on the bedside table, I did something I never did before… I wrote my phone number down for her and told her to keep in touch with me and maybe I could swing by to see her after I got back. Shit. That was dumb. What if something crazy happened and I didn't make it back? Besides, by the time I did get back, she would probably have found someone who deserved her. Someone who could offer her a stable life, the white picket fence and all that sappy shit. I reminded myself I didn't do relationships.

I just didn't.

Not with my job.

It would be stupid.

I didn't even really know this girl anyway. I ripped the paper from the notebook as carefully as I could so I didn't wake her, crumpled it, and tossed it into her trash can by the door. I stared down at the wadded-up paper amid all the other rumpled up bits of papers and trash, wishing I didn't feel like it was my heart I just ripped out and dropped in there....

What the fuck?

In one night, this girl crawled right up under my skin. I never even got her name, but knew I would never forget last night, or her.

As I quietly let myself out of her room, I ran smack into the redhead from last night coming out of the bathroom. She squealed in surprise. Great, so much for trying to keep the noise down.

"What? Who are you? What the heck!"

"Shhhhh. She's wracked out. Take care of her for me?" I gave a small, sad smile and walked out her front door, leaving her friend standing there slack-jawed.

Chapter SIX

Stephanie

May 2013

WHEN I LEFT MY SMALL TOWN TO GO OFF TO COLLEGE, I HAD BIG plans. I was going to finish college with my culinary science degree, graduating top in my class, of course, and then become a kick-ass chef who eventually owned the number one dining establishment in the nation. Yeah, they were big dreams, but who had ever made it big by dreaming small? Funny how life comes along and makes its own plans for you. For me, it came at me like a sudden raging bull, taking me out at the knees.

Like I said before, I was almost done. It was the week of finals, then graduation and my future would be laid out like a Caribbean sunset. Right?

I studied like a crazed woman. I barely slept, or ate—unless you counted Starbucks as one of the main food groups—over the last few weeks. Looking back, I realized it wasn't really my best plan and I had made myself sick as all hell. I felt like I couldn't catch a dang break! How was I supposed to keep studying and remember all the crap I was burning into my eyes when I could barely get my ass out of bed before noon and I felt like I was dying from the flu I had picked up?

So I laid in bed staring at the ceiling, counting every little, ugly, lumpy piece of that crappy popcorn texture, trying my best to keep my mind off the nausea roiling in my stomach. I tried not to think of my beat-up wicker trash can next to the bed with the two used grocery bags lining it. I tried not to think of how many steps it was across my threadbare carpet, through my door with the loose antique knob that sometimes got stuck slowing me down, into the bathroom and to the cracked porcelain god I had been worshipping for the last three days.

For God's sake, I hadn't showered in four days now. My hair was a greasy, ratted mess, my eyes were bleary and bloodshot, and no matter how many times I brushed my teeth and washed my face, I still tasted minty vomit and smelled.... Dear Lord, I couldn't even begin to tell you how I smelled. I could barely stand myself at that point.

Yeah, not helping the nausea.... Two hundred seventy-three, two hundred seventy-four....

Oh shit, not working!

I reached over for the trash can and barely kept my lank hair out of the way as I lost a whole lot of nothing from my stomach.

Yes, God, kill me now. Lightning. Flash flood. Whatever.

I couldn't take much more.

I had just flopped my exhausted body back on my equally nasty, rumpled sheets when I heard the tentative knock on my door, the rattle of the old knob, and saw Becca's worried face peek around the edge of the door. The stench of my deathbed (okay, so sometimes I was a little dramatic. Sue me. I truly thought I was dying) must have hit her like an uppercut because her worried expression quickly gave way to a look of disgust as her own face turned green and she covered her mouth and nose with one manicured hand.

"Girl, I was gonna offer to make you some toast, but you need a damn shower. Pronto. Ugh!" she complained and waved her hand in front of her face as she walked toward me. She grabbed my comforter, pulling it off me and taking my hand, getting me to a sitting position. I groaned and tried to fight her and tell her to leave me here to die, but I just didn't have the energy.

Becca softly brushed my hair away from my face as I noticed her discreetly slide the trash can as far away as she could with her foot. Her grimace said volumes as she looked me in the eye. "Come on, doll. Let me help you to the shower. I'll clean up in here and get you some clean clothes," she offered.

I moaned, "I don't think I can make it...."

Becca half dragged, half supported me as I stumbled and shuffled to the bathroom. She sat me on the closed toilet, and I leaned back against the cool tank, closing my eyes as she turned on the water and waited for it to get hot before pulling the lever to turn on the shower.

"Come on, Queen Pukey. Let's get those clothes off and get you in the shower." She helped me climb in, waiting to be sure I wasn't going to fall over. As I closed the shower curtain, I saw her plug her nose and toss my favorite red sweats and ratty Five Finger Death Punch shirt in my hamper.

"I'll be back in a minute. Holler if you need me." I heard the door click shut as she left.

I stood in the shower letting the warm water wash across my face and body in hundreds of intertwining rivulets. I had to admit, it did make me feel a little better. As the water washed across my nipples, I saw his face in my mind's eye, just like I had every day since the morning I woke up to an empty bed three weeks ago.

I pictured his slow, easy smile, the flash of dimples and how his lips felt brushing against mine. I closed my eyes, and I could feel his hands instead of the water caressing my body. My hands reached up and cupped my aching breasts, and in my mind, they were his hands. My biggest regret was not getting his number. Shit, I didn't even know his last name for that matter.

Oh well, some things weren't meant to be. At least I had some amazing memories to hold close to my heart. Of course, those memories might make every other man who entered my life have a lot to live up to.

I didn't even have the picture I took because it was on his phone and he was gone, taking the phone with him before I could forward it to myself. At least then I would have had his phone number and a picture to ogle. Obviously, he didn't want to keep in touch with me after he headed back to Georgia, or he would have at least gotten my number from me.

I sighed to myself. Georgia was a long way away anyway, and who wanted to do a long-distance relationship? I was probably just another notch to him.

The water began to lose its heat, so I hurried to wash my hair and body before it became an icy stream. As soon as I shut the water off, I broke out in goose bumps as the cool air hit my skin. I rapidly toweled myself off and carefully climbed out of the shower, holding the wall to ensure I didn't fall over. I wiped the steam off the mirror and looked at my reflection in the glass. I had dark circles under my eyes, and I looked sallow and washed out. At least I smelled better and I was clean. That was a plus.

I walked back to my room with my feet pattering on the old hard wood of the hallway. Becca was just smoothing the comforter across my bed as I walked in, nearly stumbling over the pile of dirty sheets in the doorway. I shot her a small smile as she looked up at me from her task.

"Why are you so good to me?" She smiled back and walked over, giving me a hug. She smelled like sunshine and it made me miss sitting outside in the sun to study. I needed to get better and back to studying again. Finals were rapidly approaching.

"What are friends for? Besides, I love you, girl. I feel awful that you've been so under the weather lately." Understatement of the century. "I'm going to go make you some toast. Do you want me to bring it in to you? Or do you want to come out to the table?"

"Give me a minute to get dressed and I'll come out." She nodded and walked out to the kitchen.

Dressed in clean sweats and a tee, I shuffled out to the kitchen and sat at the scarred-up wooden table, which was a hand-me-down from her grandparents, just as she carried a plate of perfectly toasted, thick-sliced bread over to me. She set it down in front of me and went to grab a can of ginger ale from the fridge for me. Then she sat at the extra chair, bringing one foot up to the edge of the chair, and rested her chin on her knee as she looked at me, chewing on her bottom lip.

"So… you feeling better, hon?"

"A little, I guess. If I can get my ass up and moving, it usually helps me feel a little better, but it's getting the energy to get up after being sick all morning that kicks my ass." I took a bite of the toast, realized I was suddenly ravenous, and made quick work of the other piece as well.

"Can I ask you a really personal question?" Becca's eyes boring into me with bright intensity made me curious about where this was going.

"Ummmm, sure?" I mean, we shared *everything,* so what could be more personal than everything?

"When was the last time you had your period, Steph?"

"Uhhhh, like a little over a month ago, or so. But I'm not usually very regular, and with all the stress of finals and whatever this bug is I have, I know I'm probably thrown off even more." I swallowed a mouthful of the cold, bubbly ginger ale.

"Do you think you could be pregnant?" She pursed her lips to the side and looked at me in question.

Ginger ale shot from my mouth and nose and the can slipped from my hand, landing so hard on the table that some of the liquid splashed out of the can onto the table. As I sat coughing and holding my hand over my mouth, I stared at the abstract blob of bubbling pop on the table. I frantically tried to remember exactly when my last period was. I felt the blood drain from my face as I realized it may have been well over a month since my last cycle. Okay, maybe almost two....

I thought back to that glorious night with Colton and realized not once did either of us even *think* to use a condom. Not that I'd had much use for them over the last several years, but crap. What the hell had I been thinking? Not to mention, he could have had an STD or something!

God, I was so stupid.

I looked at Becca with tears filling my eyes and cried, "What am I going to do?"

Becca reached across the table and grasped my hand in hers.

"First, we are going down to the dollar store to get a couple of tests. Maybe you're right and you just have the flu and lots of stress. I just know it was a few weeks ago that I ran into tall, dark, and sexy coming out of your room in the morning looking like ... well, just yum. And now here you are sick as shit, and well, I guess, I just thought...." She trailed off.

"Come on." I stood up, pulling her up from the chair, causing the chair to scrape across the floor and nearly fall over. I rushed to grab my purse and slid on some flip-flops. I threw my hair in a messy bun as I rushed out the door with Becca hot on my heels.

We both sat there staring at all the plus signs and double lines on the white sticks lined up on the counter in front of us. Neither of us said a word. We just stared. I wanted to cry, but I was in too much shock to do anything but stare and breathe.

Finally, I looked over at Becca and she looked at me. My stomach gave a little lurch and I fought back a small wave of nausea.

"What are you going to do?" she whispered to me with a stricken expression.

"I don't know. What am I going to tell my family? 'Oh, so I'm graduating soon, I don't have a job yet, and oh, did I mention I'm having a baby and I don't exactly know who the father is? I mean, I know who he is, but I never really got his name.' Yeah. I'm going to sound like a huge slut, and they're going to hate me for being a disappointment to all of them!" I buried my face in my hands as sobs racked my body. Tears quickly filled the palms of my hands.

"What was I thinking? I slept with a guy without any protection and didn't even get his name or phone number! Jesus, Becca, I feel like such a hoe-bag! Oh my God, my baby isn't going to have a father, and there is a great guy out there who will never know he has a baby!" I felt like such an idiot. I was a smart girl, but my intelligence had obviously been on vacation that night.

Shit. Damn. Crap.

"Well, you could look into an abortion, Steph. You're not that far along. I know it kind of sucks, but it's an option."

"*No!* Absolutely *not!*" I stood up, pacing in the small bathroom as Becca continued to sit on the edge of the tub. I was going to figure this out. I may have been stupid that night, but the result was a tiny, little life growing inside of me. He or she was an innocent byproduct of that stupidity, but that didn't mean they were a mistake. I held the palm of my hand to my still flat belly as though it was a shield from the horrors of the world. I looked up at Becca with new determination.

"I'm going to figure this out. I have to. Either I wait to put in resumes until after the baby is born or I get them out ASAP and get a job before I start showing. Then I'm just 'surprised' when I find out I'm pregnant." I leaned down and hugged Becca before heading to my room to try to figure out a feasible plan.

I pulled out my laptop and began to update my resume the best I could. I knew finding a job in a good restaurant coming right out of school was going to be difficult, which was why I had worked hard to keep my grades up. I knew if I could put on my resume that I graduated top of my class, it would be a boost when employers looked at my resume. Then I looked online at the websites that posted for restaurant and food preparation type positions. I fired off a few resumes to various restaurants across the state in hopes that one of them may look past my lack of experience and the fact that I hadn't quite graduated yet and give me a shot. I would be happy with anything at this point. After I finished, I closed my laptop and leaned against the headboard, pulling a small throw pillow over my stomach and clutching it tight. I slipped a hand under it to my belly and whispered, "Mommy is going to take care of you, sweetheart, one way or another. Don't worry, baby, we got this." It was said with much more confidence than I actually felt.

Chapter SEVEN

Stephanie

June 2013

GRADUATION CAME AND WENT. I, THANKFULLY, PASSED ALL MY classes with flying colors and did graduate at the top of my culinary class. Go me. At least one thing went according to plan. Becca and I had a tearful goodbye after we both finished packing up the apartment. It was the first of June. We had used the last few weeks to take our time packing and just hanging out together. After all, the rent was paid through this week. I still hadn't told my family, nor had I heard anything about a job, so I was heading home to stay with my parents until I heard something from one of the five billion resumes I sent out.

"You better keep in touch! We'll only be about three hours apart, so I expect we'll be getting together as often as we can, even if we have to meet halfway in Storm Lake for a weekend here or there," she said with a stern look. I laughed.

"Yes, Mother."

"Don't you 'yes, Mother' me," she said as she looked around to see if either of our families were around. Seeing the coast was clear, she whispered, "Have you told them yet?"

"Shhh, please be quiet! No, I haven't. There hasn't really been a good time." I knew I looked guilty, because I felt very guilty. Since Colton had been my only sexual encounter in well… forever, I was a little over eight weeks along. Still early, but I knew I would have to tell them before there was no hiding it. My stomach still seemed as flat as ever, but I knew that wouldn't last. Thankfully my morning sickness had tapered off after I figured out eating a few saltines in the morning before even getting out of bed helped settle my stomach so I could feel normal.

"Steph, there isn't going to be a good time. Are you sure you don't want to go back to CB with me for a while? Maybe you can find a job there and you can just stay with me." She meant well, but I knew I couldn't run away and hide from my family forever. Eventually, I had to tell them.

"No, I know I need to tell them, but I think I'll need to be with my mom for this. I just pray they don't hate me or disown me." I felt my face begin to crumble.

Becca reached over and gave me a hug as tears trickled down my cheeks. Her red hair tickled my nose, and I reached up to brush it back, making me think of how Colton had brushed my hair out of my face with such tenderness. I began to cry harder, and she squeezed me tighter.

"None of that now, girls. You're acting like you won't be just three hours apart. Becca can come up and stay with us any time." My dad walked over, hugging us both. He was still handsome even at fifty, with dark brown hair going gray at the temples.

My brothers and my mom came through the door, and my mom walked over and kissed me and Becca each on the cheek. She was still gorgeous, in my opinion, but to me she had always been the most beautiful woman in the world. People told me I looked a lot like her. Tall, lithe, blonde, bright blue eyes. She was a few years younger than Dad, but easily passed for a woman years and years younger. My dad looked over to her with love shining in his hazel eyes. I wondered if I would ever find the love my parents had, even three children and years later, or would it forever be just me and my little one? The thought brought a new wave of tears. The book I bought at the used book store said I would feel more emotional than usual due to fluctuating hormones, but why did I want to cry all the time? Ugh!

"Are you about ready to head out? Your brothers are securing the last of your boxes in the back of the truck, sweetheart. I figured we could grab a bite to eat with Becca and her family and then hit the road." I kissed my mom on the cheek. She was amazing, and I was so thankful for her intuition in knowing I needed a little more time with Becca, who had become my absolute best friend.

"Yes, that sounds amazing!"

Becca went to tell her parents, and I walked to my room to gather up the last few things I had piled up in the corner. I tucked the pregnancy book in my backpack, thankful that no one had come in and grabbed any of my things I had set aside here. Yikes! That would have been a great way to let everyone know. *Oh, look, Stephanie has a pregnancy book and some prenatal vitamins here with her notebook and makeup. Wonder what she has that for?*

Yeah. Not so much.

I slung my backpack over my shoulder, taking one last look around. No, this place wasn't much, but it was my first real place. Becca and I had a lot of memories, laughs, and tears here. I took in the worn carpet and the sunlight streaming through the dented blinds highlighting the dust motes floating through the air like tiny snowflakes, and gave a little sigh. It was time to start a new chapter of my life, one that would include a few major changes and alterations to my previous plans and dreams.

Chapter EIGHT

Stephanie

January 2014

"OHHHHHHHH MY GAWWWWWWD! ARGHHHHH!" I SQUEEZED my mother's hand, crushing her fingers in what must have felt like a death grip. She never once complained; she just kept holding a cool cloth to my sweat-drenched forehead and speaking in a soothing tone as she encouraged me to breathe slowly. My hair was soaked with sweat and plastered to my head. I just knew I looked awful as I tucked my head down to my chest, my face turning bright red and screwed up in a painful grimace.

"There you go, keep pushing, Miss Quinn. Your baby's head is crowning, and with one more push, the head should be out. You're doing great." The nurse was encouraging me in her ever-calm voice as she monitored my progress and all the machines beeping around me. Did these bitches take classes in that ridiculously calm voice they used? I wanted to kick her in the face. She wasn't the one shitting out a watermelon.

As the doctor walked in, taking over the nurse's spot between my spread knees, all smiles and sunshine, asking how things were going and was I ready to have this baby, I wanted to kick her in the face too. What was coming over me? I felt like a demon was inhabiting my body. I had been in labor for over seven hours. They said things were progressing very well for my first child. Yeah, fuck them. They weren't the ones being split in two.

Very well, my ass!

I fell back in exhaustion as the contraction slowly ebbed. Sweat poured down my face, burning my eyes until my mom caught it with the cool rag. I looked up at her in desperation. "Mom, I can't do this. I don't know what I was thinking. Get me the epidural. Or just make it stop. I'm not ready! Please!"

My mom gave me a small smile and kissed my cheek. She squeezed my hand lightly in encouragement and told me I was doing great. "It won't be long now, sweetheart. Your baby will be in your arms and this will be a distant memory. I still cannot believe you didn't want to know if it's a boy or a girl, but we'll know soon enough, now won't we. I'm here for you, baby." She smiled at me again, and I felt the next contraction building with a quickness, feeling like a band was tightening from my hips, meeting in the middle of my stomach. I screamed through gritted teeth as I leaned forward, nearly touching my chin to the center of my chest, and pushed.

"There we go! Look at that beautiful head of dark hair and those sweet little cheeks!" I rolled my eyes as the doctor suctioned the baby's nose and spoke of a baby I couldn't see over the still ginormous lump of my belly. *Asshole*, I thought. "Next push should have this little one out, Miss Quinn!"

How were all of these people so damn cheery? Yeah, I was gonna kick them all in the face by the end of it. Stupid fuckers!

One more brief respite and the next contraction hit. I pushed like the doctor told me and felt like I would split in two at my crotch. *Surely this baby isn't going to fit! There is no way.*

I still pushed, praying for a miracle that this giant bowling ball was going to fit through the donut-sized opening without ripping it asunder.

I heard the lusty cry of my precious baby just after I felt the fluid-like slip of the little body from mine and the pain eased. As they told me she was a girl and handed her to me wrapped in a little soft cotton blanket, I peered into her big blue eyes. I took in the full pink cheeks and pursed rosebud mouth, falling more in love with this exquisite little miracle with every breath she took. I barely felt the last of the contractions expelling the placenta that had nourished my little angel. She solemnly blinked her beautiful eyes at me before she smiled, revealing two perfect dimples, which hit me like a punch to the gut. She was her daddy's little girl for sure, and he would never know. I cried for the memories that would never be and for the gift I had been given. I cried for a little girl who would never know her daddy and for the unexpected level of amazing love I had for this one tiny person.

"So what name do you have picked out for your little girl?" the nurse asked with a bright smile as she took my tiny baby girl to clean her up better and do whatever it was they did to babies after they were born. She was so patient and kind, and I couldn't believe that minutes ago I wanted to kick her in the face. I felt a little discomfited and hoped she hadn't been able to read my mind.

"Remington Amelia... I want to call her Remi." I thought of her father and how I would have named her Colton after him if she had been a boy, but since she was a sweet little girl, I figured Remington was a close second to Colt, which was close to her daddy's name. My smile was bittersweet as I imagined how he would look holding her.

My mother held her after the nurse brought her back over, placing a soft kiss on her forehead, causing my little Remi to root around. My mother laughed as she handed her to me, saying, "I think she's ready for you, Mommy." I pulled my gaze from the window, where a soft January snow was falling, and reached for my angel.

As I placed her on my chest with the guidance of the nurse and felt the first tug at my breast from her tiny mouth, I knew there could be no greater or stronger love in the world than I had for this little precious baby. I softly ran my fingers through her silky hair and sent out a message on a prayer, thanking her unknowing daddy for the gift he had bestowed upon me.

Chapter NINE

Colton

January 2014

JERKED AWAKE FROM A NIGHTMARE OF THE LAST RIDE IN THE Humvee my spotter and I were traveling in with our interpreter and a fresh-faced young driver—a young man who, unfortunately, would never bless his family with his youthful optimism again.

I tried to catch my breath and slow my heart down before it had my nurse running in again. I squeezed my eyes closed to try to stop the tears and to erase the sightless eyes of the interpreter and our scout from my vision. I covered my ears, as if it would block the screams of my spotter, and best friend, from my ears. It seemed nothing could erase the coppery taste and crimson stains of the blood covering us all, and I relived it every fucking night. As the room slowly came back into focus after I opened my eyes, I felt like the air was different, like suddenly I wasn't alone and something had shifted in the universe. I shook off the strange feeling and reached for my water pitcher by the bed.

I couldn't tell you how many times I'd been told I was lucky to be alive. I didn't know how they figured that. I hurt every day. I had nightmares every night. Mason and I had barely survived, but we lost two good men with families who loved, and now grieved, them.

Why did I survive when I had no one? It didn't make any fucking sense. *Why me, God?*

I had my doubts there even *was* a God. How could there be? No God should allow people, with so much to live for, to die and allow someone with my sins, and no one to mourn me, to live.

I had been at BAMC—Brooke Army Medical Center—for about a month since the IED explosion along a seemingly deserted road in Afghanistan. For the first several weeks, starting with the initial stabilization by the flight medics, then the transfer to Landstuhl, Germany, and then to here was a blur of semi-consciousness. I remembered hearing screams and not being sure if they were my friends or my own. I remembered blackness. But most of all, I remembered the blonde hair, blue eyes, and gorgeous warm smile of a girl who had kept me going through everything. I clung fiercely to those memories. I couldn't believe how one night had embedded her so deeply in my psyche that she was forever etched in my heart. I didn't even know her name because I was a selfish, horny bastard who only cared about sex that night nearly a year ago. Back then, I had told myself there was no need since I would never see her again.

God, I was stupid. Such a conceited, self-righteous fuck. I hated myself more every day.

I reached down beside me, searching through the blanket for my phone, which now sported a cracked screen and what I repeatedly told myself were mud splatters on the back each and every time I scraped one off. I opened it up to the picture she had taken that night of the two of us. It was after one of our mind-blowing rounds of the best sex I had ever experienced. The pale blue sheets were tucked up over her breasts, and we both had flushed cheeks and ridiculous smiles. There was such happiness captured in that brief moment in time. It seemed fitting that the crack in the screen ran right between the two of us. I wasn't good enough for her before, and I certainly wasn't now; scarred and broken, both physically and mentally. But just the thought of her body held close and intertwined with mine, the smell of her hair, the feel of her lips against mine, and the look of complete satiation on her face kept me intact during moments that would have driven some men over the edge of sanity. For that, I would always hold her in my heart and love her like no other. Love? Shit. What did I really know of love? Maybe I shouldn't even say that shit.

The accident happened in December. Mason and I had spent Christmas and New Years in the hospital—me, pretty much in a constant haze between drug-induced unconsciousness and surgeries. His parents had come down over the holidays and stayed in the Fischer House, kind of the military's version of the Ronald McDonald House. I vaguely remembered them visiting my room with Mason. It was now mid-January and the world outside my window looked as bleak as I felt. I would almost give anything to be back in the drug-induced haze I had been in then.

Better to feel nothing than what I felt now.

I reached up, touching the scar that ran from my temple to my lower jaw. It was still thick and jagged. The doctors told me it would get better with time, but it would always be my reminder of that day.

It wasn't just my face that was scarred or disfigured in the explosion though. I had suffered nerve damage, fractures to my skull, left arm, three of my left ribs, and my left leg at the thigh and lower leg. My left leg now sported enough metal to ensure I would set off every metal detector in the airport for the rest of my miserable, worthless life. A rod took the place of the center of my femur, and I had enough plates, pins, and screws in the bones of my lower leg to build a parking garage. They said I was lucky they saved my leg.

Fuck them.

The daily therapy pissed me off. I hated the pain and the fucking optimism of the stupid fuckers that pushed me to walk and use muscles that I would have been happy to let die.

Mason had healed up pretty well, all things considering. His left side caught the brunt of the explosion as well, but the *shemagh* scarf he was wearing as a dust mask, prevented the facial lacerations I suffered from. I was thankful for that because he was always such a happy fucker and, of the two of us, the outgoing one. He was a good-hearted guy and deserved to be able to have a chance at happiness. He did, however, suffer a Traumatic Brain Injury and minor burns and breaks to both of his lower legs, but had since healed, and he used them to walk in my room and pester the shit out of me every day of our recovery. He had chosen not to re-up when his window opened and was now on terminal leave. The faint scruff growing on his face did little to hide the boyish face that still remained despite going through hell with me.

He talked non-stop about going home and prospecting for some motorcycle club. I tried not to roll my eyes as he went on about his excitement to see his family and begin the hang-around and prospect journey. I was supposed to be out of the Army in a few months as well, but it wouldn't surprise me if they extended me because I was still stuck here in this worthless shithole and would have therapy for a while. The doc said, if everything went well with the scans and tests they ran today, I should be discharged soon and moved over to the Warrior Transition Unit barracks to finish up my treatment on an outpatient basis. I didn't have it in me to stay in anymore. I wanted out. I had failed to protect the soldiers under me. I had seen more senseless deaths than I could count. I had killed more piece of shit hadjis than anyone else on my team, and yet I still felt like it didn't make a difference. They seemed to multiply like fucking rabbits to keep killing as many of my brothers and sisters as they could. I hated those motherfuckers.

Even though air entered and exited my lungs, machines continued beeping around me, and the pain throbbing through the left side of my body all told me I was alive, I felt dead inside. I had not a single thing to be alive for. I was a waste of pathetic space in this fucked-up, hate-filled world. *I* was hate filled… rotting from the inside out from the empty blackness of my soul.

Chapter TEN

Stephanie

May 2014

I LOVED MY FAMILY, BUT IT HAD TAKEN ME A WHILE BEFORE I finally told them I was pregnant. They had been great through my pregnancy, despite the shock of their "good little girl" getting pregnant and not knowing who the father was. They harassed me incessantly at first about the father of my baby. My father and brothers, seeing the situation from a man's perspective, were angry with me at first, thinking I actually knew who the father was and was just keeping the baby from him. For weeks after that day, my brothers wouldn't speak to me. My mother, bless her soul, was always supportive and never condescending. She did try to gently persuade me to share the story with her, but I remained stubbornly mute regarding the subject.

I didn't know if it was worse that my family thought me a heartless bitch for keeping a baby from its daddy or if they would think me a skanky slut for sleeping with a man whose only information I knew was his first name, he was in the Army, and he had a rocking body and a killer smile. I did try to find him, but do you have any idea how many soldiers are at Ft. Benning, Georgia? And good luck trying to find a soldier named "Colton"—no last name. I had no idea what he did, where he worked, or anything about him really. I did know his friend was from somewhere in Iowa and had friends who had been at the party, but that was another needle in a haystack considering I didn't know his friend's name either. What I did know was my little baby girl was her daddy's spitting image.

I wondered if he would be happy if he knew about her. I wondered if he would want to be a part of her life. Sometimes I made up scenarios in my mind of finding him. In my favorite, he was thrilled to have us in his life and we ended up as a happy little family, white picket fence and all. Other scenarios played out with him being angry because he thought I only found him to get child support or him wishing I had "taken care of" the situation. That was one of the worst. Still others that he hated me for keeping her from him, like I had any other option. I tortured myself daily with all of the what-ifs and if-onlys.

When I received the phone call in April from a fairly prestigious dining establishment in Des Moines, I jumped on the opportunity to tuck my tail and run from my family's censure. It took me a couple of weeks to find an apartment and get everything lined up before I packed Remi and our belongings into my little SUV and my brother's truck, which translated to mostly Remi's things. My mother waved with tears running down her cheeks and my father's strong arms holding her tight as I drove off to start a new life for me and my precious little bugga-boo. The job wasn't exactly a top-chef position. It was actually a position as a prep cook, but it was my foot in the door and it gave me the opportunity to get out of Dodge.

Remi was such a sweet baby. At times when I spoke to her, I swore she understood every word I said. She would stare at me with those big blue eyes as if she was looking straight into my soul. I prayed she never found it wanting and that she understood I was doing the best I could. I knew I was blessed to have such a calm, good-natured baby, and I thanked the good Lord above for her every day.

Since I had found the apartment, sight unseen, before we headed down, I was both excited and dreading moving in. From what I could find out, it was in a so-so neighborhood. Neither great, nor the ghetto. I just prayed it was safe enough for my little angel. It was only a one bedroom, but I figured with her being so little and us sharing my old room at my parents', it would be okay for a while. I pulled up in front of the older building that my GPS brought me to, noting the four apartments with open stairs going to the second floor apartments. My brothers pulled into the spot next to me.

Remi started to stir when I shut the car off, and I quickly went to unbuckle her from her bright pink car seat—a gift from my high school friends at my baby shower, along with the matching stroller I had crammed in the back. She opened her tiny Cupid's bow lips in a delicate yawn, rubbing her eyes as I pulled her close to me and placed a soft kiss on her downy black curls. She reached up, entwining her chubby fingers in my hair as she looked around as if to say, "Where are we, Mommy?"

"Here, Steph, let me hold her while you go get the keys." Sam said as he plucked Remi from my arms. Quiet little nonsensical sounds came from Remi and she grabbed at her uncle who was making crazy faces at her. Shoot, if I had stayed at home they would have spoiled her rotten.

The manager lived in the next building over, obviously newer and much bigger. I approached her door to collect the keys for our new home. Mrs. Burns answered the door with a ready smile. She looked to be around her early-sixties with light grayish-blue eyes, graying brunette hair, and a stature so small, she barely reached my shoulder. She walked over with us to let us in the apartment, cooing at Remi, still snuggled in my brother's arms, as we walked over.

"She's around my grandson's age. How I wish they lived closer." She smiled and unlocked the door. "If you all need help unloading your things, my husband is the maintenance slash handyman here, and he's not up to anything but watching some old western on that dang TV. I'd be more than happy to send him over if you want. That way you don't have to leave little miss, here, sitting while you unload." She looked at me with such kindness. I felt instantly grateful to be blessed with a kind apartment manager.

"I think we can handle it, but thank you so much for the offer." It wasn't like I had much and my brother's would have it unloaded in no time.

"If you change your mind, I'll kick his butt this direction!" she chuckled and walked back to her apartment tossing a "see you later, then!" over her shoulder.

Chapter ELEVEN

Colton

Lost Battles

I let the night set in around me
I poured a whiskey, hard and pure
Maybe tonight, this booze will drown me
Maybe then I'll find a cure
It's been years since I've been happy
Before these shadows found my face
It's like Pandora's box has trapped me
And I'm the perfect picture of disgrace
And come tomorrow, if you hear tonight I died
I drowned in sorrow, it ate me up inside

I don't know if you ever saw my battles behind my mask of pride
But I've been lost and drifting like a dingy on the tide
I let the night set in around me
Looking back on pictures of my friends
When the reinforcements found me
How come I lived instead of them
And though they've long been buried
They still visit me now and then
These ghosts I've carried
The scars beneath the skin
And come tomorrow, if you hear tonight I died
I drowned in sorrow, it ate me up inside
I don't know if you ever saw my battles behind my mask of pride
But I've been lost and drifting like a dingy on the tide
I let the night set in around me
I pour a whiskey, hard and pure
And if it doesn't drown me
Maybe it'll drown my memories of her
And come tomorrow, if you hear tonight I died
I drowned in sorrow, it ate me up inside
I don't know if you ever saw my battles behind my mask of pride
But I've been drifting like a dingy on the tide
~ Craig Dew

July 2014

I HAD BEEN OUT OF THE ARMY FOR GOING ON THREE MISERABLE fucking months. I hung around San Antonio, mostly because I really had nowhere else to go and no fucking motivation to look for anywhere else to go. My disability check and the money I picked up from odd jobs here and there when I needed it was enough to keep me in the lap of luxury here on the south side of SA.

Yeah, yeah, sarcasm is the lowest form of wit. What the fuck ever.

My apartment was a tiny furnished efficiency. Absolute. Shit. Hole. I could see daylight from the uneven space under the door, which had been splintered and patched up with the knob and lock moved; total evidence of someone kicking it down. Sometimes I wondered if it was the cops who kicked it in or some other nefarious excuse for a human that did it. Most times I didn't give a shit. When I was able to sleep, I slept with the lights on partly due to my fear that the cockroaches would take over and partly in fear that the darkness itself would take over. The AC ran nonstop it seemed, and yet it was still hot as fuck in here. The shades on the dirty-ass windows were broken and didn't close, so most of the time I kept the dingy curtains drawn to keep the nasty, nosy motherfuckers around here out of my business—not because I was worried they would try to break in to steal anything.

I lifted the bottle of whiskey to my lips, draining the last of it. I tossed it in a drunken arch toward the trash, amazing my own drunk ass when it hit the trash and landed with a clatter of glass on glass. Lord knew if it was hitting beer bottles or liquor bottles. I stood up, wavering on my feet for a minute before I took the three steps from my bed to the fridge. Yeah, I said the shithole was tiny.

Pulling the fridge open, I peered in with bleary eyes to see if there was a damn thing to eat.

Hmm, questionable Chinese takeout, milk that was four days expired based on the date on the jug, and about a quarter loaf of bread—yeah, I kept that shit in the fridge out of fear the roaches would get to that shit too...

Yep, looks like a beer it is.

I pulled the next to last beer from the six-pack on the top shelf, telling myself I needed to make a run to the grocery store soon. I twisted the top off using the hem of my T-shirt, adding another hole to the rest of them. Fuck it.

I sat back down on the edge of the bed and took a swig of the beer as I reached my other hand under my stained pillow, pulling out the only possession I actually valued. I set my beer on the floor by my feet and followed my routine of checking the clip, ensuring a round was chambered, and checking the safety. I rolled the pistol around in my hand. Instinct had me raising it with insane precision and speed, thumb flicking off the safety, aiming at the door when I heard a thump against it. I slowly lowered it and flicked the safety back on when I heard laughing and voices indicating it was just a drunk neighbor and his buddy stumbling by. My heart was racing and adrenaline coursed through my veins at light speed.

Fuck. Just fuck.

The gun felt natural in my hand, the cool steel warming to my touch like a living, breathing entity. The brushed stainless barrel of my Ruger 45 glinted dully in the light of the single bare bulb hanging from the ceiling. Flipping the safety off again, I stared at the pistol for what seemed like hours. My hands turned the gun over and over until the muzzle was eventually pointed at my face. I placed it in my mouth, aimed toward the roof and tilted toward my brain because I would never want to be a fucking vegetable. Slowly, I began to pull the trigger because habits die hard; you don't jerk the trigger, you squeeze it… Hot tears welled in my eyes as my hands shook. I jerked the gun back out of my mouth, flipping on the safety and tossing it across the bed like I had countless times over the last few months.

Fucking coward! I was such a piece of shit coward! I had pussied out and left my battle buddies hanging when I got out. Accepting the Medical Board because I couldn't handle the killing anymore, ate at me, yet a deep, evil, ugly part of my soul craved it. But I didn't think I could pull the trigger on anyone in my drunken, fucked-up state, and I guessed that meant on myself too.

Knowing I was sitting here broken and worthless while my brothers were still at it back in Afghanistan every day fucking tore me up. I hated myself. I was a fucking mess. Breaths continued to rasp in and out of my body. Sometimes it literally hurt knowing I was able to breathe. I fell back on the bed, staring at the ceiling as hot tears trailed down the sides of my face, pooling in my ears before running to the bed below me. *Something's gotta give because I can't live like this....*

Chapter TWELVE

Stephanie

August 2014

REMI WAS TRYING TO TODDLE AWAY FROM THE EDGE OF OUR LITTLE couch, but she couldn't quite get her balance when she let go. The look of surprise on her precious little face was priceless as she plopped on her diaper-padded behind, arms outstretched and flapping at her sides. I couldn't hold back a laugh as I dropped my arms that had been reaching for her while I sat on the floor cross-legged. At the sound of my laugh, she shot me her big, few-tooth smile, flashing those amazing little dimples as she flipped down to her hands and knees and crawled over to me so she could pounce on my lap. Looking up at me, still giggling and smiling, she clapped her hands and squealed, letting a trail of drool run over her bottom lip. She then reached her hands up to hold my cheeks and kissed me in her open-mouthed, still-lipped impression of a kiss. Her eyes were such a bright blue and always full of laughter. She had to be the happiest baby I had ever encountered.

The last few months had gone by in a blur. I enjoyed my job at the Des Moines Embassy. The people I worked with were great, and we had a blast every day we worked, whether preparing for patrons at the restaurant or special catered dinners at The World Food Prize Hall of Laureates. The chef and the director had told me when they hired me that they worked hard to allow for advancement when it was available and deserved, so I busted my butt every day. Of course, when you loved your job, it didn't always seem like work. I felt so blessed at this moment in time. My heart felt full to bursting.

For the hundredth time, I felt the little drop of sadness creep into my blissful thoughts for all the moments her daddy was missing. Guilt and anger at both of us for our foolishness that night plagued me, not because I regretted the little ray of sunshine sitting in my lap, but because our choices affected her. What was I going to tell her about her daddy when she was old enough to start asking? I rested my chin on her pretty little head as she sat babbling in my lap and playing with her own chubby little feet.

I could never replace Colton as her daddy, nor fill in that little corner of my heart I kept just for him, but maybe I needed to start dating. Reggie, one of my fellow prep cooks, had been getting increasingly overt in showing his interest in me and had blatantly told me he wanted to spend more time with me outside of work. He was handsome and lean with soft green eyes and a brilliant smile, but I didn't ever feel the fire or excitement around him that I had felt with Colton. He was more like one of my brothers to me, and I had a cozy, familial type of affection for him, but that was all. I also felt greedy and selfish because dating anyone would take time away from Remi, and I relished every single second with her.

No, I really didn't want to get involved with a coworker. It just seemed like bad juju, I guess. However, if some handsome stranger asked, I would say yes. Ha! Fat chance of that, but a girl could dream. I did need to spend time around adults too, I admitted. If I ever found anyone, I just wouldn't bring him around Remi for a while, because I never wanted to be that mom who paraded men through her home and family like there was a revolving door. Remi would have enough confusion in her life with her father in the slightly "unknown" category. I sighed and kissed my little bugga-boo again.

Cotton

August 2014

I WOKE WITH AN INCESSANT POUNDING IN MY HEAD. SHIT, I NEEDED to stop drinking so much. My mouth felt like a wad of cotton balls was shoved in it and tasted like the bottom of a dumpster, not that I really knew what that tasted like, but I could only fucking imagine. Damn.

The fucking pounding *wouldn't* stop. I swore my head might explode until I realized someone was pounding at my door, causing the door to rattle on the hinges. I reach under my pillow for my pistol, flipping off the safety, as I heard shouting.

"Oh shut up, lady, like you can hear anything over that mariachi crap you have blaring anyway!" I heard come from the other side of the door. Jesus, that door must be fucking hollow. I quietly crept to the window, moving the curtain to the side an infinitesimal amount, allowing me just enough space to see who was banging on my door at this ungodly hour of the morning but not enough for them to know they were being observed. The bastard out there was good though, because no sooner had I moved the curtain, his head whipped toward the window.

"Colton! Colton, you motherfucker, open this fucking door! I know you're in there, you bastard. Don't fucking pretend you're not."

What the fuck? Who the hell knew me and knew I was here? Who was this rude-ass sonofabitch banging on my door, wearing some ratty jeans and a leather vest? My mind whirred, trying to think of who could be out there looking for me. I was about three seconds from planting a bullet in his stupid ass. My brain felt like mush and I couldn't think straight. I slanted my view and noticed a bike parked next to mine in front of my place.

What?

"Colton! You fucking fuck. Come on, man! It's Mason. Get your sorry ass up and open the fucking door. I don't have all day, and this crazy Mexican lady next door is about to beat the shit out of me with her broom!"

Mason? What the fuck? He was supposed to be home with his family in Iowa. I unlocked the shitty-ass lock, which I was honestly surprised hadn't just fucking popped open as hard as he was rattling the door with his pounding. I tucked my gun into the back of my waistband as he pushed his way in the door, surrounding me with a back-breaking bear hug.

"Goddamn, man, it's good to see you! Don't you ever answer your piece of shit phone, bro? I've been trying to call you for months. I was beginning to think maybe you fell off the face of the earth!" If only he knew how close to the truth he was, I thought with shame. "Dude, what the fuck? You look like shit, and what the fuck kind of rathole are you living in? Jesus H. Christ!" He stepped over to my kitchen area and leaned against the counter as I shut and locked the door after looking around outside and giving the nosy bitch next door a "fuck off" glare.

I went over to the fridge, opening it to notice the fucking bulb blew. Piece of shit. Glad I went to the store last night, or I wouldn't have had anything to offer my old friend. "You want a beer, man?"

"The fuck? It's like 0900, bro. I like a cold beer as well as the next guy, but shit, I like some breakfast food in my guts first." He pushed past me to look in the fridge with me reaching for an apple out of the small bag I bought. He took a large bite, juice spraying out and running down his chin as he bit down. He wiped it off with the back of his hand as he happily chewed. The crunching echoed through my head, and I had to go sit down away from him.

I tossed down a pain pill, raised my ice-cold beer in salute to him, and took a swig. "Hair of the dog... Now what the fuck you doing down here? And what the fuck's with the vest getup?" I took in his black leather vest with a patch that read "PROSPECT" and raised a brow, waiting for him to answer me as I let another swallow of cold beer trickle down my throat and settle in my guts.

"We trailered down here, picking up a bike we're supposed to customize for some rich fuck. I've been trying to get in touch with you for damn near three months, man. When they told me you had left the WTU and you were out, I was pissed 'cause you never fucking called me or anything, bro. So when, Snow, our Prez, needed a prospect to travel down here with Gunny, my sponsor, to pick up this bike, I volunteered. I'm a prospect for the Demented Sons now." That fucker was smiling like the Cheshire cat. Truth be told, I had really missed his sorry ass. We had been through a lot of shit together, and we were probably closer than some actual blood brothers.

My head hung low because I knew I had been a straight-up shit with the way I cut him out after I left BAMC. I just didn't feel like I was human enough to function, let alone be the friend he probably needed then. I still didn't, and I really hoped he got on his bike and left soon. I just wanted to wallow in my misery alone. I was not the friend and partner he remembered. I was merely a vacant shell of that man.

"Dude. Colton, man, what have you got here? Anything? You got a woman around here or something?" Did I have a woman? Fuck. I hadn't had any pussy since the night I left the WTU with all my worldly possessions crammed in my bike's saddlebags. Truth be told, I couldn't even fuck her because I kept seeing blonde hair and blue eyes in my head and the dumb bar whore I had picked up didn't look anything like *her*. My angel was the last woman I had slept with. When I couldn't keep it up no matter how much she messed around, she laughed in my face and told me to call her when I didn't have such whiskey dick. I told her to fuck off and booted her out of my hotel room.

"Fuck no." Didn't want one either.

"Bro, ditch this shithole and come back with me. I've told Gunny all about you and everything we've been through, and he wants to meet you. He was in the Marine Corps—I try not to hold that against him." He laughed. "I told him I wanted to bring you back with me if I could find you. I hoped maybe you could look at prospecting too, if it seems like a good fit for you and the club." He seemed to get real serious as he looked down at the apple core that he'd been rolling in his fingers. "It was rough when I first got home, bro, I ain't gonna lie. I felt fucking lost. Everything I'd known was gone, and there isn't much call for a spotter in the civie's world, you know?" He looked back up at me, and for a moment, I saw the same emptiness in his eyes that I felt to my very soul.

"Come on, bro, this is the brotherhood that I know you've been missing. With the club, we say what we mean and mean what we say, and we have each other's backs. Always. I can't leave you here like this. I love you, bro."

Chapter
FOURTEEN

Stephanie

April 2016

IT WAS A CHILLY DAY FOR LATE APRIL, BUT THE SUN WAS SHINING warm and bright, so I thought maybe Remi and I could take a walk up to the park. We'd been in our new apartment in the 14Forty building for almost a year. The rent was a little higher and I hated to leave Mrs. Burns, who had turned out to be an amazing babysitter for Remi over that first year, but I loved the old exposed bricks of our new apartment and the proximity to my job and everything downtown. I was a sucker for historic buildings and being downtown, so when a one bedroom opened up at the end of my old apartment's year lease, I took it. Remi had celebrated her first birthday that January, and we moved in on the first of May. The new apartment had meant money was a little tighter, but since I was able to walk to work and Pam lived down the hall and babysat Remi for me for a great rate, it helped offset the rent. I was still setting aside little chunks of money out of my check, here and there, though. I called it my "someday" account. For "someday I was going to buy a house or start my own restaurant."

Pam was a sister to one of my coworkers, Sylvia, and charged me next to nothing because she adored Remi and said she just wanted some extra spending money. I didn't see how Pam needed the extra money since her husband had a great accounting job at Wells Fargo down the road, but who was I to judge? We still only had one bedroom, so I had Remi set up in there and we shared the closet while I slept on my pull-out sofa. Okay, most nights I was too lazy to pull it out, so I just slept on the sofa.

I bundled Remi up in her little, pink, faux leopard jacket with a matching hat. I smiled and told her how stylish she looked, eliciting a big dimpled smile as she patted her hat just like she understood every word and was pleased with my compliment. I placed her in her stroller, slipped on her little shoes, and we headed out. I knew that at two years old, she would rather walk, but it was easier to keep her corralled on the way there, and she was invariably tired on the way back, which translated to "carry me, Mommy!" and she was a heavy little stinker now. As I turned to lock the door, I noticed a man carrying a box. As he reached a door down the hall, he juggled the box to one arm and slid the key into the lock. I couldn't help but notice how good-looking he was. He paused and I realized he caught me gawking at him.

"Uh, hi! Are you moving in today?" Wow, that was smooth and brilliant sounding. I felt my face heat all the way to my ears, and I knew I must match Remi's hot pink stroller. I had obviously lost all ability to be suave and flirt since graduating college and becoming a mother. I tucked my hair behind my ear and prayed my face calmed quickly. How embarrassing!

"Why, yes, I am. Why? Are you offering to help?" He laughed as he set his box down and came down the hall toward me. He extended his hand to shake mine. "Michael. And you are?"

As we shook hands, I noticed his sandy hair was a little in need of a haircut, and I wanted to touch it to see if it was as silky as it looked. His eyes were a soft green and his smile was slightly crooked. My belly gave a little flip as I experienced the appreciation of a good-looking guy standing so close to me. Heck, I was human after all, what could I say?

"Oh! I'm Steph, and this is my daughter. My little Remi. We were heading out to the park to enjoy the sunshine. I don't mean to keep you. Welcome to our little corner of the world. We've been here about a year, and we love it." I let go of his hand and still felt the warmth of his grasp. As I leaned over to cover Remi again with her little blanket she had kicked off, he knelt down to her level and smiled at her in greeting. When he touched her chubby little fingers and told her he was pleased to meet her, she lit up and giggled.

"Dimples on a dark-haired, blue-eyed princess... Ahhhh, I'm slayed." He held his hand over his heart and rolled his eyes back in mock dismay. This elicited further giggles from Remi, and I couldn't hold back a small chuckle of my own. He smiled and gave Remi a small wave before he stood, meeting my eyes. Remi waved and said, "Bye-bye!" not realizing he wasn't actually leaving when he waved.

"I don't exactly have any of my kitchen things unpacked, and thought I would go grab dinner somewhere tonight. So, if it wouldn't be too presumptuous of me, it sure would be nice to have the company of two beautiful ladies. And did I mention, I'm new to the area and don't really know anyone? Have pity on a poor, lonely guy? I promise I don't bite."

At those words, I was taken back to a night outside a college party—one I wasn't even going to attend—and a set of dimples, paired with blue eyes that matched perfectly to my beautiful little girl's. I looked down as I felt my smile slip. After composing myself, I met his eyes again. I revived my smile and took a deep breath.

"We might be able to do that. We can meet you at the little diner up the road if you'd like? It doesn't look like much, but they have amazing food, great staff, and it's clean. It's up about six or seven blocks. Will that work?" I looked at him, expecting him to back out any minute.

"Sounds perfect. Say, around six? I figure that will keep you from having your little one out too late. Unless you would like to do five instead?"

"No, six is great. So, I guess we'll see you there?"

"It's a 'not date' dinner, then." He winked.

Until dinner that night, I hadn't realized how long it had been since I had sat down and had actual adult interactions. Michael and I sat and conversed in an easy banter through dinner, dessert, and coffee. We were still sitting at the old Formica flecked table with the glittery red 50's style booth seats talking as little Remi began to rub her eyes, dropping her cookie she was still working on.

"Well, that looks like my cue. I didn't realize so much time had passed," I said as I looked at my watch, noting the late hour. I suddenly noticed the diner was nearly empty and the waitress was wiping down the tables around us. As I stood and gathered Remi's little toy cellphone and her jacket, he stood and unbuckled her from her booster chair, lifting her until her head rested on his shoulder. The simple paternal gesture tugged at my heartstrings.

"You're good with children," I noted as I watched Remi grab his shirt with a grubby little hand, which I tried to loosen and wipe with a water dampened napkin. "I am so sorry, she got cookie all over your shirt!" Shit, I felt bad that she had just messed up his clothes.

"No worries. I'm used to it, after my nieces and nephews. They made it their singular goal in life to christen me with anything and everything they could! Man, I'm going to miss them," he said with a look of longing. I knew from our conversation that he came from a large, but close, family down by Davenport and he had moved here to take a supervisory position with a construction company that had expanded to the Des Moines area. I missed my family too, and I understood his ache for home.

I tried to pay for my and Remi's meals, but he intercepted the waitress when she tried to hand me my order slip. I felt guilty because I never intended for him to pay for our meals, especially after he had made it sound like our "not date" was definitely just two people sharing company over food.

"No, you don't need to pay for us. Please, I can get it."

"Of course not. Just because I said this wasn't a 'date' per se, I still invited you. It's my treat. Please, I insist."

He held Remi while I put her coat on her and then offered to carry her to my SUV after the waitress brought him his receipt. I slipped on my jacket, grabbed her bag, tucking her bib, toy, and sippy cup in it before slinging it over my shoulder.

"Thank you again, Michael."

"It is my absolute pleasure," he replied as he held Remi with one arm and opened the door for me with the other. I glanced at him and walked out the door and over to my SUV with him next to me in a companionable silence. I couldn't believe what a good night it had been. He was so polite and handsome. His personality was almost too good to be true as well.

I buckled her in her seat, tucking her blanket around her legs, and she mumbled sleepily as her eyes fluttered open and then closed again. Her little head dropped off to the side of her seat as she snuggled into her small cuddle blankie and I gave her a gentle kiss on her head, running my hand against her cheek.

"You're a good mother, Steph." His soft voice startled me as I had almost forgotten he was there. He stood behind me with his hand resting on the top of the door. When I turned, I realized how close we were standing. I felt a little self-conscious as we stood there without speaking, and I shifted from one foot to the other.

"Ummm, so, thank you again for dinner."

"I told you, it was my pleasure." He reached over and tipped my chin up so I was looking at him instead of the ground. As I met his green eyes, I thought he was going to kiss me. He leaned closer, placing a gentle close-mouthed kiss to my cheek. "Thank you for the wonderful company." He stepped back, allowing me room to close the door and get in the driver seat to start my SUV. With a shy smile, I backed out to head home and gave him a little wave, which he returned with a smile of his own.

Well, that was an unexpected end to a beautiful day....

Chapter FIFTEEN

Stephanie

June 2016

MICHAEL AND I BEGAN SPENDING MORE TIME TOGETHER. OVER the past couple of months, we had dinner a few times here and there, but mostly watched movies at my place so Remi could go to bed and not disturb her schedule. He frequently texted me to tell me he was thinking about me and hoped all was well or asked if I was having a good day. I thought it was sweet that he checked on me like that. We had developed a comfortable relationship that had as yet to truly be defined.

The first night we took our relationship to the next level, we were watching a suspense film and I had jumped after the main character was caught going through her maniacal boyfriend's briefcase just when we thought she was safe. Of course, that caused me to laugh nervously after it made me feel silly. Michael chuckled and drew me closer with the arm he had around my shoulder. I turned to him, and we both stopped laughing as we looked deep into each other's eyes, and my heart raced for a minute in anticipation. He leaned forward, and his lips touched mine hesitantly. When I parted my lips slightly, he ran his tongue along the opening of my mouth, sliding it in past my teeth and touching mine in smooth strokes. As his hand caressed my shoulder, I placed a hand on his chest and leaned in a bit.

His other hand slid up from my hip to the side of my chest. He gently rubbed my breast along the side and then slid it over and squeezed. For a second, I was taken back to a night that seemed like ages ago and remembered calloused hands running over my entire body in worship and ownership. It didn't take long for reality to return and realization to sink in that this wasn't *him*.

I didn't know what I had expected or hoped for, but other than the anticipatory increase in my heart rate at the actual touch of a real living, breathing man and not my imagination, I really didn't feel much. Of course, we were still new in our relationship, I told myself. Being nervous about being with a guy for the first time in three years was bound to make a girl tense. Right?

I also felt a crazy sense of betrayal to a man I truly owed no allegiance. I pulled back, pressing my lips together and looking down at my hand resting on his chest. I gave him a pat, trying to make light of what suddenly felt like an uncomfortable situation.

"Steph, I'm sorry. I hope you don't think I was being too forward. I've tried my very best to be patient with you. You are a special woman. I want you to know that." He tipped my chin up, raising my gaze to his. I thought I saw a flash of irritation in his eyes, but it was gone so quickly I must have imagined it.

"No, it's just… well, I'm not sure I'm ready for… well… you know." I felt my face heat, and I was at a loss for words. "I mean, there hasn't been anyone at all since Remi's…." I didn't know what else to say. How did I describe Colton? He wasn't ever her dad, nor my boyfriend, but he held a spot in my heart just the same. I didn't want Michael to get the wrong idea and think I was a cheap tramp. Thankfully, he remained ever the gentleman as he stood and held my hand. I knew he was a little frustrated, and I could see a slight bulge in his jeans, which caused my face to flame again as I quickly tried to look away.

"It's okay, Steph. I understand. And when you're ready to talk about him, I'm here. You think I haven't noticed her father never comes by, nor has any visitation? But that's your business and I won't pry. I think it's time for me to head home. I have an early morning anyway." He dropped a quick kiss on my head and turned to leave.

He walked out my front door, and I heard him close the door to his apartment down the hall.

Why couldn't I just let go of Colton? He and I only had one single night together three years ago. He could be a total ass, have a girlfriend, or be married for all I knew, and I needed to stop carrying around this stupid romanticized image of him. Hell, he could be dead by now! God, that thought almost brought me to my knees. Jesus. My heart ached, and I fought to calm my breathing.

I needed to forget about him. I was never going to see him again, and holding every man up to this fabricated image I carried around was pathetic.

I got up to tidy the kitchen and get ready for bed. I had a busy day tomorrow too. We had a huge executive dinner lined up, and I knew everyone wanted to make sure everything was perfect. I heard my phone ping and picked it up after I dried my hands on the kitchen towel and hung it on the stove handle.

Michael: I hope I haven't offended you. I'd like to stop by after you get home tomorrow.
Me: It's okay, really. And sure, no problem. :)
Michael: Great. See you then. Sleep well.

I smiled and then climbed on the couch, pulling my fuzzy blanket tight over my shoulder and snuggling my head into my pillow. I didn't even remember falling asleep before the alarm on my phone was going off.

Chapter SIXTEEN

Stephanie

July 2016

TODAY'S CATERING JOB HAD GONE OFF WITHOUT A HITCH, BUT WE had all worked fast and furious to get everything prepared to the high standards we maintained. June and July were always busy months due to all the weddings, and this year had been the busiest on record according to all the other prep cooks and the sous chef.

It was later than usual by the time I got home, and I was so thankful for Pam's offer to leave Remi at her place since she was already sleeping. She was so sweet. She didn't want me to worry about disturbing Remi's sleep and then trying to get her settled again at home. I left Pam's apartment and was digging through my purse for my keys as I walked down the hall. When I slammed into a solid form, it caused me to stumble back until my arms were gripped in a tight, almost painful grip. I looked up into Michael's angry expression.

"Where have you been? I've been worried sick! You didn't answer your text messages or calls! What the hell, Steph?" He loosened his grip on my arms, and I felt sorry I had worried him, but damn, he had really hurt my arms. I figured he didn't realize how hard he grabbed me.

"Michael! Crap, you frightened me! I'm sorry, I didn't have my phone on me all day, and we were so busy, I never thought to check it at all. After I got off, my battery was dead because I had forgotten to plug it in to charge last night. I'm sorry, I never meant to worry you. Then I stopped to pick up Remi, but she's asleep and Pam and I got to talking." I felt like I was rambling, but I felt so bad I was apologizing all over myself.

"It's okay. I forgive you. Just don't do that to me again. I hate being worried about you. You really shouldn't walk home alone when you get off late. It's not safe." Geez, I felt like I was in high school again with my dad lecturing me. I fought rolling my eyes.

"I didn't walk all the way by myself, Michael. Reggie walked most of the way with me, so I only had to walk about a block by myself." I thought I saw his nostrils flare and his jaw tighten. "I know we said we would hang out tonight, but I'm really tired. We were so busy today and I'm exhausted. I think I'm just going to go to sleep early." I felt my fatigue increasing by the second.

"Fine. No problem, Steph. We can make up for it tomorrow. Get some sleep and I'll see you tomorrow night. Do you want me to give you a ride to work tomorrow?"

"No, I'm good, really. I enjoy the exercise, and the weather has been cool enough by the time I get off that it's a beautiful walk." He didn't look pleased by my response, but I knew he had been worried about me. I kissed him gently on the cheek and unlocked my door to go in. When I tried to push the door shut, Michael's foot stopped it from closing.

"Please don't be upset with me for worrying about you. I really care about you, Steph." He reached out, pulling me into his embrace. I tried to loosen his hold, but he held me tight. I can't lie, I was starting to get a little claustrophobic and panicked for a minute until he let me go abruptly, pressed a kiss to my lips, and stepped back.

He then turned and stepped out into the hall, waiting for me to lock my door before he left.

I hung my coat on the pegs inside my door and set my bag on the kitchen counter. Reaching for a glass from the cupboard, I wondered what the heck that was all about. Michael had seemed very worried about me, but shit, I'd been walking home from work just fine for quite a while. It *was* pretty late though. I needed to make sure I charged my phone tonight. I was usually very responsible. I could have missed calls from Pam if something happened to Remi. Of course, she knew how to get a hold of me at work too. Oh, well, I was too tired to even think anymore. I sat on the couch, plugged in my phone, flipped on the TV to watch a little of the news, and dozed off sitting up still dressed in my clothes.

Chapter SEVENTEEN

Stephanie

REGGIE, SYLVIA, PAUL, AND I WALKED OUT OF THE EMBASSY laughing over how red Chef Jonas had gotten when he and the sous chef had argued about the menu for next week. Jonas was a redhead, and when he got mad, his face tended to match his flaming red hair. It happened quite often and had us holding back our laughter to prevent his ire from being targeted at us. We tossed around the idea of stopping for a drink since it was Friday night, but decided we were all too tired and Remi was waiting for me.

We started down the road toward the bus stop where Sylvia and Paul would part company from Reggie and me. I heard someone call my name and turned to see Michael striding purposefully toward me. He looked angry, and I couldn't imagine what had happened to get him so upset. My friends stopped with me, Sylvia looking at me in question and concern. As Michael reached us, I told them to go on without me and assured them everything was probably fine and I would see them Monday.

Reggie gave Michael a look of irritation and then asked me if I wanted him to wait. I knew he still had a thing for me, but he had accepted when I didn't encourage his hints about us going out for dinner. I was about to tell him everything was cool when Michael placed his arm around me in a proprietary manner.

"She's fine. I'm going to give her a ride home. She's not your concern." I heard him mutter "asshole" under his breath, and I looked sharply at him and then imploringly to Reggie in apology for Michael's snappy, rude behavior. Reggie didn't look convinced, but when I smiled and nodded, he grudgingly turned to walk home.

"What the hell was that all about? What happened to put you in such a foul mood?" I couldn't believe he'd acted like that in front of my friends. To be perfectly honest, I was shocked because he'd always been so sweet and caring toward me.

"Who the hell was that guy? Jesus, are you fucking him? Is that why you're holding out on me? Is he the real reason you were late last night?" He seemed to get more irate as he spit his accusing questions at me. I was so shocked, I couldn't even find words to reply.

"Get in the truck, Steph. I'm giving you a ride home. These streets aren't safe enough for you. You need to be more careful. What would you do if I wasn't here to take care of you?" I tried to jerk my arm from his punishing grasp, but he only tightened his hold and pulled me to his truck, opening the door and waiting impatiently for me to get in. I didn't want to argue out here, so I got in and buckled up.

"Michael, I think you have the wrong idea and I don't know where the heck you came up with that crap. They are my friends and I work with them. That is it. If you can't handle me working with men, then maybe whatever this is isn't fucking working." I was getting more and more pissed off the longer I thought about what had just happened.

"Don't say that word!" he shouted, "Steph, you are a lady. Ladies do not swear like sailors. I don't ever want to hear you using language like that." I was stunned at his outburst and sat quietly during the short ride home.

When he pulled into the parking garage and parked his truck, he took a deep breath and seemed to collect himself.

"I'm sorry, Steph, baby. I just get so worried about you, and I think I'm really falling hard for you. The thought of something happening to you drives me crazy." He gently placed his hand on my cheek and leaned over, pressing a kiss on my lips.

"It's okay." I looked at my hands twisting in my lap. He took my bag as he got out of the truck, and I slowly followed him toward the building.

He walked with me to Pam's to pick up Remi and carried a chattering Remi down to my apartment. After taking my keys from my bag, he opened my apartment and set Remi down. She toddled off into her room where she started to pull blocks out of her toy box.

"I should give Remi a bath and get her ready for bed." I thought Michael would take that as a hint that I wanted to be alone tonight, but he walked into my kitchen, grabbed a beer from my fridge, and set my bag down by the couch as he sat down and turned on the TV. I figured I would let him chill and I would talk to him after I finished with Remi.

"Mommy!" Remi came running out of her room with a block in each hand and a smile on her face. I scooped her up, burying my face in her sweet-smelling hair. I kissed her dimples, which had become a routine with us since she was a baby. I called them "Mommy's kissy spots," and it always made her giggle. She dropped the blocks, slapping her hands to either side of my face, planting a big slobbery kiss on my lips. "Luss you, Mommy!"

I laughed, hugging her tight as we went into the bathroom,

closed the door, and I started to run the water. A big sigh escaped as I let my hair down from the tight bun I wore it in for work and replaced it with my messy bun. Grabbing sweats and a tee from the hook on the back of the door, I quickly changed while the water ran but kept a close eye on my angel as she leaned over, splashing her hand in the water. My work uniform got tossed haphazardly in the hamper and I stripped Remi of her clothes, placing hers in the hamper with mine.

Remi splashed and giggled through her bath, and I was as wet as she was by the end of it. Dressed in her fuzzy, blue, footed PJs with Cinderella on them, she ran out of the door as soon as I opened it. She raced to the living room, struggling to climb in Michael's lap. I saw him drop my phone on the couch as he reached for her to hug her and kiss her cheek. I couldn't help feeling uneasy with him holding her after his recent outburst. I walked up to them and picked her up from his lap.

"Tell Michael night-night." Remi waved her little hand and then placed it spread wide open over her mouth before rapidly pulling it away. I laughed at her attempt to blow kisses. Lord, I loved this baby girl. I couldn't believe she was two years old already. I took her to her room and sat in the glider to read her a bedtime story. By the time I was done, she was already nodding off to sleep. I sat there for a minute, enjoying the feel of my baby girl snuggled up in my arms and tried to collect my thoughts. Was I overreacting to what happened? Maybe I was just tired and I was blowing things out of proportion. After all, he had never lost his cool like that with me before.

I placed Remi in her crib, careful not to wake her. Leaning over, I kissed her sweet-smelling hair, breathing in the scent of her baby shampoo, her lotion, and the sweet smell that was just Remi. When I raised the rail of the crib, I told myself I was going to have to start looking for a toddler bed for her.

When I walked out to the living room, I wished I had kept my bra on because my shirt was soaked from Remi's splashing and sticking to my breasts. My nipples were erect from the wet shirt and the air conditioning, and I crossed my arms over my chest when I saw Michael staring at them and licking his lips. Eww. For some reason, that just felt creepy. After I saw my phone sitting on the coffee table, I remembered he had been looking at it earlier.

"Why did you get my phone out?" I asked him.

"Huh? Oh, I was just checking to see what version of iPhone you had. I have a bunch of cases I never used from mine, and I thought you could use them if it was the right one. But you have a 4s, mine was a 5. That's all."

It seemed a little odd that he didn't just ask me, but he was a real sweetheart most of the time and that seemed like something he would do, so I bought his explanation. He stood up, wrapping his arms around me and pulling me close. I couldn't meet his eyes. He kissed my forehead and stepped back, bending a little at the knee to look me in the eye.

"We good, baby?" I gave him a half-hearted smile and nodded.

"Yeah, but I think I'm going to go to bed." He stood up straight and motioned toward the couch.

"Do you want me to stay with you since neither of us work tomorrow? I can help you pull out the couch. I'll just hold you. No pressure, babe."

"Actually, I need to do a few things. Then I'll probably just crash, but thanks." I was hoping he would go. I just wanted to call my mom and unwind. I hadn't talked to her in forever. He didn't look happy, but he nodded and started for the door.

"Good night, Steph. Sleep tight." He let himself out, and I plopped on the couch, reaching for my phone to call my mom. I saw the app store was open on the screen. Weird, I didn't remember opening it, but I must have hit it accidently before I closed it earlier.

I called my mom and she answered on the third ring. She was so happy to hear my voice, and I felt guilty for not calling more often. Despite the text messages and pics or videos I sent of Remi, I'd been bad about calling. There was no denying I knew I was still hiding, and I also accepted I needed to stop. She begged me to come home over the next weekend because my brother was having a cookout and they missed Remi—oh, and of course me too. I laughed, promising to see what I could do. I didn't even tell her about Michael. Of course, I wasn't really sure what to tell her as our relationship was still pretty undefined, despite all the time we spent together. He did seem to be acting like there was more to our relationship than I thought there was though.

I placed my phone on the charger and lay down, falling asleep almost instantly. Why my dreams were once again filled with blue eyes, dimples, inky hair, a deep voice, and a perfect smile, I had no idea....

Chapter EIGHTEEN

Reaper

"HEY, REAPER, YOU ABOUT DONE WITH THAT OIL CHANGE, MAN? The dude is back early and was wondering if by chance his bike was ready?" I was wiping my greasy hands on a rag and looked over at Gunny when he spoke as he walked into the shop.

"Yeah, bro, I actually finished it a few minutes ago. I was just cleaning everything up. I'll bring it around for him." I hopped on the customer's bike, starting it up and pulling it out of the garage. Damn, summers were hot here. Sometimes I wondered if I was crazy or if it was really hotter here in northern Iowa than back home in Tennessee.

Shit.

As I parked it up front, the guy came out of the office with a smile. He loved his Indian and he had been bringing it to us for all his maintenance for years, according to the guys. It was a sweet ride, but I was partial to my baby. Nothing could beat a Harley in my opinion. We shook hands and he drove off. *Another satisfied customer,* I thought to myself.

Fuck, it had been a long day. I leaned back, stretching my back. My left leg was a little achy today after all the crouching I'd done. The garage the club owned and ran was one of our "legitimate" businesses, and we were always busy with bikes this time of year. During the winter, we worked on more cars and trucks, but work stayed steady. I was ready to wrap shit up and head over to the Oasis for a cold beer and maybe a game of pool. I headed to the next bay to see if Mason, more commonly called Hollywood now, was ready to go.

"Hey fucker! Get your slow ass moving! I'm ready for a fucking beer. I'm heading to the Oasis. Not in the mood to drink at the club. Gretchen won't quit fucking with me, and I just don't want to deal with her shit." I kicked his feet as he lay under a Camaro on a creeper. He rolled out from under it with his trademark grin in place. He was still such a pretty boy, even covered in grease. I shook my head and laughed when he jumped up and went to the sink to wash his hands.

"Reaper, dude, you are the one who messed up there. She thinks she's special to you and is telling people it's only a matter of time before she's your old lady. You should have never gone back for seconds, man. You went and got her hopes up since you never mess with the same broad twice." He laughed at me as he watched me through the mirror while he washed his hands, arms, and face and dried off.

"Man, fuck you, Hollywood. I was fucking drunk and she crawled into bed with me. I couldn't have told you who the fuck she was that night. Stupid bitch wants to be sneaky, then she deserves to be disappointed. I don't want a fucking old lady, and if I did, it sure as hell wouldn't be a club whore who's fucked every brother in the club at least fifty times each. Nasty bitch. I'm just glad I was in control of my faculties enough to use a condom, or the next thing she'd be saying is she's pregnant." I got on my bike and started it up, waiting for Hollywood. He got on his bike, and we headed downtown to the Oasis.

We pulled up in front of the Oasis and backed our bikes up next to the other three already parked there. Looked like some of the brothers beat us here. Of course Pops was here. Wondered if Mama Jean had made up some of her homemade pretzel bites…. Mama Jean and Pops had owned and been running the Oasis for the last thirty years or more. Pops was one of the original members of the Demented Sons MC, and he was head over heels for Mama. They never had any kids, and she took all of us boys from the club in as her "boys," as she called us. I tried to pretend I hated her calling us boys, but truth be told she was a great person and it felt good to have someone who was like a mother to me. I missed my mother every fucking day, even though it had been almost nine years since she died thanks to a drunk driver. If he hadn't killed himself in the accident that day, I would have put a fucking bullet in his skull. Piece of shit asshole. I fucking hated drunk drivers as much as I hated hadjis, and as much as the Prez hated hard drugs, since his little brother OD'd on meth seven years ago.

I walked in through the old door that had to have been original to the old building. The bar was dim and smelled like smoke, beer, and a little like old musty building, but it was all part of the appeal. The exposed brick walls gave it a warm almost prohibition-era feel. The pool tables in the back were already in use. Smoke and Pops were in the middle of a game on one and some young preppy college pukes on the other. Hollywood and I walked over to the beat-up bar and each pulled up a creaking barstool to wait for the college fucks to finish their game.

Mama Jean ambled up and placed a cold Corona, complete with a lime sticking out the top, in front of me and a Bud Light in front of Hollywood. Yeah, she knew us all well. I grabbed the Corona with a smile for Mama Jean, shoved the lime inside and took a deep drink. I set my beer back down on a little cardboard coaster that had seen better days.

"So how's life treatin' you, Mama?"

She smiled at the drawl I could never really shake and leaned across the bar to give me a rough kiss on the cheek. Mama was a big busted woman who, despite her nearly sixty or so years, still had coal-black hair. I had a sneaking suspicion it was from a bottle, but I sure as shit wasn't busting her out. She had deep lines on her face that spoke of the many years on the back of Pops's bike and the cigarettes that also gave her that raspy voice she still had even though she quit the smokes a few years ago.

"Shitty, thanks for asking, Reaper. My back is killing me and my feet are gonna fall off one of these days. I been after Pops to sell this joint so we can travel more before we're too damn old to do it. It's just this old place has been the only baby we ever had. I would have to find just the right people to take over. It would break my heart to see it close down." She scowled and I laughed at her. I knew she wouldn't let this place go no matter how much shit she talked. She loved it, and she loved us coming in here to see her.

Hollywood started batting his eyes in a crazy-ass imitation of a little kid and begging Mama Jean for some of her pretzels and beer cheese dip. She swatted at his arm and laughed when he told her how beautiful she was and how she made the best beer cheese dip in the world.

"Cripes, kid, you don't need to lay it on so thick. You know Mama will hook you up, but don't think you're getting them for free just 'cause you're good at baffling me with bullshit." She sauntered to the back to get the pretzels, laughing the whole way.

After she brought them out and we sat drinking our beer, I reached over and grabbed one of his pretzels, dipping it in the cheese before he could pull it away.

"Hey, you shit, order your own!" Hollywood dragged the plate over to the side out of my reach. He continued shoving pretzel bites in his face as I smirked and finished my beer. Mama walked up, setting a plate of them in front of me, telling me they were "on the house" for me as she gave a sidelong look at Hollywood and tried to hold back a smile.

"What? That's not fair! Why is he so special?" Hollywood pouted like a two-year-old, and I couldn't help but laugh at him. I held up my empty bottle and asked Mama for another. She set another one in front of me and we enjoyed the rest of our pretzel bites before getting up to grab the pool table the preppy fucks had vacated. I tossed a generous tip on the bar for Mama along with the money for my beer.

As Hollywood racked 'em up for the game, I picked out a pool cue, chalking the tip and blowing off the excess, creating a brief green cloud. The game was close, and he only kicked my ass because I sank the fucking cue ball with the eight ball when I saw a tanned, blonde-haired chick walk in the bar. When she turned around, she looked at me with her big brown eyes, and I resumed breathing. Fuckin' A. Why did I think it was *her*? Why did I care? But I knew the answer. It was the same reason I only fucked women from behind. Because it was easier to pretend they were her if I couldn't see their faces. Because she was still under my skin after three fucking years.

"I gotta run, man." I put the pool stick up and hugged Hollywood, patting the patch on his cut firmly even as he razzed me for being a fucking pussy and leaving because I lost. Motherfucking little shit. "Shut the fuck up, bro, respect your elders. I need a ride to clear my head. You can join me if you want."

"Aww, fuck you, bro, you're only a year older than me. And yeah, I'm game. I'm always up for a little wind therapy. Let me settle up with Mama." He walked over to the bar, taking the opportunity to flirt with blondie and her friend. Typical Hollywood. I looked the other way and walked outside to wait on him, trying to think of anything but how she had felt underneath me... riding me... snuggled up against my cock with her back pressed to my chest and my hand tucked around her tit. Jesus. What the fuck was wrong with me? She was probably married by now and hadn't given me a second damn thought. She probably didn't even remember what the fuck I looked like. She sure as shit deserved better than me anyway.

I told myself these things, but since coming back up here to Iowa, at least once a week, I talked myself out of riding down to her old house to see if by chance she was still there. Besides, what would I say when I knocked on the door? 'Oh, hey. Is there a great looking blonde here with amazing sky blue eyes, legs that go on forever, and the perkiest tits this side of the Appalachians?' Yeah, that would work. They would probably call the cops on me. That would piss Snow off. What I needed to do was quit thinking every fucking blonde I saw was her.

That's what I needed to do.

We raced down the road, handlebar to handlebar, as the sun began to set in the sky behind us. My hair blew in the wind, flipping wildly, as our bikes continued to eat up the miles on the asphalt. There was absolutely nothing like the freedom of the wind whipping against my clothes and plastering my cut to my chest. It was so easy to think and clear my mind. I could breathe. I could outrun my demons. At least temporarily.

As darkness descended, I figured we better turn back. I just rode without any idea of exactly how far we had gone. I pulled over at a gas station to fill up and take a piss. As Hollywood pulled up to the pump opposite me and got off his bike, he looked at me without saying a word before opening the cover to his gas tank and reaching for the gas pump to fill up.

"So, you wanna tell me what's on your mind?" Hollywood asked as he returned the nozzle to the pump. He walked over toward me, slapping me on the back as he stopped next to me and looked me dead in the eyes. This was a man who had been through the depths of hell in Afghanistan with me more times than I could count. The same man who dragged me from the edge of oblivion, rescuing me from myself and bringing me back with him to what I now I considered my family. He knew me better than anyone, and he knew I was a fucking mess right now, but I didn't have the words to tell him what was eating me up inside. I didn't know how to explain that I was fucking obsessed with someone I would never have. Someone I didn't fucking deserve. Someone I couldn't get out of my fucking skull no matter how much I drank, no matter how many whores I fucked, no matter how many miles I rode.

"No." I didn't meet his eyes.

"Well excuse the fuck out of me."

"It's nothing I can talk about right now, bro. Just fucking drop it, okay? I just need to sort through some shit, that's all." I walked off into the shitty little gas station to piss and grab a Gatorade. The cool AC in the store hit me at the same time as the smell of burnt grease assaulted my nostrils. Shit, did they ever change the grease in their shitty-ass fryers? Damn. I took a quick pit stop in the men's room to piss, washed my hands—yeah, thanks, Momma, for drilling hygiene into my damn head—and walked over to the cooler and grabbed a blue Gatorade. No clue what fucking flavor it was and didn't care.

Fuck it.

I placed it on the counter and pulled out some cash, peeling off enough to pay for the bottle and telling the pimple-faced cashier to ring up Hollywood's too and I would get it. After dropping the change in my pocket, I pushed open the door, going back out in the heat and across the lot to the pump with Hollywood on my heels.

I sat on my bike as I cracked open the bottle and began drinking the cold liquid. It felt good running across my tongue and I held the side of the bottle to my forehead. Condensation formed quickly on the cold bottle in this heat; it ran down my face before dripping to the ground.

"You know we have church tomorrow, right? And then the get-together down at the Oasis for Mama Jean's birthday?" He took a long guzzle of his Gatorade. "Man, that shit hits the spot! Thanks, bro."

"Yeah, no problem," I drawled, "and no, I didn't forget. We have that run to Des Moines we need to iron out. About that delivery for the South Dakota chapter around the end of the month, right? That's gonna have to be a quick run, and we're gonna need most of the brothers in on this to flank the truck and drive look out. We don't need to be fucking around down in Des Moines too long. The cops are dicks there and have a grudge against bikers. I don't want them harassing us and snooping through the trucks before we can get them dropped off."

"Snow knows all this, and that's part of what I think he wants to go over tomorrow night. Man, I'm glad Snow did away with this kinda shit, but even the occasional guns for other chapters is starting to make me nervous. Fucking ATF is really tightening shit down. This isn't some biker TV show. It's getting harder to fly under the fucking radar. It's too easy to go legit these days. Don't know why they want to fuck with that shit. Quick money, I guess." He tossed his empty bottle in the trash and sat on his bike. "You ready?"

"Yeah, let's hit the road." I tossed my bottle in the trash as I lifted my kickstand and started my bike. We pulled out together as one, but I purposely roared ahead to fuck with him, and he downshifted to catch up, flipping me off with a smile when he caught up to me again.

By the time we pulled up to the clubhouse, it was well after eleven. We walked in to Metallica blasting on the old jukebox Gunny had picked up at an estate sale. I fucking loved that thing. I saw Butch and Gunny sitting in the corner sectional getting lap dances from two of the club's strippers from our strip club and some other skanky-looking chick I didn't recognize, and briefly wondered where they dragged her up from. They could keep her. One of the prospects, Soap, stood close by watching over the room.

The club whores must be "servicing" because I didn't see them around. The whores were just that, whores. They lived at the clubhouse voluntarily and were free to leave when they wanted. They serviced the brothers when they wanted it and in return they had a place to stay, three hots and a cot, basically, and the protection of the club.

It smelled like cigarette smoke and ass… and what the fuck had I stepped in? Jesus, I was gonna have to get after the prospects to clean this shithole up tomorrow. As I walked past the bar toward the hall leading to small rooms set up for the brothers to crash in if they got too drunk or if it had just been a long night, I felt tits press to my back and saw a set of bright red manicured nails reach around and run across my abs. Fuck. I didn't even have to turn around.

"I'm not in the mood, Gretchen. I told you I don't need your fucking services. Go hit up Hollywood or Butch." I pulled her arms off me, trying to walk away, but she grabbed my hand, placing it on her mound, clearly defined in her tight spandex boy shorts. She rubbed her fake tits on my arm as I jerked my hand from her crotch.

"Come on, Reaper, baby, I've missed you. You know it was good between us. No one has ever made me come like you do… Your cock is the only one that can satisfy me now. The rest of them are just bumbling boys compared to you in bed. Don't make me go to bed alone and unsatisfied, baby." She batted her brown eyes and flipped her bleached-blonde hair over her shoulder.

"Gretchen, there is no 'us.' There will never be an 'us.' I've tried to be nice, but you're too fucking stupid to get it. Fuck. Off. Go blow someone else's cock. I'm not your 'baby' and I'm not interested!" Stupid fucking bitch. Did I have to draw her a fucking picture? I jolted away and stomped off as she stood glaring daggers into my back, I'm sure. I didn't give a flying fuck.

I entered my room, locking the door. This was my sanctuary and my home for the time being. I hung my cut over the back of the old office chair and sat on the bed to remove my boots. I tossed them over by the closet one at a time and hung my head, resting my elbows on my knees. I ran my hands through my hair. It still felt strange to have hair. I had grown it out after getting out of the Army because I was too fucking lazy and drunk to go get a haircut. After I hooked up with the club, I thought I would grow it out long, but I could never hack it getting longer than my hairline at the back of my neck. So I kept the sides and back buzzed short, and the center at the top was long and slicked back. I scratched my short beard. Time to trim this up. It was too fucking hot for a full beard in the summer, so I kept it clipped short and trimmed up, but I rarely shaved clean. Fucking Army made me do that for too long.

I flipped on my iPod, blaring STP's "Creep." Yeah, that was my song. It sucked to feel like you were half the man you used to be. I grabbed my hair on the top of my head in both fists, closing my eyes tight, trying to push the demons back.

As Shinedown's "Cut the Cord" began to play, I ran both hands down my face and rose, padding barefoot to the bathroom to take a shower before bed. I loved that the clubhouse used to be a warehouse with this back area where the executive offices were located, so we each had a bathroom with a shower. One day I'd get a place of my own, but part of me was afraid to be alone. A lot of the reason was fear that the fucking memories would take over and I would start to slip away again. As long as there was enough to keep my mind and body busy, I could mostly forget.

I reached over my shoulders, grabbing my black tee shirt at the back and pulling it over my head. I caught a glimpse of myself in the mirror and trailed a finger over the scar on the left side of my face before glancing at the scars on my torso and left arm that I had covered with tats. Most of them had healed well, and the one on my face was a thin, but jagged, white line now, though it was a constant reminder of all the fucking scars I carried both inside and out. A reminder of how damaged I really was.

Chapter NINETEEN

Stephanie

THE NEXT WEEK WENT BY PRETTY UNEVENTFUL WITH MICHAEL working late on a big project he had at work until Thursday. My phone pinged and I looked at it to see a message from him.

Michael: Hey babe, I just got home and I thought we could go grab dinner

Me: I'm already making something for myself and Remi, but thanks. Maybe tomorrow?

Michael: You got enough for a third?

I really didn't want to spend time with him tonight. I was still a little upset with his behavior Friday night. I didn't answer him right away; instead, I set my phone on the counter as I went to check on Remi in her room. She was busy playing with her Little People and stacking blocks around them. I could only imagine what she was building. Perhaps she pretended it was their castle. I smiled at her and turned back toward the kitchen. As I walked down the hall toward the kitchen, I heard my door open and turned to see Michael pulling a key out of the door. What. The. Ever. Living. Hell?

"You have a key to my apartment?" I asked in shock.

"What? Oh, you gave it to me weeks ago, remember?" Michael sauntered in, flipping his long bangs back out of his face as he tucked the key in his pocket. He reached where I stood frozen to the floor, wrapped his arm around me, and kissed me on the cheek. "You didn't answer my last text, so I thought I would come down to see if everything was okay or if you needed help with anything."

I knew damn well I hadn't given him a key to my apartment. What I wanted to know was how he had gotten a copy of it. I didn't want to ask him and risk starting an argument since Remi was playing nearby. I left it alone, making a mental note to speak to the manager about getting my apartment re-keyed. That pissed me off. He was beginning to make me very uncomfortable. Actually, truth be told, he was starting to scare me a little. He had gotten possessive and strange over the last few weeks. Even though neither of us had actually said we were "boyfriend and girlfriend," it seemed we had just fallen into the assumption.

When I hollered for Remi to come up to the table, she came running to the kitchen, standing by the sink for me to lift her up to wash her hands. She played in the bubbles as I soaped up her hands and rinsed them clean. After several failed attempts at climbing up in her chair, I helped her up into her booster and then grabbed another plate, adding it to the two that I already had on the counter. Michael grabbed a beer from the fridge and sat at the table teasing Remi. The way he made himself at home made me grit my teeth as I dished up the plates.

After we finished eating, I took Remi in to bathe her without saying a word to Michael. I was trying to think of how I was going to break things off with him. Things were just getting too weird. I remained preoccupied as I bathed Remi, soaping up her hair and body as she played with her floating ducks and fish. Once she was rinsed clean, I drained the tub, pulling her out of the tub and wrapping a fluffy towel around her to dry her. As I fluffed her hair, she pushed the towel off her face, hollering "Mommy! Me no see!" with a frown on her face and bottom lip protruding. I gently flipped her lower lip with my finger, telling her not to pout like that or a chicken would poop on her lip. That made her giggle.

"Mommy! You say *poop!*" Remi continued giggling as I dressed her in her jammies.

Our bedtime routine was complete with a bedtime story, tucking my bugga-boo in, and kisses on her precious dimples. Taking a deep breath as I left her room, I quietly closed her door. I slowly walked out to the living room, shuffling my feet on the wood floor, to find Michael flipping through the channels while he sat on my sofa. He didn't even look at me as he said, "You really need cable. There is nothing to watch."

Really? Oh my gosh, he was pissing me off!

"Michael, I think we need to talk." I sat on the edge of the couch and folded my hands in my lap. I was still not sure exactly what to say to him. I pressed my lips together and bit by lower lip. When I glanced up, he was looking at me in question with his brows raised.

"About?"

"About us."

"What about us?" he asked slowly as he muted the TV and turned to face me on the couch.

"Well, we have never really discussed our relationship, and it just seems like things have evolved a little further in your mind than mine. I was thinking that maybe we needed to take a break from each other to think about what this is"—I motioned my hand back and forth between us—"and where it's going." I could feel sweat breaking out on my upper lip, and I saw his jaw clench.

"What the hell are you saying? Is this about that guy Reggie? Are you trying to ditch me so you can hook up with him instead? You sure haven't had a problem holding out on *me*, but maybe you've been getting it from him, so you haven't needed it from me."

"What? What in the heck are you even talking about?" I asked in shock.

He stood and threw the TV remote against the brick wall, shattering it, then turned to me. He stepped closer, pointing his finger in my face and yelling as I leaned back in the couch to get away from his finger.

"I'm tired of you acting like the born-again virgin with me while you laugh and flirt and act like a slut with those guys you work with! You think I haven't seen it? You have Remi, so I know you aren't a damn virgin! I have been patient with you. I have been a *gentleman!*" His eyes took on a demented look and spittle seemed to gather at the corners of his mouth. Then he reached down, grabbed my upper arms in a brutal hold, jerked me off the couch and shook me. I was terrified he was going to hurt me or, worse, wake Remi, bringing his suddenly insane attention to her. My heart was racing and I could feel my entire body shaking. Nausea welled up in me.

"Michael, you need to leave," I said in a tone much more confident than I felt at that moment.

He let go of me, raising his hand like he was going to hit me, and I fought from flinching. No way would I let him see how he had affected me. He took that hand and clenched it in a fist. Then he took some deep breaths, seeming to pull himself together and regain his calm. He flared his nostrils and backed away from me.

"We'll talk about this tomorrow night. You're obviously tired and not thinking clearly. You need to go to bed. I'll come by tomorrow when I get home. I'm sure you'll be thinking with a clearer head by then, Steph." He turned without another word and left my apartment. After I heard the door close on his apartment down the hall, I raced to the door, locking the safety hasp and the deadbolt. Of course, if he had a key, he could open the deadbolt too, but it gave me a false sense of security.

Jesus, I needed to get away from here. I leaned against the door, wracking my brain for what to do. Think, think, think… Yes. I was going home. Mom had been bugging me to come home anyway. I would call in sick tomorrow, and Remi and I would leave after I knew he was gone for work. That way I wouldn't have to risk seeing him. I would call the management office in the morning and get my apartment re-keyed while I was gone too. Shaking, a nervous thought came to me and I raced over to the glass dish on my breakfast bar. The spare key I had kept in there was gone. He had gone through my things! I felt violated and sick as I replaced the glass lid with shaking hands, causing the glass to rattle.

I quietly went into Remi's room, opened the closet, and took my suitcase down from the top shelf. Remi wiggled and rolled over in her sleep. I stood still until I heard her even breaths again. I pulled open drawers as quietly as I could, shoving Remi's clothes in, then moved to the closet and pulled mine off the hangers and stuffed them in the suitcase. I rolled the suitcase to the bathroom, packing toiletries into the pockets until there was no more room. Fuck it, anything I forgot I could buy there. When I caught my reflection in the mirror, I saw a pale, frightened little girl staring back at me. Noticing the bruises already forming on my arms, I began to cry as I leaned over the sink, feeling ill.

What the hell had just happened to my happy, ordered life?

I washed my face with new resolve. I looked at my watch; it was almost 9:00 p.m. If I left immediately, I could make it home by about midnight. I knew I wouldn't sleep anyway. Remi would sleep in the car, I prayed. I could call my mom after I got on the road to tell her we were on our way. Later I would think of something to tell her about what happened to bring me home in the middle of the night.

Chapter TWENTY

Stephanie

WHEN I CALLED MY MOM TO TELL HER WE WERE COMING, SHE was surprised but excited and said she would wait up for us. I told her she could just leave a light on and she didn't need to wait up, but this was my mom we're talking about. It was dark and the highways were mostly deserted this time of night. Remi was asleep in her car seat, and I snuck glimpses of her in the rearview mirror as I drove. I only had about forty miles before I hit Grantsville, then another three miles past town to the turnoff for my parents' farm.

I was getting kind of sleepy and felt my eyes becoming heavy. I passed a bike going the opposite direction and I was alert again. The bike's passing made my thoughts drift to the ride on Colton's bike. Dammit! There he was, sneaking into my head again. Shit. Maybe I needed to see a counselor. Surely this was an unhealthy obsession. On the other hand, I did share a child with the man, whether he knew it or not. I gripped the steering wheel tighter as I remembered holding him close as we rode back to my place that night. I still remembered the cut of his six-pack as my fingers wandered along each indentation of muscle. The man was made for sex, and his body had been a sculpted masterpiece. I could lick his pecs, abs, and arms every day....

Ugh! Stop it, Steph! What the heck is wrong with you?

I saw the lights of G'ville come in to view. The restaurants and stores were all closed this time of night, but the feeling of home and the memories came flooding back. I remembered stopping at the Dairy Queen when my dad would pick me up after school on Fridays; it was the one day he wouldn't make me ride the bus. There was the library and the downtown square where the Corn Festival was held every fall. The Catholic Church at one end of town and the Lutheran Church at the other—as if they had to maintain a separation of the two for fear of contamination. It always made me laugh a little. I hated to admit it, but I missed this small town, despite how I always swore I was going to get as far away from it as I could growing up.

Going through town went quicker than I realized, as I was lost in thought. Before I knew it, I was slowing down at the large oak set back a bit from the road right at the top of a small rise in the road. I turned into the packed gravel driveway and parked under the carport my dad had built years ago off the side of the old square two-story farmhouse. I shut my SUV off and sat listening to Remi's soft breathing and the utter quiet out here. The stars seemed so bright and so much more abundant than in the bright lights of downtown Des Moines.

The floodlights came on at the corner of the house, and I saw my mom come out onto the front porch in her bathrobe. She rushed down the stairs and over to my SUV as I opened my door and got out. She hugged me and then leaned back, holding my shoulders.

"Let me look at you! My baby girl! Do you have any idea how much I've missed you? And where is that beautiful granddaughter of mine?" She looked in the windows for Remi who must have sensed there was a major source of spoiling nearby and woke with her eyes popping wide and her mouth open in surprise. "There she is!" My mother squealed like a teenager and quickly opened the back door, unbuckling Remi and scooping her out of her seat in one smooth motion. Remi's squeals mirrored my mother's as she returned my mom's hugs and clapped her hands in excitement for whatever unknown joys she was thinking of. So much for her going back to sleep.

Thanks, Mom.

"Come on inside. I'll have your brother come out and get your bag. He stayed here waiting for you to arrive, but I think he dozed off watching TV." She bustled up the steps, chattering away to Remi and Remi to her. I saw my younger brother, Sean, standing in the doorway with a big smile on his face.

"No, I'm not sleeping, Mother, but I figured I'd give you your moment with Steph and Remi." He kissed Remi as my mother reached the doorway and snatched her from Mom. "Come see your Uncle Sean. You probably don't even remember me since your momma is so stingy with you." He winked at me, causing me to grin, and then Remi started babbling a hundred miles a minute to him like she knew exactly what she was saying and they had just seen each other yesterday. He patiently listened to her while nodding and responded with "oh really" before explaining he was going to give her back to her grandma so he could go get her things. He jumped down the stairs two at a time to go grab the suitcase from the back of my SUV.

"I'll go put it in your old room. Mom has it waiting for you. Dad is sleeping since he needs to get up early in the morning, but he said he loves you and he'll see you tomorrow." My "little brother," who was a good head taller than me, looked the spitting image of our father with his dark brown, close-cropped hair, hazel eyes, and ready smile. He gave me a big hug and then headed up the stairs with my suitcase.

I glanced into the living room and saw it looked exactly as it did when I left—cozy and inviting but spotless like a room out of a Better Homes & Gardens ad. My mom was always a meticulous housekeeper, even when we were kids and sabotaging her efforts at every turn. I followed my mom's voice down the hall from the entryway into the kitchen where she had Remi sitting at the table helping her eat some homemade banana bread and drinking some milk.

"Mother! You are spoiling her already! She needs to get back to bed." I rolled my eyes as my mother had the nerve to look contrite. I laughed before kissing my mom's cheek and telling her I was going to run up and get ready for bed while she spoiled her granddaughter. She chuckled and told me she would bring her up shortly.

My feet dragged as I tiredly trudged up the stairs and into the third room on the left closest to the bathroom. As a teen, I had raised a fuss arguing that as a girl it was important for me to have the bedroom closest to the bathroom. Looking back, it wasn't much of an argument, so I could only assume my brothers really didn't care which rooms they had. I laughed to myself, shaking my head at the memory.

My room was much as I had left it when I went to college, with the exception of the posters all having been taken down and replaced with some of my mom's amazing cross stitch, which my dad had framed for her. My double canopy bed still had the quilt on it that I made with my grandma the summer after 8th grade. The squares were a little crooked, but every single one was made up of her old clothes and sewed with love by me, with my grandmother's guidance. The walls were now a soft yellow instead of the pale pink of my youth.

I went to my suitcase resting in the corner of the room and pulled out some sweats and a tee to sleep in. After getting changed, I looked around once more.

I shouldn't have stayed away so long. It was good to be home, but I couldn't escape the irony that I ran to the one place I had run from.

Chapter
TWENTY-ONE

Stephanie

WAS WAITING IN LINE AT THE FAREWAY GROCERY STORE AND getting irritated because there was only one cashier. *Dang it, I thought, I knew I should have gone to Hy-Vee.* I also should have grabbed a dang cart, but I didn't expect to grab so much for myself and Remi, and I wanted to make sure Mom and Dad had enough Pull-ups for Remi overnight. She had been doing great with daytime pottying, but the nights were still a challenge. I didn't really feel up to going out tonight, but my older brother, Samuel, had stopped by and asked if Sean and I wanted to join him down at the little town bar, the Oasis. It was Mama Jean's birthday party tonight and nearly everyone showed up there at the end of July for her big birthday bash. They closed off the town square, brought in a band, and had dancing in the street in front of the bar. Mama Jean was like a fixture here in G'ville, and her and Pops were loved by everyone, despite Pops's big bad biker presence. Everyone knew he was a teddy bear at heart.

Speaking of bikers, at least I had a nice view while waiting in line. I was staring at the very nice butt of one of Pops and Mama Jean's "boys," as she fondly called them. The MC had been in the area for as long as I could remember. I think everyone knew they were into some shady shit, but they never bothered anyone in town and they kept the riffraff to a minimum here in G'ville. They were also huge supporters of the Adolescent Drug Prevention and Rehabilitation Center that had been built on the north edge of town my freshman year of college. They ran a big annual fundraiser every fall to raise money for it. In fact, they were one of the biggest contributors to its development and subsequent construction after their president's baby brother overdosed about nine or ten years ago. I didn't really know him well, as he was a several years older than me, but it was a huge scandal back when it happened.

The sexy biker seemed a little more patient than I was as he messed with his phone while waiting to pay for his Gatorade and an energy bar. I felt myself leaning slightly toward him as I inhaled his light, but rich-smelling cologne along with the leather of his vest and a faint smell of oil or engine grease. I desperately wanted to touch his midnight hair to feel if it was crunchy or pliable where it was slicked back up top. And I would have loved to just "accidently" bump that butt to see if it was as firm as it looked. When I realized what I was doing, I felt my face flushed scarlet and I looked around to see if any-one had noticed. Thankfully, the young girl behind me was too busy popping her gum and reading one of the gossip magazines that they place by the checkouts. Sheesh! The last thing I needed to do was go sniffing after some sexy biker. Besides, a guy on a bike was my down-fall once.

Get a grip, Steph! You're a mom, for God's sake. Behave yourself! Self-motivation and castigation were not my strong points, since I rarely listened to myself.

We moved up in line and he reached in his pocket to get cash to pay for his items. As I tried to get my racing heart under control, I attempted to distract myself by looking over at the magazines sitting on the rack and reading the covers. I dipped my head so my hair fell over my face, hiding my flaming cheeks and ears.

"Excuse me? Ma'am? Are you ready to pay for your items?" the cashier said in a sarcastic tone. Little high school brat. I hoped I wasn't that rude when I was her age. She was probably just ticked because the sexy biker ignored all her childish attempts at flirting with him as he paid for his items.

I moved up to slide my debit card and saw the biker walking out the door.

Mmmmmm, straight-up sexy there. Okay, yeah. So what? I could look. Moms weren't dead; we just had responsibilities.

I grabbed my receipt from the snotty cashier and gathered up my bags, trying to hold the Pull-ups under my chin on top of the bags I had over my arm. The little snot could have called for a carry-out for me.

Little wench.

Going out the door, I saw two bikes sitting off to the left and Mr. Sexy-biker was pacing down the sidewalk in front of the store with his phone pressed to his ear. Just as I passed the two bikes, with another biker sitting on one, the Pull-ups fell from under my chin. Great. I knelt down trying to pick them up, but I was having a hard time with the other bags around my arms. I saw a set of tattooed arms grab the pull-ups, and I looked up into a familiar face.

"Erik!" I said with a smile as I recognized one of my oldest brother's, Sam, buddies from high school. I hadn't seen him in years! He was still handsome as ever, with those beautiful blue-green eyes, dark messy hair, and that one slightly crooked tooth that only seemed to give his smile more character.

"Well, well, little Stephie! All grown up. Where the heck have you been hiding, girl?" He gave me a one-armed hug as we stood. "Let me help you get these to your car, babe. Where you parked?" I gestured over to my dad's farm truck that I had taken to town, and we walked over to put the bags in the back. He looked at the Pull-ups as if he had just realized what he was holding.

"Oh! Dang! Grown *and* a mom, huh? Shit, some guy is a lucky dog." He laughed. I didn't bother correcting him that there was no "lucky" guy. "Don't tell Sam I said that. He'd probably still kick my ass. He's always been protective of you, and all the guys on the team were threatened with broken legs if we so much as spoke to you! I doubt that's changed...." He laughed again as he dropped the package over the side of the truck.

"You coming to the birthday bash tonight?" he asked.

"Yeah, Sam is dragging me and Sean with him. I really wanted to spend my weekend chilling out at the farm, but you know how it is. Sam doesn't take no for an answer." I smiled as I prepared to climb in the big Ford F350 dually. Erik gave me a big bear hug, and I noticed the patch on his vest read "Hacker." I poked him on the nametag and asked him what was up with the name.

"Well, I went away to college for computers, but I got bored, dropped out, and joined the Marines for a bit." He shrugged. "I do the computer and security systems now. It's fun and pays good," he said with a crooked grin.

Pecking a quick kiss to his cheek, I thanked him again for his help. "See you tonight!" I said as I climbed in the truck. I closed the door, started the big diesel up, and slowly pulled out of the lot. Dang, this truck was big and I hadn't driven it in years. I should have just moved it and then drove my SUV. Bleh!

I drove the few miles home with the windows down and the radio blaring an old KISS song. For a farmer, my dad sure loved his classic rock. I chuckled at the thought of Dad jamming out to his old rock in the farm truck and out on the tractor.

It really did feel good to be home.

Reaper

I hung up from the call with Snow, telling him we were on our way to the clubhouse, just as Hacker was getting a kiss on the cheek from some homegrown farm chick in short, cutoff, jean shorts. As usual, it made my heart jump at the curly blonde hair and I had to tell myself, *it's not her.* After she drove off, he walked back to the bikes and climbed on his bike, sliding on his shades. I climbed on my own bike and looked over at him with a teasing grin.

"Sooooo... that one of your old hos, Hacker?"

"Fuck no, I wouldn't be alive if it was! That was the little sister of my old buddy from high school. Sam would have strung my fucking ass up if I would have messed with her back then. Besides, she was a year behind us and I was too busy trying to chase college pussy my senior year." He laughed as he started up his bike.

The rumble of our bikes as we pulled out of the lot drew the attention of people walking down the sidewalk of Main Street, and Hacker gave a casual low wave to those who waved to him. This was his stomping ground and people still loved him as a war hero and the high school football star that took the team to state his senior year. I shook my head with a smile. He had grown up here in Grantsville, and Hollywood was from a small town down the road about an hour from here. They had met during football and had been friends ever since, even with Hollywood joining the Army and Hacker going off to college and the Marine Corp. I was a little jealous of their ties to family and community, but I was thankful they pulled me into the fold and for making me feel like I had always been a part of the club family at least.

We pulled up to the clubhouse, parking in line with the rest of the bikes. I grabbed my Gatorade and energy bar from my saddle-bag and headed into the dimly lit interior of the clubhouse. The murmur of voices and the music on the jukebox hit me, wrapping around me like my momma's arms welcoming me home. I sat at the bar and cracked open my Gatorade. Half the bottle was gone in one long swig, and I wiped my mouth with the back of my hand. It had already started to warm from the short ride in the July heat, but it was cold enough to hit the spot.

"Church!" yelled Snow, heading to the old board room that was now our "chapel," or meeting room. I got up from the bar, draining the last of my Gatorade, and setting the empty bottle down in the wet ring on the bar. Cammie, our bartender, grabbed it from the bar and wiped down the counter as I climbed off the barstool. As Snow's old lady, no one fucked with her. Period. But she was a sweetheart and looked out for us sorry fucks. She gave me a sympathetic smile as I stretched my left leg out to work the muscles again. Almost three years, and the fucking thing still sporadically got tight if I sat or rode too long.

I entered the chapel and sat in my seat as the rest of the brothers filed in, some laughing and joking, some quiet, but all patted each other on the back patch as they passed each other to take their seats.

Bang, bang, bang resounded through the room.

Fuck.

Snow pounded his fist on the old, thick wood table to get everyone's attention. Vinny, the VP, sat to Snow's left. The remainder of the officers, Cash and Dice, flanked them.

"All right, all right, come on, boys, we have a lot to discuss before we head over to the Oasis for Mama's birthday," hollered Two-Speed, our Sergeant-at-Arms. This brought a fond smile to Pops's face. Yeah, he loved that woman. The thought of having that someday made me smile for a second before I beat it back, telling myself that shit wasn't for me. Some of the brothers had old ladies, and most of them were devoted and faithful to them. There were a couple who still fucked around with the club whores and, deep down, that pissed me off, but hey, it wasn't my place to tell someone else how to live their fucking lives.

I looked around the table at the men who had been my brothers for over a year since being patched. We were a smaller club, but our chapter was tight. We had four other chapters—one each in Montana and Nebraska and two in Missouri. We were the original, or mother, chapter. The majority of the founding members had been prior service and formed the club to recreate the brotherhood and comradery they experienced in the military. It was no surprise that the club ran its businesses with military precision.

"We are set to meet with the Black Souls MC in two weeks in Des Moines. I don't fucking trust them, but we promised to help with this delivery as a courtesy to our chapter up in Montana. They're hoping this will help create a truce among us. I don't know if I'm in total agreeance, but our Montana prez and I go back a long way, so I agreed. We need to be on our toes during this drop off. We're getting a 20 percent cut of the profits from the deal for our escort and delivery. We'll meet up with the Montana delivery crew in Sioux Falls where we'll take possession of the truck. From there we'll drive straight through to Des Moines. We don't want to draw attention to the truck, so the bikes and our van will keep a fair distance in front and back. No cuts. We want to appear like random weekend warriors in a couple of small groups in front and back of the truck. Three riders in front, then the van, followed by the truck with four riders in back. Dress like you would expect a group of civie riders out riding for the weekend to dress. Reaper and Hollywood, you two will be the advance party to set up as an eye in the sky to make sure the drop off location is secure." Snow continued with the remaining details of who was riding where and looking each member in the eye to try to read them for dissention.

"All right then, any other issues or concerns anyone has to bring to the table?" Snow patiently waited for anyone to voice their bitches or questions. No one spoke up. "Next meeting we will discuss more about the status of our prospects. Soap has been prospecting for almost nine months, and he has been a kick-ass fucking prospect. He's done everything we've asked without complaint, and he's had every member's back at some point or another. Think about your feelings about it and we'll take the vote on patching him in at the next meeting." Everyone nodded and Snow brought an end to the meeting.

We all stood and bullshitted in the room for a few minutes before Hollywood shouted, "Come on, fuckers! What are we waiting for? Let's go party!" Everyone shouted, laughing and hugging with slaps to their back patches as we filed out and climbed on our bikes. The prez started up his bike, followed by the rest of us. We pulled out of the clubhouse lot in formation as a single unit, two by two, with the gate sliding closed by remote sensor as the last man pulled out.

We rode to the downtown square. We were the only vehicles allowed within the barriers blocking the street, and we all backed in one at a time until we were all parked, lined up and down the street on the side where the Oasis was located on. We were early, but the band had already begun to warm up and the sun was beginning to drop lower in the sky. There were several civilians already at the bar as I walked in to greet Mama. She had temporary bartenders for the event and they were already hopping, taking everyone's orders. I grabbed myself a Corona and turned, crushing Mama in a big hug, telling her happy birthday. She kissed my cheek with a big smile and raised her glass to my Corona, to clink them together. I usually kept my drinking to a minimum, but shit, I was looking forward to letting go for a little bit.

Chapter
TWENTY-TWO

Stephanie

WE ARRIVED AFTER THE PARTY WAS IN FULL SWING. EVEN though I hadn't been home forever, the amount of people that showed up for Mama Jean's birthday bash each year never ceased to amaze me. We pushed our way into the bar to order drinks and then fought our way through the crowd to go outside to listen to the band. The night air was sultry and people all around us were laughing, drinking, dancing, and having a great time. The laughter was infectious, and soon my brothers and I were taking turns dancing in the street while one of us watched our drinks at a picnic table. While Sean and I were dancing with some friends, I looked over to see Sam standing in the shadowy outskirts talking to Erik at our table. When they looked my way, I waved. They smiled, returned my wave and resumed what I was sure was their reminiscing of their football exploits. The next time I looked over, I saw my brother shaking hands with the hot-ass biker I had ogled in the grocery store earlier today.

Oh my gawd. Just thinking about my blatant ogling was embarrassing. I prayed he didn't notice me making a fool out of myself today. Sheesh, I had actually *sniffed* him.

I felt someone dance up behind me, placing their hands on my hips, and I looked over my shoulder to see my old friend Chas from high school. With a huge smile, I reached my arms up over my head, tousling his hair in a teasing fashion, and slid lower against his body as I swung my hips from side to side. He was a damn hottie, but I knew there was no harm dancing like this with Chas since he was gay, so it was all in fun. I was so glad I had let Sam talk us into going because I was having a blast! It felt good to let loose for once, knowing Remi was in good hands with my parents and they weren't rushing us home.

As I glanced over to the table again, I noticed the sexy biker glance towards the dance area. I didn't know what came over me, maybe it was the alcohol, but I began to dance for him and him only, using Chas as a mere prop. From here and with him obscured by the shadows, he reminded me of Colton and I felt myself getting worked up as I thought of him dancing with me.

Uh-oh.

The closet wanton was coming out again. That hadn't been such a great idea the last time, no matter how hot the memories were that were burned into my brain. I just couldn't seem to help myself. I felt drawn to him in this insane way. Maybe it was the dark hair and fantastic build. Hell, I always had been a sucker for the tall-dark-and-handsome ones. A bead of sweat ran in a slow trail down my spine as I slid my hands from my hips, up my sides, along the sides of my breasts, to my neck, and into my hair, lifting the heavy curls above my head as I continued to sway and grind.

When I looked over again, he was gone. Damn. I scanned the

crowd but didn't spot his considerable height anywhere. I looked up at Chas, thanking him for the dance and bussing his cheek. I tapped my brother on the shoulder as he danced with a cute, but young-looking, brunette who I vaguely remembered from school. She must have been several years behind me. When he looked up at me, I yelled in his ear that I was going to the bathroom and then to grab another beer. He nodded with a smile, giving me the thumbs up sign. There wasn't much worry of me walking by myself since we had known everyone here forever. I wound my way through the crowd into the bar.

I finally saw Mama Jean alone with Pops and went up to give her my birthday wishes. She hugged me and, to be heard above the crowd, exclaimed in my ear about how much I had grown and asked if I was back in town for good or just to visit. I told her I actually wished I was back for good, but I had a place and a job back in Des Moines. She pulled me off to the side to sit at a tall table, and I noted Pops kept a fond eye on her from where he stood drinking and laughing with another man wearing the same vest as he had on.

"So what are you doing down in the big city anyway, sweetie?"

I explained what I had gone to school for and what I was doing. She got a speculative gleam in her eye when I told her my dreams of running my own restaurant someday. She asked me if I would stop by to see her tomorrow as she had something she wanted to run by me. I asked if I could bring Remi and she said of course, no one would say anything about her being there in the day and they were slow after the lunch rush. I apologized, explaining I really had to pee and I still needed to grab my beer. She hugged me again, and we separated as she went back to Pops where he folded her in his arms, kissing her head while his long, thick, gray beard must have tickled her nose. I saw her laugh and brush it out of her face. I prayed for a lasting love like that someday. My heart was heavy as I somehow doubted I would find it.

I figured I should go pee before I got my beer since I didn't know how long the wait would be to the restroom. I walked around the corner, noticing the long line for the bar bathrooms, so I quickly made my way out to one of the porta-potties set up over by one line of barriers.

I used the facility as quickly as I could, availing myself of the hand sanitizer and flinging the door open to go get another beer and return to my brothers. As I rushed out of the door, I ran smack dab into a solid wall of leather with a patch that read "Reaper" right at my lips. I tried to step back and apologize, but felt my smile melt away and my vision go cloudy as I looked into the same crystal-blue eyes that had haunted my dreams for the last three years. The same eyes I looked into every morning in my little girl's face. I started to shake and my knees buckled underneath me as the music and laughter became muffled and slipped away.

Reaper

I walked over to bring Hacker his beer. He'd asked me to grab him another when I went to get my own. He introduced me to his old high school running buddy, Sam. I liked Sam straight off. He seemed like a cool fucking dude, and I stuck around while Sam and Hacker shot the shit telling tales of their glory days on the football field. I had played football in school as well, but after my experiences over the last several years, it seemed like a lifetime ago.

I was scanning the crowd, trying to account for all of my brothers and, in my mind, ensuring their safety. Of course I noticed the curly blonde dancing almost immediately. *It's not her*, I told myself right off the bat. I wasn't going through that same shit again. Of course, that didn't mean I couldn't admire her long, tan legs topped by some short frayed denim shorts that sat low on her hips and a snug peach-colored tank top that accented the swell of her magnificent tits. Fucking A, I could imagine her bent over while I reached around and squeezed those tits in my hands as I pounded the shit out of her. *Yeah, she would work as a fill-in for my memories tonight*, I thought with a slow predatory smile.

Blondie looked like the chick Hacker was talking to earlier today at Fareway, but I wasn't sure. Wished I had gotten a better look at her. Hmmmm, if so, maybe he could give me the hook-up.

That's when her dickhead boyfriend came grinding up on her. Figures someone like her would be with a pretty boy douche like that. I saw her look over her shoulder at him, grinding and swaying against him. Crazy thing was, after she looked my way, I could have sworn she was dancing for me.

Jesus. What. The. Fuck. I felt my cock jump in my jeans. Little fucking tease.

I watched as she ran her hands along her body in a sensual dance. She held her hair up over her head, raising those glorious tits up like an offering. Damn, she reminded me of my angel, but I knew it was an illusion of the flashing colored lights from the stage and the same trick my eyes always played on me. Jesus, I couldn't take it any-more. Trying to discreetly adjust my wayward cock, I turned around and walked off to find someone who could help with the ache in my balls since it wasn't going to be her. The thought of that preppy puke with his hands, mouth, and cock on her tonight just plain pissed me the fuck off.

What was up with that? I shook my head.

Hollywood intercepted my prowl around the crowd, pestering me to play a game of darts with him. Pops and Jean had a row of them set up along the side of the bar for the night, and we headed over to wait for one to open. I figured *fuck it*, it was as good a distrac-tion as any from the sex kitten on the dance floor. There was plenty of time to find a willing chick for the night. We stood by a tall table, drinking our beer and talking about a lot of nothing.

Damn, were any of these fuckers gonna finish their games?

"Bro, I gotta piss. If one of them finishes, grab the fucking board. I'll be back in a few, unless I find me some warm legs to wear as a belt." I laughed as I headed over to the porta-johns along the barrier between the bar and the building across the street. After pissing, I walked out of my john and turned to head back to Hollywood, but the door on the john next to me flew open and a sweet-smelling blonde chick slammed into me, smashing her face into my cut. I steadied her by the arms as she pulled back, and I realized it was Sex Kitten. As her smiling gaze raised to mine, her apology died on her lips and I saw her face go white, her smile fade, and those eyes that had kept me going through mortar blasts, sniper missions, and the IED went wide and unfocused before her knees buckled.

I grabbed the body that was etched in my mind and lived under my skin and scooped her up, carrying her over to an empty table off to the side of the street. My heart felt like it was going to explode as one beat melded to the next in a rapid-fire succession. I was finding it hard to breathe as I smoothed her hair back from her brow, flicking the few strands back that were plastered to her forehead with sweat. My fucking hands shook for Christ's sake. I didn't know what the fuck I had done in this shitty world, for whatever God existed, to drop this angel in my lap... almost literally... but I couldn't help the thoughts that raced through my head swearing to never let her go again.

Chapter
TWENTY-THREE

Stephanie

A S I FELT MYSELF REGAIN CONSCIOUSNESS, THE MUSIC, LAUGHTER, and blended voices pounded in my ears. I felt myself cradled next to a firm body with my face pressed against leather. And was that a...? Oh God, please tell me that wasn't a hard penis under my ass. I thought I might die. Then the visual of those eyes flashed back through my mind. I raised my gaze to skim up the leather vest, up the thick column of his neck, over the scruff of a beard, firm lips, and a noble chiseled nose, finally resting on those blue, blue eyes. It couldn't be. I raised my hand to cup his cheek.

"Colton?"

Those lips curved into a half smile and the gravity of the situation came crashing down on me. I scrambled out of his lap to a standing position. My breath coming in ragged gasps, I held my hands to my chest, trying to gain some semblance of order to my heartbeat and respirations. Oh my God. Oh my God! *Oh my God!*

"Colton! Oh God, it *is* you! But how? Here? How? Why are you…?" I couldn't get my brain and mouth to communicate to form a complete sentence as my brain ran in circles.

Holy shit.

Oh my God.

How the hell did I even begin to explain? I tried again to regain my composure, but that was easier said than done.

"Don't. Not yet," he groaned as he stood, framing my face with his strong, calloused hands and lowered his lips to mine in a wild and frantic kiss. I placed my hands over his with the intent to break his hold on me and end the kiss, but my body betrayed me as I felt my breasts press into his chest and my mouth open in subservience to the thrash of his tongue. I heard a moan that I soon realized came from my unrestrained body as my hands moved to his face. I felt the faint ridge of a scar on his left cheek, and I briefly wondered what had happened before all thought escaped me. As I leaned my body further into his, I also felt the hard ridge in his pants pressing against my pubic bone, and I was now certain of what I was feeling. A tingling, pulse began between my legs as he pressed his hardened member against me firmly and our kiss deepened as his mouth ravaged mine in a desperate plea for more.

We broke free, gasping for breath, his forehead braced against mine as we looked deeply into each other's eyes. My lips were swollen from the bruising kiss, but I wanted him to kiss me again. With every breath I took, I felt my nipples raise and graze against his chest, driving me insane. He reached down, grabbing my ass. I wrapped my legs around his waist as he walked around the back of the bar, entering through the back screen door and taking the first left after the screen slammed behind us. He kicked a door shut and reached back with one hand, turning the lock. He allowed me to slide down his body, catching on the tip of his cock encased in his jeans. He closed his eyes briefly and captured my mouth with his again as we tore at each other's clothes. I was vaguely aware of being in an office of sorts, lit by a small lamp on the desk, spreading a golden glow across the room and casting the corners of the small room in shadow.

Within seconds, we were stripped naked and I felt the firm contours of his body melding perfectly with my soft curves. He laid me down on a small cot with a thick, soft blanket spread neatly over it and my head met the pillow. He ran his gaze reverently over my body, and I couldn't help covering my breasts with one arm and my mound with the other in what now seemed misplaced modesty. I knew my body wasn't as taught or lithe as it was three years ago, and even though they were barely noticeable, my stretch marks made me feel ugly.

"No. Don't ever hide your body from me." He touched my face gently and leaned over to nip, kiss, and suck along my neck and shoulder. His short beard scrapped my sensitive skin in an incredibly erotic way, causing me to break out in goose bumps. I felt him reach over to the floor, rustling around for something. A plastic wrapper crinkled as he briefly took his lips from my skin. I watched as he raised up to roll the condom over his thick, pulsing cock. Then he looked in my eyes with an unspoken question as he waited for my answer, poised at the edge of my slick entrance.

"Yes. Jesus, Colton, yes."

"Thank fuck, because I honestly don't know if I could hold myself back from you." He briefly slid the tip back and forth in my slickness before plunging into my core, filling me to the point where it bordered on pain as he stretched me to accommodate his girth. My head tipped back as I closed my eyes and hissed in a deep breath through clenched teeth. He held himself still, and I opened my eyes to see his head bowed, his eyes closed, and his muscles straining for control. His eyes opened and met mine.

"Oh my God, baby, you are so tight. Am I hurting you?" I shook my head no, breathing erratically. "I don't know if I can hold off for long. I've lived out this moment for the last three years." His voice rasped with emotion.

"Then don't hold back. You won't break me," I whispered.

With a pained expression and a rushed exhalation, he stroked in and out of my wet sheath in a frenzy of movement. I could feel the familiar tingle and throbbing of my climax building. I dug my nails into his shoulders and wrapped my legs tightly around his as I grasped at him in an attempt to ground myself before my body shattered and flew away in a million pieces. I floated aimlessly above the earth before I gathered back together underneath him.

He stroked deep into me a few more times before I felt him swell even more. He finally slammed deep into me as he roared. "Yessssssss!"

Then he collapsed down on me before he slid his weight to the side, pulling off the condom and tossing it in the trash. He pulled me over so I lay with my cheek against his chest and one arm and one leg lying across his body while the other was tucked up next to his warmth. We both were breathing deeply, and I could hear his heart pounding under my ear as I listened to his breath become even and slow as we dozed off in a tangle of sweat-slicked limbs.

I awoke with a start a few minutes later, and his arm reflexively tightened around me, but I could tell by his breathing he still slept. Oh my God, what had I done? I hadn't seen this man in three years and I just had sex with him in a bar office. It was confirmed. This man made me into the biggest slut that walked. He sucked the brains God gave me right out of my dang head! I felt mortified at my behavior as I carefully extricated myself from his limbs and climbed off the cot, searching for my clothes that were scattered across the floor. I found my bra dangling from the corner of a shelf.

Nice.

I quickly dressed and took a minute to study him as he lay

sleeping. He looked so peaceful and sweet with his dark, thick lashes fanned across his cheeks. His body that of a sculpted Adonis, he was truly a beautiful man. Just looking at him made me want to crawl right alongside him again and plaster my soft curves against his rock-hard contours.

Shit, shit, shit.

I just stripped down and screwed him without even telling him about his daughter. Dropping my head in shame, I covered my face with my hands. I hadn't had sex since the last time with him three years ago, but it was like all my inhibitions flew out the window when our bodies were close. My sense of control completely dissipated when he came close to my airspace.

Biting my lower lip, I stood there trying to think. I needed to get away from here so I could clear my head. There was so much to tell him, but I had to gather my thoughts first. At least I knew how to get a hold of him. I fumbled through his jeans and found his phone. When I swiped his screen open, I almost passed out. My heart raced and my lungs struggled to fill with air. Staring back at me was the picture I had taken on his phone on our first night together. It was a different phone, so not only had he saved it from one phone to another, but he intentionally saved us as his home screen.

My mind didn't know what to do with this unexpected knowledge. My brain felt like it was a reeling blob of mush. Taking a deep breath, I called my phone from his, silencing my phone before the ringing could wake him. I then sent him a text as I set his phone back on his jeans and quietly unlocked and opened the door, closing it with a soft click.

Me: Colton. This is my number. We need to talk, but I need some time to gather my thoughts. I'll be in touch soon - Steph

Reaper

I woke stiff and cold as I realized she was gone. I sat up quickly, throwing my feet to the floor and looking around in confusion. Where the hell did she go?

When I realized her clothes were gone, I frantically started to dress, stuffing my phone in my pocket and pulling on my boots. I raced out the door with the side zippers of my boots still unzipped, my fly still open, and my cut dangling from my fist. I slammed out the back door. No sign of her. I went back in and through the hall up into the bar. The crowd had started to dwindle and I caught Hollywood's eye. He raised his eyebrows at me, taking in my disheveled appearance with a grin. When I saw no sign of her, I went back to the office to dress properly.

The pieces started to fall into place as I realized my angel, the blonde at the grocery store Hacker helped out and the sex kitten on the dance floor *were* actually one and the same. That meant the guy, Sam, he introduced me to was her brother, because I remembered him saying she was the little sister of his former teammate. My angel. Jesus, Hacker knew her this whole time! I pulled out my phone to call Hacker when I saw I had a text message.

Unknown number: Colton. This is my number. We need to talk, but I need some time to gather my thoughts. I'll be in touch soon. Steph.

I fell back into the office chair, my phone dropping to the floor with a thump when it slipped from my slack fingers. What the fucking hell? How did she just get up and leave me? Put aside the mind-blowing sex, there was the matter of our insane history. Did it not mean a damn thing to her? Fuck. I needed to talk to her.

Then a sick feeling settled in my stomach as I remembered the guy she was dancing with. Fucking hell. She was with someone else, just like I fucking told myself she would be for the last three motherfucking years. It shouldn't be a surprise to me. There shouldn't be this vicious ache in my chest. I buried my head in my hands, clenching my hair as I fought the burn behind my eyelids.

Fuck. Just fuck.

Chapter
TWENTY-FOUR

Stephanie

FELT LIKE A TOTAL PIECE OF SHIT FOR THE WAY I RAN OUT ON HIM. As I lay in bed, I tried to come up with a scenario that worked out without him hating me. I had his child and she was over two years old. He had missed two years of her life. In what world was that okay? In my defense, how was I supposed to find him when I had so very little to go on? I had his first name and very little else. Even now.

I continued to lay there staring at the ceiling, thinking about the end of the night…

My brothers looked at me like I lost my mind when I came rushing up to them begging for them to take me home. Sam was still sitting with Erik, who jumped up, asking if someone had fucked with me, and threatening to "take care of whoever it was."

"No!" I burst out in horror. Oh dear God, I couldn't have him going after one of his brothers because he thought he had done something. Jesus, God in heaven. "No, I just started really missing Remi. I haven't been away from her like this before, and it got me worked up." I tried to appear calmer and together. With the skeptical look I received from Erik, I wasn't sure how well I pulled it off.

My brothers didn't question me further, and we drove home in silence. As I walked toward the house, Sam called out to me.

"Steph, if you need to talk, you know you can call me, right?" I smiled and nodded.

"Of course, I do. Thank you for everything." I gave a small wave and slowly walked up the stairs and through the front door. I paused in the entryway, taking in the silence of the old house before heading up the stairs, avoiding the creaky ones as well as I did when I was a teen sneaking in late. Remi must be with my mom because she wasn't in my room. I peeked in my brother's old room, seeing my dad lying in the bed softly snoring. I smiled as I gently closed the door and went to my room.

So I lay there, staring at the ceiling with no answers to my dilemma. Maybe I should ask my mom.

No.

She would only worry and tell me I just needed to *tell* him. Well, that I already knew. Maybe I would just head back to Des Moines tomorrow after I met with Mama Jean to see what she needed help with. It would give me time and space to think, but I knew I couldn't put it off too long.

I tossed and turned, trying desperately to go to sleep. I wished I could have showered after I got home, but I was afraid of waking everyone. I smelled him all over me. It was like he was wrapped around me, and every time I moved, I smelled a faint whiff of his cologne or his leather. Or sex. Yeah, I smelled a *lot* like sex. I needed to shower first thing in the morning before I ran into one of my parents. They may not notice, but that would still be awkward.

I punched my pillow in an attempt to make it more comfortable.

No good. I flipped it over, looking for the cool spot. Nope. I tried counting sheep. Who the hell came up with that crappy idea? It didn't work for shit! Ugh! I lay wide awake most of the night.

I must have dozed off somewhere around dawn because I vaguely remembered hearing my dad get up to start his day. All I knew for sure was that my dreams were haunted as I fitfully slept with the recent memory of Colton's touch, kiss, and the feel of his body against mine.

Chapter
TWENTY-FIVE

Reaper

F
IRST THING IN THE MORNING, I KNOCKED ON HACKER'S DOOR. I
waited as long as I could, barely sleeping all night. I needed to ask
him how to find her. Yeah, I could call her, but I had a feeling she
wouldn't answer her fucking phone; besides, this was something I
needed to talk to her about face to face. The last thing I wanted to do
was cause trouble with her guy by calling her or showing up on her
doorstep, but I needed to see her. Anyway, how good could things be
between them if she could be with me like that last night?

I pounded on the door again when he didn't answer. I stood listening for his steps or for any sign of life behind his door.

"For fuck's sake! I'm coming. Shit! There better be a motherfucking fire." I heard him mumble the last part, along with thumping

and rustling behind the door, before the door flew open and Hacker glared at me with bloodshot eyes, dressed only in his boxers.

"What the fuck, man? It's like 7:00 a.m., bro!"

"Hacker, I need to talk to you. It's important."

He leaned against the doorframe, arms crossed and eyebrows raised. "At seven in the morning? Shit. You're killing me."

"It's about Stephanie. I need to talk to her. I need to know where I can find her." I appealed to him, pleading with my eyes. Jesus, I felt like a fucking lunatic. No, I felt like I was beginning to unravel and it was bullshit.

The words had no sooner left my mouth and he rushed me, grabbing me by the front of my cut and slamming my ass against the wall across from his doorway. His face in a vicious snarl, he slammed me against the wall again before I could even think to defend myself.

"It was you! You motherfucker, I should gut you now. What the fuck did you do to her? I knew something had happened!" He looked like he would strangle me any second, and I grabbed his wrists, shoving him away from me, which was no easy feat since the fucker was my size and still as fit as he was during football and in the Marine Corps.

"Get your fucking hands off me! I didn't fucking do anything to her she didn't want." His fist connected with my jaw before I even saw it coming. Jesus H. Christ! I punched him in the gut on reflex, and as he doubled over, I pushed my hair back out of my face and stepped back.

"Goddamn, man, I don't want to fight with you. I just need to talk to her," I said in defeat.

He remained bent over with his hands on his knees, breathing deep, head bowed. He lifted his head to look at me.

"Just leave her alone, Reaper. She's like my little sister. She has a kid, man. They don't need your kind of shit baggage. Just… just stay away from her."

A kid? What? What the fuck was this stupid motherfucker talking about? My head shook back and forth in denial. She didn't have a kid. He was fucking crazy. Unless that was what she wanted to talk to me about? Shit, she was married and had a kid. She wanted to gather her thoughts to tell me she was attracted to me sexually, but what we did was a horrible mistake because she was married with a baby. Fuck me. I leaned against the wall, sliding down until I sat with my arms propped on my knees and my hands dangling loose.

All these years of holding her in my mind, staring at that damn picture, praying I might find her again… They say be careful what you wish for. Now I wished I had never seen her again. At least then, I could have continued to feel like there was still hope. I felt like the blackness in my soul, which I fought so hard to keep at bay, was creeping in to swallow me.

Stephanie

When I rolled out of bed, my bleary eyes could barely focus. Stumbling to the bathroom, I climbed in before the water was even hot. After a cursory wash, I got out of the shower and went back to my room to change. My phone lit up as I entered the room. Damn, since going to bed last night, I had missed five calls and had seven text messages. Shit. I wasn't ready to talk to him yet. But as I opened the messages, I saw they were from Michael. Crap. That was worse.

Michael: Where are you?
Michael: Call me
Michael: Call me. Please
Michael: Steph I'm worried about you. Call me
Michael: Call me. Now
Michael: I have been trying to see you all weekend. You weren't

home last night or this morning. I tried to give you some time but this is getting ridiculous.

Michael: Steph. Answer your god damn phone!

The last message was seven minutes ago. I checked and saw that all the missed calls were from him as well. *Yeah, asshole, and I bet you had a big surprise when you tried to get into my apartment and the lock was changed, huh?* God, I loved my management company. I tossed my phone on the bed, having no intention of answering him.

I dressed quickly and threw my hair up in a messy bun to head downstairs, following the smell of bacon cooking to the kitchen. Warm sunlight flowed in through the lace curtains at the kitchen windows. My mom was at the stove cooking, and Remi sat quietly at the table coloring with a fat purple crayon while she patiently waited for her breakfast. She looked up as she realized I stood in the doorway. Her face lit up and she scrambled down from the chair, running to me and wrapping her little arms around my legs and squeezing.

"Mommy! Wemi miss you so, so much!" she exclaimed. I scooped her up, sharing a good morning kiss with her and repeatedly kissing her dimples, which were a straight punch to the gut for me after last night. I squeezed her in a great big hug. "Mommy! You squish Wemi!" She giggled. I laughed with her as I placed her back in her chair at the table where she happily resumed coloring after I sat next to her. I smiled and shook my head a how cute she was even when she struggled with her R's. I glanced over to my mom and asked if she needed any help with anything. She said no thank you, smiled, and went back to flipping bacon and stirring eggs.

"I need to head to town this afternoon. I'm going to take Remi and get some I-C-E C-R-E-A-M after I run a couple of errands." I spelled out the ice cream part or I would never get her to eat her breakfast.

My mom laughed and asked if I wanted company. She seemed a little disappointed when I told her I needed to take care of some things alone. I assured her I would be back afterward and I would be here at least through tomorrow.

"At least until tomorrow?" my mom asked with confusion. "Don't you have to work on Monday?"

"Yes, but I may need to call in." I didn't want to get into why I was reluctant to head home. She started to question me more, but I held up my hand. "Please, Mom, it's a long story that I don't want to get into right now." She pressed her lips together in annoyance, but didn't say anymore. I didn't let myself be fooled into thinking that meant she had dropped the subject. After all, I had known this woman my whole life.

We took Remi out to gather eggs and she laughed and giggled and tried to catch the chickens, but they ran circles around her. As we were leaving the chicken coop, I saw Sam pull up in the driveway and get out of his truck. He had a troubled expression on his face as he leaned against his truck with his arms crossed. Of my two brothers, Sam and I looked the most alike. We had both inherited our mother's blonde hair, though his had darkened with age and was now more honey colored than blond, and her clear blue eyes. The irritation and concern I saw in his eyes had me on edge, and I wondered about the reason for his visit this morning. Once we walked closer to the house, he stood up, dropping his arms. He hugged our mom and kissed Remi, promising her he would be in to see her soon. Then he turned to me, intercepting me by catching me by my arm and quietly stating, "We need to talk."

"Okayyyyy... what about? Is everything okay with you?" I wasn't sure where this was leading, but I didn't think I was going to like it. I followed him as he began to walk down the driveway and cut across the front yard to sit on the bench under the big oak tree. I sat down next to him, and he turned to me.

"You wanna tell me what happened with you and Reaper last night?" he said without preamble.

His use of Colton's road name threw me for a second. Oooh, oh okay, that's where this was going. Shit. Not a conversation I wanted to have with my older, very protective brother. And how the hell did he know Colton? I stood up, crossing my arms, turning away from him so I didn't have to look into his eyes, so like mine.

"Nothing happened, Sam. I don't know what you're talking about." I tried for calm nonchalance, but I knew I failed miserably when he continued.

"Really. Then why the hell was he asking Erik how to find you this morning? How would he know who you are, Steph, if nothing happened? Even though he's quiet as hell and a little pensive, he has always seemed like a pretty decent guy any time I've seen him in town. And I really liked him when Erik officially introduced us last night, but looks can be deceiving and I need to know if I read him wrong. Was he the one who put those bruises on your arms you tried to cover with makeup last night? Tell me what's going on. Do you know him, Steph, or not?" His tone was getting sharper and I could sense his frustration.

"No! God no! He didn't do that to me! I swear!" I started to sob and I covered my face with my hands. I turned abruptly toward him and, shoulders sagging, told him about Michael and how he had started out such a sweet, great guy but had steadily been progressing to a possessive psycho. Tears continued to run down my face as I stared down at my shoes.

Sam gathered me in a big hug. "I'm going to fucking kill him, Steph," he ground out in a low voice. "And Reaper? Where does he fit in this? And don't give me that crap about nothing happened. I don't fucking buy it. A man doesn't want to find a woman, with the desperation Erik described, if there is nothing between them."

I raised tear-filled eyes to his and whispered in a tortured voice, "He's Remi's father, but he doesn't know it…"

"*Holy Shit!* Are you fucking kidding me? That little girl is over *two* years old! And you never told him? How could you do that to her? And how in the hell could you keep a father from his own daughter, Steph?" He looked at me with an incredulous expression, like he didn't know who I was anymore. I pulled away, turning from him.

"It wasn't like that," I answered. Then I proceeded to tell him the whole sordid story, minus the details of our night together. There were some things a brother did *not* need to hear.

"Fuck, Steph. He's lived here for a while. How have you never seen him?" He ran his hands through his hair in frustration. "Jesus, you have to tell him. If you don't, I will. It's not fair to either of them."

"You think I don't know that? You think I didn't pray every day that things had been different and I could have told him? And if you remember correctly, I haven't been home much in the last couple of years," I cried out. "I just don't know what to say to him now!"

"Just tell him! He'll understand." He stood up and walked toward me, giving me another hug. "I love you, little sis, but you have to do this sooner than later."

Chapter TWENTY-SIX

Reaper

LEFT THE CLUBHOUSE ALONE AND WENT FOR A RIDE. I NEEDED some wind therapy. The sorry thing was, even the wind whipping past me as I flew down the highway did little to still or calm my crazy fucking mind. My thoughts were all over the place. I felt angry. I felt betrayed for some stupid goddamn reason. I felt hopeless... and for the first time in a long while, I felt like giving up.

As I approached a sharp curve in the road, it crossed my mind to just keep going straight. At the last minute, I slowed, leaning into the curve and accelerating on the throttle as I continued through the curve. I took the next turn and followed the road as it curved again, past the lake, pulling into a boat loading and unloading area.

I hit the kill switch and put my kickstand down as I sat on my bike, leaning over my handlebars and staring out at the sun reflecting and glittering on the water. I took a deep breath. I didn't know what to fucking do with myself...

I leaned against a crumbling wall, gunfire and explosions coming from all around us. Mason sat next to me and took a quick glance through a hole in the wall. There was no sign of our extraction team yet. We had taken out our target and had made it to the rendezvous spot. We looked at each other and leaned our heads back against the shitty wall again.

I pulled my phone out. I didn't have service, of course, but I brought it with me and kept it charged just so I could look at the picture of her smile. I told myself, when I got home, I would find her no matter what it took.

I would tell her that it may sound crazy, but she had kept me sane while I was gone and I was pretty sure I loved her. In my mind, she would hug me, telling me she loved me too and she had been waiting for me. I kissed the screen, turning the phone off and tucking it back into my IBA. I looked at Mason and he shook his head and smiled as we heard the sound of the Blackhawk getting closer. Mason and I raced up to the top of the hill, and I sent up a thank you to my angel for getting me through again.

I shook my head, clearing out the memory that had taken over and felt so incredibly real. I needed to just fucking move on. I needed to accept that she wasn't my damn guardian angel anymore and the dream that had kept me sane had come to an end.

I had a job coming up that required me to have my fucking head screwed on straight if I didn't want to let my brothers down. It was time to get all my fucking shit in one sack and deal. Hell, I didn't know how much more crap I could handle on my plate, but I had dealt with worse before and came out just fucking fine.

Fucking A.

I leaned back, starting up my bike again and heading back toward town. I needed a fucking beer.

Shit.

The closer I got toward town, the clearer my head was beginning to feel. Fuck her, I didn't need her shit in my life if she was going to fuck around on her guy with me anyway. She obviously wasn't the girl my imagination built her ass up to be. Reality never lived up to fantasy.

Before I knew it, I was pulling up to the Oasis. Backing my bike up to the curb, I hit the kill switch, and flipped down the kick-stand. After getting off my bike, I slid my shades off and stepped into the dim interior. I walked up to the bar and Mama handed me my Corona then asked me who fucking kicked my puppy. A self-depreci-ating laugh escaped me.

"Let's just say I've come to some realizations and life isn't always what you think it's gonna be." I took my beer to a booth in the back where I could sit in the shadows and not have anyone bother me.

I had been nursing my beer for a while when I heard the door open and someone come in and a child squealed in laughter. It was a melodious sound and it made me smile as I took another drink of my beer, realizing it had begun to grow warm. I drew lines in the condensation as I absently listened to the murmur of voices from up front. Suddenly, there were quick little footsteps running toward me, and a little kid scrambled up into the other side of my booth. As she placed her hands flat on the table, she peered at me, giving me a big dimpled grin and said "Hi!" just as I heard a familiar woman's voice coming closer.

"Remi, you cannot just run off! And you can't just hop up and bother people... I'm so sorry, sirrrrr...." Her voice trailed off, and I looked up to see Stephanie going white as a sheet for the second time in two days as she stood stock-still by the table. My heart raced just seeing her. It made me wish the traitorous chunk of muscle in my chest was still dead inside.

I didn't know what finally clued me in, but I looked from her to the little girl who was obviously around two years old or so. I took in the dimples, the ice-blue eyes, the dark head of hair—though with curls just like her mother—and I tried to do the math.

No. No fucking way. I flashed my eyes to Steph who was trying to pick up the little girl she called Remi, but the little one was having none of it. I reached out, placing my hand on her arm.

"Leave her. Sit." My tone left no room for argument. My nostrils flared. My breathing sped up. She slid into the booth next to the little girl, twisting her hands on the tabletop and staring at them so she didn't have to meet my eyes.

"Is she…?" I couldn't say it. The words got stuck in my throat, and I couldn't swallow.

"Yes," I barely heard her whisper.

I was in shock. This bitch had my baby? And kept her from me to have some other asshole raise her? I clenched my jaw as I struggled to maintain my cool so as not to frighten the little sweetheart sitting at the table organizing the ketchup, salt, and pepper containers.

On that night so many years ago, I had told her I had no family I knew of and I wished it were different. I didn't discuss a lot about myself, but I remembered that being mentioned. How could she think it was okay to keep her from me, knowing I had no one? I wanted to throttle her, and I didn't hurt women. Never did I hurt women. I felt like I had just been dealt the deepest betrayal anyone could have given me. I had made her into an untouchable guardian angel these past few years, and I now realized how incredibly foolish that unrealistic ideal had been.

As I stood, I looked her dead in the eye. I felt indescribable anger toward her, and I was having a hard time reining in my rage. I wanted to scoop the little girl—*my* little girl—up and run off with her, but I knew I was in no state of mind to be around her.

"So you had my baby, didn't even try to find me, and then just replaced me in her life?" It came out an angry whisper. I could only shake my head in disbelief. Ignoring the look of shocked incredulity on her face, I walked around her and stormed out the door. She had no right to look shocked. No right at all. I also ignored her franticly calling my name when she burst out the door of the bar as I revved my engine to drown out her voice and rode off like a bat out of hell down the street and out of town.

I was the one who needed to gather my thoughts now. And when I was done, she and I were going to sit down and I was going to get some fucking answers.

I found myself back at the boat landing. I was lying on the end of the ancient small dock that jutted out into the lake, staring at the pale blue sky with the clouds drifting slowly past. The color reminded me of the sheets we wrinkled and scattered off the bed that night so long ago. I imagined them tucked around her full tits in the pic I still carried with me on my phone's memory card. What a pathetic piece of shit I was. No matter what I did, I couldn't fucking reconcile the angel of my memories with the woman she really was, and it was fucking killing me. I slammed both fists down to the dock beside me, feeling the ancient boards rattle and shake with the force of the connection.

I sat up, leaning my head on my crossed arms as they rested on my knees, and closed my eyes, focusing on the sound of the birds, the water lapping gently against the pilings of the dock and the shore, and my breath as it entered and exited my body. It felt like I had been transported back to my time in the hospital—feeling dead and disillusioned inside, but knowing I was alive by the sounds around me.

After my mind calmed, I felt a little guilty for the way I treated her. I was a real dick. Sometimes I just couldn't control my anger, despite working so fucking hard at holding that part of my wicked inner demons at bay. It was as if the dam didn't just burst, it fucking exploded.

I pictured the little girl... *my* little girl. Damn, I just couldn't wrap my head around the fact that I was a father. She had my dark hair and the same fucking dimples that chicks seemed to go apeshit over, not that I had ever used that to my advantage.

Yeah, whatever.

Her eyes were the same blue as mine, not pale and soft like her mother's, but clear and vibrant, with the darker blue flecks I saw every time I looked in the mirror. More than those few things, I couldn't recall because I began seeing red soon after she had climbed up to the table with me and things clicked into place.

One thing I knew for a certainty was I wanted to have a relationship with her. Tough shit if her mother had replaced me in her life. My child was going to know me. I would never have her growing up like I had, not knowing her father. I needed to talk to Stephanie now that I had calmed the fuck down and pulled my stupid hot head out of my ass… sort of.

I removed my phone from my back pocket and pulled up the message she sent me. I shot off a reply and stuck it back in my pocket after I received her brief response.

> **Me: We need to talk. Tonight. Meet me at the Oasis. Dress for a ride.**
>
> **Stephanie: I'll see what I can do.**

I needed to get back to the clubhouse and talk to Hacker. We needed to fix that shit from this morning. We were brothers, and I couldn't have shit like that hanging over us and coming between us. He needed to know that the "kid" Steph had was *mine*. My kid. My *daughter*. I also needed him to look into what she had been up to over the last three years. I wanted to know who the preppy fuck she was with was and everything about him. I wanted to know the first time he took a shit and who changed it. I wanted to know what he ate for breakfast. I wanted to know what his throat felt like as it was being squeezed by my bare hands because he had touched her. I wanted to know how and where she had been raising my child.

My daughter.

Fuck. I had a daughter.

I was a fucking father.

Jesus, help me.

Stephanie… My Stephanie. I finally had her name, and yet she wasn't mine and never would be. She had moved on just like I knew and hoped she would. I was never meant for her. I was damaged and evil. My soul was black and rotting. I had snuffed out the lives of human beings without batting an eye. I was scarred and broken. No good for her. I could only hope that I could be a better father than I was a man.

Chapter
TWENTY-SEVEN

Stephanie

SHOCK CONSUMED ME AS I STOOD OUT ON THE SIDEWALK STARING down the road. I couldn't believe what just happened. Of all the scenarios I imagined of me telling him about Remi, that was definitely not one of them. And what did he mean *I replaced him*? I had wanted to arrange a time to talk to him and explain. I wanted to introduce Remi to her daddy. I just thought… shit, I don't know what I thought.

I turned and re-entered the bar in a daze. I walked back to the table where Remi sat with Mama eating a plate of chicken nuggets and fries. "Thank you for sitting with her." Mama looked up at me with concern as I dropped into the seat across from them. As I stared at my shaking hands resting loosely together on the table, my mind felt like it was circling and I was fighting to keep the heavy tears pooling in my eyes from falling.

Mama reached a small, but strong, hand over and placed it on top of mine, squeezing them in a reassuring manner.

"I only heard a little of the situation back here but enough to know you and Reaper have some things to talk about and work out, hon. I think maybe what I wanted to talk to you about can wait. You have a lot on your plate right now." She patted my hands and began to pull away, but I caught her hand and met her gaze as I choked back my tears.

"No, Mama, I'm good." I sniffed and smiled a wobbly smile. "Really. Please, talk to me. Is everything okay? I'll do what I can to help you if there is something you need."

"Ummm, well." She took a deep breath. "I was going to talk to you about taking over the Oasis. Pops and I have been talking about 'retiring' so we can travel more while we're still able, and I can't let just anyone take over the Oasis... It's the only baby I've ever had besides those boys. You are part of this town, Steph, and you grew up with the Oasis. When you told me what you went to school for, well…." She trailed off.

Well, that was the last thing I expected. I thought maybe she needed help with reorganization or menus or something. I didn't know what to say. The wheels in my head started spinning at about 200 mph as my mouth flopped, open and shut like a damn fish but I couldn't help myself. Mama took in my expression and burst out in her raspy, raucous laugh.

"Girl, you look like the little bass I caught last week out at the lake! We can talk more later. You just think on it." She started to leave the booth.

"Wait! Mama, I don't know. I mean, what I meant to say was I don't have that kind of money. I wouldn't know where to begin! I… well… I'm so flattered, but I'm so… wow." I was scrambling for words as unbidden ideas for the bar popped in my head one after the other.

"Well, we could probably work something out. You know the club takes care of their own, and the way I see it, after the bit I heard earlier, little Miss Remi here is a connection of the club, whether you like it or not. You give that boy time to cool off and then talk to him. He's usually a quiet one, but he has a level head. He'll come around." At the sound of her name, Remi looked up with a mouthful of chicken nugget and shouted, "Wemi!" patting herself on the chest.

We both laughed as I hugged her close and kissed the top of her dark, silky curls.

Mama and I spent the next hour or more going over thoughts and plans for how I could take over the Oasis. The more we talked and the more I thought about it, the thought of coming home just felt right. A warmth begun at my very core and was spreading outward.

We had decided that, if I could come up with a down payment, we could draw up a contract where I could make monthly payments to her and I would have the option to refinance the bar when I was able. I could make changes to the bar menu and I could remodel as long as the changes met Mama's approval until it was refinanced in my name. The longer we sat talking, the more excited I was to go home and discuss the opportunity with my parents.

I began ticking off everything in my life that needed to be addressed. My apartment was on a month-to-month lease because I had been there past my one-year-lease term and I hadn't gotten around to signing a new lease to lock in my rent. I could turn in my notice at work and pack while I worked out my days at the restaurant. I didn't really have a lot to pack, and I was pretty sure everything would fit in my SUV and a small trailer if I could get a one-way rental.

Colton was furious with me, and though it ripped out my heart, I really didn't expect him to ever forgive me. I just prayed he would come around and want to be a daddy to Remi. He and I set aside, Remi deserved to have her mommy *and* her daddy in her life. I knew if we were able to sit down and talk, we could work out a visitation schedule. He wouldn't really need to interact with me unless it had to do with Remi's care or future. My chest ached as if there was a gaping hole where my heart had been at the thought of being so close to him and yet not being able to touch him and *be* with him. Fate was a cruel bitch.

My phone pinged with a message as Remi and I pulled up in front of my parents' house. When I saw the message was from Colton, my heart gave a lurch. I opened the message with shaking hands.

Colton: We need to talk. Tonight. Meet me at the Oasis. Dress for a ride.

Oh shit. I closed my eyes, trying to gain control of my raging emotions, before I quickly stamped out a reply.

Me: I'll see what I can do.

Gathering Remi from the car, I carefully set her on her feet and held her until I knew she had her balance. Hand in hand, we walked across the brick-paved sidewalk to the steps that she took one at a time. As I opened the door, she pulled her hand from mine and ran into the house shouting, "Gama! Gampa!" I couldn't help my sad smile as I heard her squeal as my dad must have tickled or teased her. I hung my keys on the hooks by the door, took my shoes off, lining them up neatly on the mat inside the door... anything to delay the conversation I needed to have with my parents.

Taking a deep fortifying breath, I walked down the short hall to the kitchen where I could hear the murmur of Remi's chatter and my parents' responses to her. I stopped in the doorway, leaning on the doorframe, absorbing the domestic warmth that always emanated from my mother's kitchen. My parents both looked up at me from the table where they sat having coffee. Remi sat in my dad's lap, and he was letting her scoop sugar in his cup as he directed her on how much and prepared to catch her hand if she spilled. After my dad took the spoon from her, setting it on a folded napkin, Remi leaned back into my dad and rubbed her eyes as her Cupid's bow mouth stretched in a little yawn.

"I'm going to lay this one down for a short nap. If you both have a minute, there are some things I need to talk to you both about."

"Of course, honey. We'll be right here when you're done." My mom gave Remi a wave and blew her a kiss as I carried her out to the living room where we had set up a pack-and-play for her naps. I lay her down, tucking her snuggle blankie and her favorite stuffed elephant up under her chin. Dang, she was barely fitting in the thing anymore! My baby girl was getting so big. She rubbed her face in the blankie and her eyes drifted closed. Our day out wore her clean out.

I returned to the kitchen and sat at the table. Feeling the need to do something with my hands, I started twisting a napkin. I had a hard time meeting either of my parents' eyes as I began to recite the same conversation I had with my brother earlier today, telling them about Michael and Colton, but also adding the conversation I had with Mama earlier. By the time I had finished, I had bits of napkin in a pile in front of me on the table and tears running down my cheeks and neck, soaking the collar of my tee shirt. My parents had yet to say a word. I hesitantly looked up at them and my dad reached out for me, pulling me from my chair, rocking me in his lap and hugging me tight in his arms like I remembered him doing when I was young. My mom reached over, rubbing her hand on my back in a soothing manner.

My dad spoke first.

"Stephanie, I wish you had told us all this when you were pregnant and everyone was beating you up about being selfish. We could have tried to help you better if we had known the truth. I know your brothers and I were hard on you back then, and I'm sorry for that. So sorry. We love you. We want what's best for you, and while we would have preferred things to work out in a different order for you, we wouldn't trade that little girl out there for the world. She was the best gift you could have given any of us." He looked at my mother, seeming to have a conversation without words.

I told them that Colton wanted to talk to me tonight and asked if they would mind watching Remi again. They assured me it was no trouble and agreed it was best to talk to him and get things sorted out ASAP.

"Why don't you go wash your face with cool water and lie down for a bit? I want to talk to your mother about a few things, and we can talk again tonight, okay?"

I nodded, then after accepting a kiss from my mom, I trudged upstairs, skipping the bathroom and collapsing on my bed. God, how had my life become such a train wreck?

Chapter
TWENTY-EIGHT

Reaper

I SAT ON MY BIKE IN FRONT OF THE OASIS WAITING FOR STEPHANIE to arrive. She had sent me a message saying she could be here by 2000. It was 1955. Then I saw an older SUV turn into the square and park two spots up from where I sat. Slowly, she got out, tucked her key into her tight pocket and walked over to me. She was tugging at the hem of her shirt nervously, with her bottom lip held by her teeth. Those beautiful eyes looked up at me, and I handed her the helmet I had been holding on my leg for her. She took it from me, cinching it down tight.

"Get on."

She didn't question me and threw her leg over the back of my bike, settling her chest against my back and wrapping her slender arms around my torso, locking her hands over my abs. The feel of those plump tits pressed into my back made my cock jump. It was difficult to ignore how good they felt pushed up against me. Fucking hell. That's not what tonight was about.

Down, boy... she has someone else. Too bad he didn't want to listen. Traitorous bastard.

I started my bike, flicked it in gear with the toe of my boot, eased off the clutch and onto the throttle, and we took off down the road. I knew exactly where I was taking her. I needed us to be alone without interruptions.

When I pulled up to the boat landing and hit the kill switch, she hopped off my bike like it was on fire and headed over to the picnic table under the tree, taking off the helmet as she walked. I followed her, trying to keep myself from staring at the full globes of her ass in her tight jeans—that didn't fucking work, by the way—and sat on the top of the table, resting my feet on the bench seat. Resting my elbows on my knees, I ran my hands through the hair on the top of my head. I had to keep my distance from her and keep my fucking hands from reaching out to pull her curvy body close to mine.

Shit.

"I don't—"

"I'm sorry, Steph—" We both started to speak at the same time.

"Umm, you go ahead," she said quietly.

I took a deep breath, blowing it out hard, and looked at the section of seat between my booted feet.

"I'm sorry, Stephanie. I was a dick today, and I fucking know it. You didn't deserve that nor did you deserve my shitty thoughts. I've had time to cool my shit and think today. I was a fucking douche for accusing you of keeping our daughter from me. I realize now that you had no way of contacting me. What you don't know was the morning after, as you were sleeping, I wrote my name and number down for you, but I felt stupid and threw it in your trash. Earlier, I wasn't remembering pitching it in the trash, just that I wrote it and my fucked-up head latched onto that part and pronounced you guilty. I can't even imagine you going through all of that alone, and I feel like a complete piece of shit for doing that to you." I looked into her beautiful blue eyes. "I need you to know I had never before, and haven't since, been with anyone without a fucking condom. Ever. I don't even know why I didn't with you. I have no excuses, Stephanie. That was a real dick move on my part. I'd like to say I'm sorry, but after seeing... her... I just can't be."

She didn't look like she was overly happy when I said there had been other chicks after her, but fuck, it wasn't like we had been together back then. Besides, there was no way she hadn't been with anyone else in the last few years. She had a passionate nature, one I remembered very well. Hell, she was with someone now. God, why did the thought of her fucking someone else piss me off so bad? I actually felt knots building in my stomach at the thought. Jesus, I needed to stop thinking about it. And I certainly wasn't a fucking monk. Never claimed to be.

"Colton—" she began, but I cut her off.

"It's Reaper. Just Reaper. I don't even feel like Colton exists anymore." In all honesty, I tried to keep him buried. Colton was fucking weak and stupid. Colton held on to a ridiculous notion of love for a woman in a goddamn cell phone pic.

"Okay... ummm, Reaper..." She seemed unsure as she said my road name. "You're right, I had no way to get in touch with you. I only knew your first name because your friend called out to you as we left. I knew very little about you, which didn't give me much to go on to track you down. Trust me, I would never have chosen for things to play out like they did. I didn't try to get pregnant, I didn't try to keep your daughter from you or you from her, but I wouldn't change it for the world. She *is* my world. If you want the honest-to-God truth, Colton—I mean, um, Reaper—I thought about you every damn day." Her voice cracked on her last word, and I looked over at her just in time to see her discretely touch a finger under her eye to catch the lone escaped tear.

"Stephanie, it's okay. I get it now. And I don't fucking blame you for finding someone else. I just hope he is good to you and our daughter." It killed me to say that. Fuck, did it rip me apart.

She looked confused as she reached out her hand to rest on my forearm. A jolt shot up my arm at her touch.

"I'm not with anyone, Reaper. I came here this weekend to get the hell away from the guy I was seeing, but I don't know if you would say we were even really 'dating.' He ended up not being who I thought he was." She looked me in the eyes with a distressed expression.

"Stephanie, I saw you dancing with him at the birthday bash. I figured that was why you took off after we hooked up; you felt like you betrayed him by being with me. It's okay though. It was nothing. I know things got out of control, we were both half drunk and not using sound judgement. I won't say anything to him or anyone else. I swear." Jesus, it gutted me to make it sound as if Friday night didn't mean the fucking world to me, as if I didn't feel whole when her body was next to mine. I wanted to punch my-damn-self for lying like that.

She stood up, then knelt on the bench between my boots, cradling my face in her soft hands. She lifted my head to look at her, and when I looked into her beautiful pale blue eyes, I felt as if someone ripped open my chest.

"Reaper, first of all, Chas—the guy you saw me dancing with—is an old friend from high school, and he's gay. So what you thought you saw was definitely *not* what it actually was. Funny enough, I was behind you in line at Fareway the other day, but I didn't know it was you at the time, and I thought you were hot as shit. Then when I saw you standing over by Erik and my brother? Well, maybe it was the alcohol—no, definitely the alcohol—but I was dancing for *you*." She laughed. "Shoot, I should probably be asking if *you* have someone."

She wasn't with him.

He was fucking gay, for Christ's sake.

Holy shit. *Way to jump to conclusions, you dumbass.* Now I really felt like a dumb fuck.

"Jesus, Stephanie, no. There isn't anyone else. I'm not going to lie to you and tell you I've been a monk. But every fucking one of them? Every one of them I pretended was you."

"I think I would prefer *not* to imagine that." She laughed again and leaned in to kiss me gently on the lips. As soon as our lips touched, it was as if a fire was ignited between us. It was like a kiss couldn't just be soft and gentle between us. Our kisses were desperate, frantic—a battle of tongues, lips, and teeth.

Grabbing her ass, I hauled her up to straddle my lap and pulled her jean-covered pussy tight against my cock as it strained against my own jeans. I felt the sharp intake of her breath against my mouth, and she moaned as I ground her against me. With my arms wrapped tight around her, I pressed her into my chest and threaded my fingers deep into her tangled blond curls. When I broke from the kiss, both of us gasped for air, and I pulled her head back by her hair to have better access to her neck, where I began to kiss and nip on her soft, smooth skin. Damn, she tasted better than I remembered.

One of my hands slid down, slipping under her shirt and lifting it above the top of her bra. I almost lost my mind when I saw them swelling up over the top of her lacy bra as they heaved with each breath she took. I pushed her bra down, leaning over to run my tongue along the top curve of her plump tit and then sucking the nipple into my mouth. She held my head close to her chest, showing me it felt good, but she didn't keep me from going back and forth between her puckered nipples. Pulling back abruptly, I released her nipple with a popping sound before capturing her mouth with mine again and squeezing both luscious tits in my hands. When I felt her breath quicken and her back arch, I knew she was going to come just from our juvenile actions. Her body stiffened and she stopped grinding her hips to press herself tight to me. Then she buried her head in my shoulder as she groaned into my neck and then bit down at the spot where my neck met my shoulder.

"That's right, baby. Don't hold back. Come for me. Don't stop."
I held her tight as I rained kisses on her head and nipped her ear
through her curtain of hair.

Holding her by her ass, I slid down off the table and dropped
to my knees, laying her back as gently as I could into the soft green
grass. As I knelt between her legs, I looked down at her flushed face
and her wild tangle of curls spread out on the ground. Her lips were
parted and her eyes were bright and wide in the glow of the setting
sun behind us as it glittered over the water. I could smell the earth
around us, and it seemed to call to me on a primitive level.

God, she was fucking beautiful. I had no idea what this shit was
between us, but she felt like eternity and I didn't want to let her go.
Ever. And I was going to show her how much I fucking *needed* to feel
her wrapped around me.

I grabbed her shirt, pulling it up over her head and setting it to
the side. Her tits were still resting over the top of her bra like an offering I couldn't resist as I leaned over to run my tongue across them
and sucked lightly on each nipple. Reaching down, I pulled off her
boots and unbuttoned her jeans, pushing them down her legs until
she kicked them off her feet and ankles. My lips never left my worship of her body as I slipped my hands under her when she arched
her back, giving me better access to the hook and to her nipples. Her
bra came loose and I tossed it to the side before dragging her panties
off as fast as I could. After she was completely nude, I knelt there between her spread legs and took her in to compare and memorize her
body now against the first time I saw it. She was abso-fucking-lutely
gorgeous. Perfect. Just fucking perfect.

Her tits seemed a little fuller than I remembered and her hips
had widened slightly into a woman's hips. She still had her belly button pierced and her belly, though slightly curved, was still taut, and
I ran my fingers lightly along the few faint silver lines I had missed
the last time—evidence of when our child had grown inside her. I
imagined her belly swelling with my child, our daughter, and I felt

an instant pang of regret that I hadn't been there to see it, but quickly pushed it aside. There was no room for regret between us. Regardless of where things went from here, in that moment and for as long as I could keep her, she was mine.

I ran my hands in a featherlight caress across her belly, to her hips, across her groin—causing her to shiver—and finally, across her mound and down her wet folds. I leaned over, pressing light kisses to each of the faint marks from our baby. When I raised up, I cupped her wet pussy firmly as I leaned over her with my weight held on one arm so I could look her in the face.

"This pussy? It's mine. No one else's. I do not share. No one touches this but me. Say it."

"It's yours," I heard her breathlessly whisper. I groaned as I leaned in to kiss her and my fingers separated her slick, wet folds, teasing her before sliding first one finger then another into her in an imitation of what I would soon do to her with my cock. She moaned, clawing at my back through my shirt and pressing her pussy into my hand as I circled my palm on her clit and fucked her with my fingers.

Her walls quivered before they tightened and pulsed around my fingers. Her creamy cum soaked my fingers and hand. Sweet fucking hell her body was made for me. There was no way this woman could respond like this to anyone else, and I was going to make sure she never did. This pussy? This body? My soul knew it was mine. Touching her was like coming home. Being inside her was like a healing balm that soothed my blackened soul.

I couldn't believe the things he did to me. It should be against the law for a person to feel this good. He played my body like a master pianist played the piano, bringing forth music that shattered the soul. When he pulled his fingers from between my legs and raised them to his full lips, I couldn't believe it. Oh. My. God. He wouldn't... He did. I watched him lick his fingers before leaning in to kiss me.

"Taste how your body responds to me," he whispered before kissing me gently and running his tongue across mine. I never, ever, in a million years would have thought that would be a turn-on, but I became a shameless hussy with him. Pulling away from the kiss, I begged him to remove his clothes. I needed to feel him, touch his skin... taste him. My hands wildly grasped at his shirt and jeans, plucking and pulling at them.

He gently extricated my hands from his clothes and stood above me. I knew I looked wild and savage as I lay sprawled out on the ground, panting as I watched him undress. He wasn't moving fast enough, and I heard myself whimper. Holy crap, he was driving me crazy!

Reaching over his head, he grasped his shirt by the back and pulled it over his head in one swift sweep, tossing it to the ground. He unbuckled his belt, unfastened his jeans, and slid them down his legs, stepping out of them as he kicked them to the side. When I saw the defined ridge in his boxer briefs and the small damp spot on them at the top, I licked my lips before biting the lower one in anticipation as he slid them off, his thick cock springing out as he freed it from its confines.

I noticed the bold tattoos that twisted and wrapped his arms from wrist to shoulder, some I remembered from before, but many were new since then. He had a large eagle across his chest with the tips of the spread wings touching the front of the swirling abstract designs wrapping around his shoulders. A set of dog tags tattooed within other abstract designs and words ran all along his left side and matched the real set glinting around his neck. The tats did absolutely nothing to detract from the sexy, sculpted muscles he still maintained, and I actually might have started drooling.

Sweet Mary, mother of God.

The muscles in his legs flexed and bunched as he crouched then knelt back down to the grass. He even had tats on his left leg, but I wasn't able to see what they were before he was lying over me, bracing his weight on his forearms so as not to crush me. He brushed my hair from my face and looked piercingly into my eyes.

"Do you know how many times you saved me? Kept me strong? Brought me back?" he asked me in a low voice. I shook my head. His lips brushed softly along mine as he whispered, "You are my angel, Steph. You were with me the entire time."

"God, Colton—I mean, Reaper… I feel like I'm going to… I want to tell you…" I couldn't form a complete sentence. It was like my brain had turned to mush. He did that to me.

"When it's just us like this, baby? Use my real name. Only with you, like this, can I be the man you remember from that first night. You deserve so much more than what I am. God, Steph, I'm so fucked up inside." My hand caressed his face.

"Even though we haven't been together these past few years, you were never out of my thoughts. I don't want to scare you away or make you say anything you don't feel or want to say, but I need you to know where my head is before we go any further. Colton, I think I'm falling for you. I can't help it. You've always been in my heart," I said breathlessly. My heart raced as I worried I would chase him away with my confession.

"Fuck that. You aren't making me say or feel anything I don't want to. I love you, Stephanie. It sounds insane, but I've loved you since the first time we were together. I loved you while you were a figment of my crazy fucking imagination in that shithole country. I loved you while I was delusional in the hospital after the explosion. I don't deserve you, but I love you now, and I will love you till I take my last fucking breath. *You* need to know where *my* head is before we do this." He looked at me, motionless, waiting for… what? Possible rejection? He must be crazy. I wrapped my arms around him, pulling him down to kiss me again.

His lips ignited a fire in me when he pressed them to mine. This was no soft, gentle kiss. This was a fierce claiming. We both explored every aspect of each other. We nipped and collided. His strong forearms framed my shoulders as his fingers threaded through my hair, anchoring us together.

He ended the kiss and reached over to his jeans. I heard the crinkle of the condom wrapper and watched him rip it open with his teeth, lift up, and roll it on. Holy hell, that was hot. Then I watched as he held himself at the base and stroked a couple of times before guiding it to my entrance. His eyes never broke contact as he flicked his tip through my wetness then plunged to the hilt. I sucked in a hissing breath as he filled me completely, and it took a minute for my body to acclimate to his invasion.

My entire body tingled and quivered as he slid in and out slowly at first, and then gained speed. I felt my muscles tensing up in expectation and the telltale pulsing begin at the deepest core of my body. Every muscle felt tight, and I pulled desperately at the grass before grabbing his ass and raking it with my nails. I screamed as my climax ripped through me, sending my soul flying through the air and floating to the ground, finally landing in the incessant throbbing of the finale of my orgasm. I noticed fine beads of sweat break out over his forehead and across his chest. After he had prolonged my pleasure until I thought I might truly shatter, he resumed stroking into me in a rhythm as old as time.

"God, Stephanie… you unravel me…" he rasped, before his own muscles tightened. He groaned, and I felt his cock thicken and pulse as it filled the condom. He collapsed over me, wrapping me tightly in his arms, kissing my head and temple reverently. Our hearts seemed to pound in unison. Nothing about this felt wrong. It was like falling together. Like finding that lost piece of myself.

Chapter
TWENTY-NINE

Reaper

"WHAT DID YOU MEAN WHEN YOU SAID 'IN THE HOSPITAL AFTER the explosion'?" She was lying replete with her head pillowed on my bicep and my arms wrapped around her. Her fingertips ran lightly over my forearm where it rested across her chest. Fuck, as soon as those words were out of my mouth earlier, I regretted them. I had never talked about the accident with anyone. I didn't want her to know exactly how fucked up I was, but I didn't know how to hide it from her now. I took a shaky breath and my chest ached.

"It was in Afghanistan before Christmas the year we met. I was riding up front. Mason—Hollywood—my spotter, was sitting behind me with Kamil, our interpreter, behind the driver." I felt myself drift back to that day, remembering it like it was yesterday.

The Humvee rocked and jolted along the shitty-ass trail they called a road in that God forsaken hellhole they called Afghanistan. We were in a small convoy headed to our rendezvous point where we would meet up with a trusted informant. We would then take that intel and break off to get into position. Our target was a key member of the fucking piece of shit Taliban. It had begun to feel like a hopeless cause, because it just seemed like when you killed one, another sprouted up to take his place, but I had my mission. There hadn't been a soul on the road as we traveled, and it gave an unnatural eerie feel to the land. Everyone was on edge and vigilant, watching for anything that seemed out of place or suspicious.

We had been about fifteen clicks out from the rendezvous point when we hit a large rock, causing us to swerve off the road. Suddenly, there was a loud explosion and I couldn't hear anything. We were flying through the air, tumbling over and over. I frantically fought to hold my phone. Even though it was powered down and I wasn't supposed to have it, I knew my angel's picture was in it and I clutched it with a death grip. It felt like the fires of hell rained down on us. Debris in the Humvee was flying around inside like missiles, hitting us repeatedly before working their way out the windows as we tumbled. Something must have busted open because it splattered across my face and chest.

We came to a jolting stop and my hearing slowly returned along with a constant ringing sound as we sat at an angle against a bunch of boulders and rocks. Everything was still muffled, but I could hear screaming and then realized it was me. I tried to catch my breath as the pain surged and seared through the left side of my body. Hearing a moan, I looked over into the baby face of the driver. He was covered in blood and looked at me with fear in his young eyes as he mumbled, "Help me, Sarge." Then he coughed, followed by a gurgled sound before blood ran out of his nose and mouth. I kept saying "No, no, no, no, no, no, no!" as his sightless eyes bore into me. His blood ran down and dripped on my shoulder. I desperately tried to unbuckle, but my left arm wouldn't work right. I twisted slightly in my seat to see the interpreter *staring sightless at the roof of the Humvee with his one remaining eye and his head flopped to the side. Twisting hurt so bad I couldn't catch my breath. Mason was screaming behind me, but I couldn't see him. I yelled for him to hold on as I shoved my phone back in my IBA with my right hand and tried to move to get to Mason, but the pain was excruciating. I began praying to my angel and whatever God she served.*

It seemed like hours had passed before I heard voices yelling and gunshots exploding around us as bullets pinged off the rocks. I had no idea who was shooting or if the rest of the convoy was safe. The gunshots stopped, and I heard more yelling and boots running in various directions. It was frustrating as fuck not being able to protect myself with my own damn weapon. I tried to see outside the Humvee, but something ran in my left eye, burning, and we were lying on my side of the vehicle. All I could see around us was dust, rock, and dirt. "SSG Alcott! SGT Lange! SPC Thompkins! We're coming in to get you!" It was getting harder to breathe, and I could barely keep my eyes open...

"The last thing I remember was hearing Mason moan, and I prayed it meant he was alive and would make it. I thought I was dying. I didn't expect to see anyone ever again. I remember briefly regaining consciousness in Germany, but no real details. The next time I was lucid, I was in a hospital room in BAMC, the Army Medical Center down in San Antonio, wrapped up and wired up to so many machines I thought I was in a Sci-Fi movie. Mason was in a wheelchair dozing next to my bed. He had both lower legs in some kind of funky casts. He jolted awake and told me I had suffered multiple fractures to my left arm, three of my left ribs, and my left leg had a rod at the thigh and the lower leg had pins, plates, and screws. I found out what I thought was mud from the dirt and a busted canteen was actually our blood being splattered around inside the Humvee. They said if we hadn't hit that rock, we would have all been killed instantly, but it set us off track just enough, I guess. He told me I had internal bleeding and for a while they didn't think I was going to make it. There were many days and nights after that where I wished I hadn't.

If Mason hadn't found me again after I got out..." I couldn't speak anymore. The telling was nearly as draining as the events themselves. "Let's just say, between Mason and the MC, they pulled me back. Mostly."

"Is that where this came from?" She tilted her head back to face me and ran a fingertip along the scar on my cheek. In a knee-jerk reaction, I reached up and grabbed her hand, halting its progress. It was a burning reminder for me, and just her touching it made me angry inside.

"Yes."

"I'm sorry," she whispered.

"No, don't be sorry for me, baby. There are other people who deserve your pity and empathy. I don't deserve any of that." I stared up at the stars that were beginning to come out. They were barely visible through the leaves of the trees above us. The night sky was darkening, and I could hear crickets and frogs in the shadows of the lakeshore awakening. I had no idea what time it was, but I knew we should probably get going.

"I think it's time for me to take you back."

"Where do we go from here, Colton?"

"I want to spend time with you and Remi. I want to get to know my daughter. I want us to see where the fuck this goes. Shit, I can't lie. I want to keep you forever, baby, but there are things you need to know about the life I live before you make a decision." I hugged her tight, kissing the top of her head before I reached over and grabbed her clothes to hand to her.

"Do you want to follow me back to my house after you drop me at my SUV? Remi should still be awake. She took a late nap today." She looked nervous, and I noted her hands shook as she pulled her jeans up over her sexy-ass legs. It was then that I noticed the bruises on her upper arms.

"I didn't do that last night, did I?" I felt sick to my stomach that I might have hurt her in my insane, lustful frenzy last night. She looked at me briefly, nervousness flickering in her eyes, before she seemed to focus intently on buttoning her jeans and pulling on her boots.

I squatted down next to her as she sat on the ground pulling on her last boot. My hand gently tipped up her chin, forcing her to look at me. Hurting my angel was the last thing I ever wanted, and if I had done that to her, I needed to know.

"Steph?"

"No, you absolutely did not, but I would rather not talk about it right this minute, okay? So, ummmm, do you want to go see your little girl?" Her eyes filled with anxiety, and she pulled her bottom lip between her teeth. I would get my answers about those bruises later. I wasn't dropping this. No one treated my angel like that, not as long as there was a breath in my body.

"I would absolutely love to."

Stephanie

The ride back to my car was as stressful as the ride out to the dock, but for different reasons. Remi was going to meet her daddy. Her daddy was finally going to meet her and, hopefully, be in her life. Would he think I had done a good job with her? Would he feel the deep love like I had for her, even though he had missed the first couple of years of her life? The questions ran nonstop through my mind.

The feel of his warm body as I snuggled up to his back had me wishing we had more time before we went to the house. I stroked his abs as my hands slid slowly toward his pecs… yummmm. His hand stopped the roaming of my hands, and I felt him chuckle.

Oh my gawd! We were on the way to unite my baby with her daddy! Could my body not behave for just one short ride? Ugh!

He rolled to a stop next to my SUV, and I carefully slid off his bike and moved to hand his helmet to him. As I did, he grabbed my arm, pulling me closer and capturing my mouth in a deep kiss. The helmet hung suspended loosely from my fingers as he slowly ended the kiss with a smile.

"How do I get to your place, baby? I need to run by the clubhouse and check in first. Then I'll head over. I'll only be a few minutes behind you." He ran his thumb along my bottom lip, and I wanted to grab it between my teeth.

There I go, again! Ugh! I was hopeless!

After I gave him directions, he nodded and winked at me before pressing his bike into gear and roaring off with a burst of the throttle. I stood listening to him work through the gears as he raced off, the rumble of his bike fading as his taillights became specks in the distance. I touched my lips where he had kissed me and squealed like a school girl. I couldn't believe it! Things were falling into place.

Was this really my life?

As I backed out of the parking spot and pulled up to the stop sign, a pair of headlights behind me pulled me out of my musings. Crap, I hoped I hadn't been sitting long at the stop sign lost in thoughts. They probably thought I was an idiot.

As I headed out to the edge of town toward home, I called my mom to give her a heads up that Colton would be coming, and she assured me Remi was still wide awake and waiting for me to get home. I thanked her and told her I would see her soon. As I slowed for the turn and rolled up my parent's driveway, I was surprised to see truck headlights turn in after me. Wonder what Sam was doing here again… I parked and Sam pulled in behind my SUV. When I got out, his headlights blinded me. *Dang, Sam, you ass!* I held my hand over my eyes, waiting for him to get out so I could tell him I had talked to Colton.

I heard the truck door open and slam shut.

"Sam, you don't have to be pissed anymore. I talked to him." I lowered my hand in time to be pushed up against the back end of my SUV. My head hit the rear window and bounced off. *What the heck?*

When my vision cleared I saw Michael glaring at me with gritted teeth bared in rage.

Oh God, oh God! I tried to scream, but he grabbed tight around my neck with one hand and shook me hard. My head whacked against the window again.

"I cannot believe you! You would barely let me touch you, but you are all over some nasty-ass biker? I saw how you looked at him when you watched him ride off. You fucking slut! You're fucking him, I know you are. Don't even try to deny it! How could you do this to me? To us? I was *good* to you! But you ran off to this little shitty town to hook up with a dirty-ass *biker!*" He looked like a crazed maniac with spittle flying out of his mouth and his eyes wild and angry. I was terrified. *Where was Colton? Please, God, let him get here soon and please don't let anyone bring Remi out to meet me.*

"Michael! What are you doing here? How did you know where I was? I just needed to get away for the weekend. That's all. I wasn't running off, honest!" My words were raspy as he continued to hold my throat. I desperately clawed at his fingers as I tried to placate him and get him to calm down. I was afraid he was going to really hurt me before anyone even knew I was out here struggling. I had no idea how he had found me. That, in itself, was terrifying. How long had he been following me?

"I was worried about you walking home late at night after work, so I installed an app on your phone. I just wanted to keep you safe, Steph. You and Remi are so special; I just needed to protect you and watch out for you." Holy Jesus, he was insane! How could he think something like that was okay? I wondered what else he had done besides stealing my key and tracking my phone.

Just then, I heard the rumble of a motorcycle and saw a headlight come around the curve of the driveway before suddenly skidding to a stop. The bike was still running as I suddenly felt Michael's hands ripped from my neck as he flew backward.

I was shaking and felt nauseous as I dropped my hands to my

knees, breathing ragged breaths. Looking up through the curtain of my hair and the dust billowing from the bike's sudden stop on the gravel, I saw a fist connect with Michael's jaw. He staggered back before catching himself and charging toward my rescuer.

"You sonofabitch! Don't you *ever* touch her again!" I heard Colton rage before he grappled with Michael again. They were evenly matched in height, but Michael had insanity behind him, while Colton had sheer power and a fighter's instinct. I watched them struggle before they fell to the ground, Colton straddling Michael, beating him over and over with his fists. As I ran to stop Colton before he killed him, I heard the front door bang open and my father yell out to me. He scrambled down the front steps and wrapped his strong arms around me before I could get to Colton.

"No, Dad! I can't let Colton kill him. He'll go to jail! I need him! I love him! *He's her daddy!*" I was frantic and thrashing in my dad's arms to get loose.

My dad sat me on the steps, telling me he would take care of it and not to move as he ran to grab Colton.

"Son! Stop! My girls need you! Don't do this!" My dad tackled Colton in a bear hug. I watched Colton fight my dad's hold, and I prayed he wouldn't hurt my dad in his blind fury. Something seemed to finally click in his mind, and he stopped struggling, but he was still panting in great heaving breaths. He held his bloodied hands up to my dad to signal he was calm and wouldn't continue to fight.

As my dad and I walked Colton toward the steps and into the house, blood dripped from his hands. It was also splattered across his face and chest. I noted Michael rolling around on the ground, groaning. I pulled out my phone to call the sheriff once we got Colton inside and cleaned up. Jesus, I prayed my mom had Remi distracted somewhere.

I was about to call the sheriff when I heard a truck roar to life and gravel spraying as it spun out of the driveway and down the road. Thank God. I debated having the sheriff take him in and put the fear of God in him, but I was pretty sure he would think twice before messing with me after the beating Colton just gave him. I was surprised he could still drive.

Asshole.

"Son, let Steph get you cleaned up and put some ice on those hands." My dad looked up at me, giving me a nod to take him inside. I wrapped my arm around Colton's waist and walked him into the kitchen.

"Baby, I'm fine. I just need to wash my hands. Really. Honestly, I'm okay." Colton closed his eyes, taking a deep breath before he placed his hands under the cold water I had started. I saw him suck in a sharp breath when the water hit the small nicks and cuts on his knuckles. He used some dish soap to scrub the blood from his hands and arms until the water ran clear.

My dad walked in and handed him a clean white T-shirt and reached out his hand to shake Colton's.

"Son, I owe you a debt of gratitude. I don't know how to thank you. If my intuition is correct, I would say that was the young man who has been giving my daughter a hard time." He turned to me with a questioning look to confirm of his statement. I nodded yes. "I was in the shower and Stephanie's mother had Remi watching a movie, so I didn't even hear anything until your bike pulled up." My dad looked slightly defeated, and I knew he felt he had failed me.

"Dad! It's not your fault! I had no idea he was here either. I actually thought it was Sam pulling in behind me, or I would have gone straight into the house. Do *not* blame yourself."

I filled plastic zipper bags with ice and wrapped them in a towel as Colton changed out of his leather cut and bloody shirt into the shirt my dad had handed him. I saw my dad's eyebrows raise when he took in Colton's tattoos, and I gave him a silencing glare just as Colton's head was popping through the tee. My dad just smiled and raised his hand in acquiescence to me.

I felt Colton's eye boring into mine as I placed the ice on his hands while he rested them on our kitchen table. I knew we were in for a long, uncomfortable discussion after tonight was wrapped up. Great. Nothing ever went as planned with this man and me. This was not exactly how I intended on telling him about Michael.

"Do you still feel up to seeing Remi or do you want to wait until tomorrow?" I was worried after everything that had happened tonight. What if he hated me for having his daughter around a man like Michael?

"I don't want to wait, baby. I think I've waited long enough." He pulled a hand from under one of the ice bags to tuck my hair behind my ear. His cold fingertips caressed my cheek as he slowly pulled his hand away. Stepping back, I grabbed his dirty shirt from the floor and gave him a small smile before I turned to place it in the washing machine off the kitchen.

"I'll go get her... if you're sure." He raised his eyebrow and his expression said *What do you think?*

I went through the hall and up the stairs to my parents' room where Remi was contentedly watching an animated movie with my mom. I stood soaking in my precious baby girl for a quiet moment. Her silky dark hair hung in fat ringlets against her rosy round cheeks. Her blue eyes, so like her father's, reflected the flashing colors of the movie that held her attention. They seemed wise beyond her young years. It wasn't long before she realized I stood in the doorway.

"Mommy!" She jumped up to her knees, jumping up and down on the bed when she saw me. My mother chuckled and paused the movie. Remi stood and walked across the bed with my mother prepared to catch her if she fell. She jumped in my arms and wrapped her little arms around my neck. "Wemi miss you, Mommy!" She gave me a big kiss.

"Mommy has a big surprise for you, my bugga-boo," I said to her as I smiled at my mom over her shoulder, waving her to follow, and turned to head back downstairs. Lordy, I felt as nervous as a long-tailed cat in a room full of rocking chairs right about now.

Here goes everything....

Chapter THIRTY

Reaper

MADE SMALL TALK WITH STEPHANIE'S DAD WHILE SHE WENT upstairs. I liked him. He really cared about his daughter and struck me as loving, but very protective. I imagined I would be the same as I thought of the little raven-haired baby girl I would officially meet soon. I started to get nervous. Fuck. Was I doing the right thing? Should I even corrupt that precious baby and my angel with the fucking ugly blackness that consumed my body and soul?

Would she even want anything to do with me? She had blithely jumped up into the booth with me earlier today, but what about when she found out I was her daddy? Her daddy. It sounded strange, but I fucking loved it already. Would I be worth a shit as a father? It's not like I had an example to follow. My dad had never been around while I was growing up, having shit-canned my mom when I was a baby. He never contacted us again.

Just as the silence in the kitchen began to border on uncomfortable, I heard footsteps on the stairs and the small giggles of what I assumed was my daughter. My daughter. Ready or fucking not…

I couldn't stand. My legs felt like leaden weights as I watched them close in on me. A woman there was no denying was Stephanie's mother, entered the room behind them and I barely registered the brief look of censor she gave me before standing next to Stephanie's father. My ink and scruffy appearance probably weren't winning me any favors. Her father whispered in her mother's ear and I watched her expression relax.

Stephanie walked right up to me holding Remi in her arms. I took in her raven ringlets, her clear blue eyes, and her solemn expression as she held several fingers in her mouth. Then she pulled her fingers out, covered in drool, as she cracked the biggest grin, revealing two dimples which were the miniature of my own. Fuck if that didn't melt my heart. I knew mine were in full affect as she leaned over quickly, reaching for me.

I pulled her in a tight hug, but I loosened it quickly for fear of scaring her.

"Remi, baby?" Stephanie knelt in front of me and spoke softly to her. "This is your very own daddy." I heard her voice waver as she said "daddy." I damn near started crying as her bright blue eyes turned to me and her hands grasped either side of my face. She still had slobber on her hand, but I just didn't give a shit. She stared deep in my eyes in such a solemn manner it was nearly unnerving. I swear that little girl saw straight to my soul, and I prayed she wouldn't find it lacking.

"Wemi daddy!" she suddenly exclaimed. I had no fucking clue if this little girl understood what hearing her say "daddy" did to my galloping heart. I couldn't keep the smile from my face. It felt like my face might actually crack in fucking two, my smile was so big. My heart swelled with love for a child I had never held before this moment. I was a motherfucking father. I actually helped create this beautiful, precious, little princess. Fucking hell. I was a goner already.

"Thank you, Stephanie. Thank you for this gift. You have no idea... Thank you for taking such good care of my princess when I wasn't there to do it. She's beautiful." Stephanie continued to kneel at my feet with tears silently streaming down her face. I had no idea when her father had soundlessly left the room, but I was thankful for the minimal audience as I felt tears break free from my eyes. I swiped at them quickly. Fuck, I was getting soft.

We spent the next hour sitting in the living room surrounded by the soft glow of a floor lamp while Remi showed me all her toys and treasures. I felt my face fucking flame when she stuck a small silver plastic tiara on my head, looking so proud of herself. Stephanie burst out laughing, quickly covering her humorous outburst with a hand, but she couldn't hide the laughing twinkle in her eyes. Little shit. *I'll get her for this later*, I thought with a smirk.

"Daddy princess!" Holy shit. Who the fuck would have thought Colton Alcott, former sniper, current big bad biker, would be sitting there with a plastic tiara on his head while a gorgeous blonde giggled and a raven-haired princess glowed?

And he was fucking loving it.

Stephanie

Colton had been so sweet and tolerant with Remi. It was amazing to watch him with her. It was bittersweet seeing how well they connected despite the time they had missed. There was little I could think of that was better than knowing they were finally able to be together. I wondered what the future held, and I prayed he didn't break her heart... or mine. I had yet to tell him, but I had admitted it to my father. I wasn't just falling for this man, I loved him. Absolutely and irrevocably. We didn't even really know each other, so maybe it was a little crazy, but looking at him, my heart felt warm and full. When I looked at him with our baby girl, I thought it might burst.

When Remi climbed in his lap and began petting his short beard, I saw him smile. I noticed Remi's eyes appeared heavy and she snuggled closer to his chest as if listening to his heartbeat. While she was curled into his chest, his shirt fisted in her chubby little hand, she began to drift off to sleep. As he held her close, he slowly ran his fingers through her dark curls and across her little cheek. Closing his eyes, he rested his scarred cheek on top of her head.

"Do you want to help me put her to bed?" I whispered. His gorgeous blue eyes met mine and his dimples flashed, causing my stomach to flutter. He stood slowly, careful not to wake his precious bundle. I turned and led the way to the stairs, climbing the old wooden stairs, listening to the familiar creak of the steps from his weight as he followed me to the top. I turned into my room and motioned to the pack-and-play set up in the corner.

After he laid her, ever so gently, in her bed and covered her with her fuzzy pink striped blanket, he turned to me, gathering me in his arms. I laid my head on his shoulder and wrapped my arms around his waist. He placed one hand on my head, cradling it to him as he rested the other on my hip. The domestic quality of the moment was not lost on me, and I fought the silly tears that struggled to escape my eyes. *If only I could stay like this forever.* If I died tomorrow, I would die a happy woman.

"Thank you again for tonight, Stephanie. I cannot even begin to tell you what this means to me. I've been alone for so fucking long…. To be blessed with this precious gift? You just have no fucking idea. When I think of all the other possibilities you could have chosen after finding out you were pregnant, my heart aches. This is just so much. I want to kneel at your feet and fucking worship you, and yet I'm sure even that wouldn't be enough."

I reached up and kissed him softly, letting it linger until our lips merely feathered against each other. I took a deep breath, stepped back, and grabbed his hand to lead him back down the stairs. He walked to the door and I followed him out onto the porch, my hand still held securely in his. He stopped at the top of the porch steps, staring at the stars scattered brightly across the dark night sky.

"God, I want to stay with you tonight, Stephanie. But I won't disrespect your parents' home like that. When do you plan to leave? I need to see you both again. Fuck, I don't want you to leave at all, especially with that asshole out there. We need to talk about where we go from here. God, I feel like you're both an addiction in my veins already." He turned to look at me with the moonlight reflecting in his eyes.

I pressed my lips together, biting them in my teeth. I didn't want to leave either, but I had a job and a life that weren't... well, they just weren't... here. I needed to think about my options and decide what would be feasible and best for myself and my baby girl. The apartment management had called, telling me they had changed my locks, but I still had the situation with Michael to deal with. I cursed the day he moved in down the hall.

"I really need to head back tomorrow afternoon. Would you like to have an early lunch? We can talk then, if that's okay?" I felt my exhaustion sinking in just looking over where, a short while ago, I had been assaulted by Michael and rescued by Colton. Jesus, it had been a long damn day.

"Yes. What time and where? Do you want me to pick you up, or do you want me to meet you somewhere?" He placed soft kisses to the top of my forehead as he spoke.

"Well, considering I don't think both Remi and I will fit on your bike with you, how about we meet you at 11:00 at the café downtown?" I said with a smirk.

"I do have a truck, you know. But I can meet you since I don't have a car seat for Remi yet." He chuckled. Dang, I loved the sound of him having a car seat in his vehicle for Remi. Silly, I know. Like I said, I was tired and it must have shown because he lifted my chin gently with his hand, kissed me softly, and told me to go get some sleep and he would see us tomorrow.

I watched him walk to his bike, climb on and start it up. I loved the rumble of his exhaust, and I knew he intentionally didn't rev his motor, slowly easing onto the throttle, trying to be as quiet as he could as he pulled out. For the second time tonight, I watched his taillights disappear.

I prayed that someday, God willing, I wouldn't be watching him drive off at the end of a night together, but rather snuggling up in the same bed.

The next morning, over coffee and breakfast, my mom and dad approached me with an offer that would change the direction of all of our lives.

Chapter
THIRTY-ONE

Reaper

I FOUND MYSELF KNOCKING ON HACKER'S DOOR FIRST THING IN THE morning. Déjà vu. I just prayed it wouldn't end the same way it did last time, 'cause fucking A, he could pack a punch. I needed his help finding this Michael motherfucker. He was going to regret laying his hands on Stephanie like he did. She may have thought I was letting this lie, but that was the farthest thing from the truth. I couldn't stand a man who abused a woman, but he really fucked up when he hurt *my* woman.

Hacker answered the door in his boxers again, with a wry look.

"Reaper, man, we gotta quit meeting like this. Do you have something against a motherfucker getting some sleep?" Hacker ran a hand through his hair and briskly rubbed his face.

"Fuck, bro, put on some damn clothes. I need your help." I brushed past him, dropping down in his recliner.

"Oh, sure. Come on in, make yourself at home, Reaper. Shit. Fuck you. What if I had company? You're damn lucky I didn't answer buck-ass naked, you fuck." He walked back over to his bed, flopping down and pulling a pillow over his face.

"Man, what the fuck ever." I laughed. I had never known this fucker to keep a bitch overnight. He fucked them, then kicked their ass out. No cuddling, no pillow talk, just wham, bam, thank you, ma'am.

"I need your help tracking down this crazy fucker who is stalking Stephanie." My humor ended with this announcement. I looked at him, waiting for his response.

At those words, he sat straight up, the pillow falling to the side. "The *fuck?*"

"Yeah. I don't know exactly what happened, but she had damn bruises on her arms and he showed up at her parents' last night. He had her slammed against her SUV when I pulled up. I swear to fucking Christ, if her dad hadn't stopped me, I would have fucking killed him then and there. I put a beating on him, but he hauled ass before I could go back out to finish him off. I'm glad she didn't call the cops though, because that would have just complicated things when I find this motherfucker. You know?" I could feel my rage building just talking about that piece of shit. I had to make a conscious effort to unclench my fists.

"Dude, you can't just go after this guy like that. And you know if Snow finds out I helped you find this guy, I'm a dead man too. You have to bring it to the table, bro. You need to think of the potential blowback on the club if you do this. I'm not saying I don't want to help you or that I don't want to beat him within an inch of his life too, but, man, we gotta be smart about this." I knew Hacker was right, but it sure as shit wasn't what I wanted to hear.

"I'm worried as hell about her, man. She's going back to Des

Moines today, and I can't be there to protect her. I have obligations to the club right now. It feels like I'm being torn in two." I leaned forward in the chair, holding my head in my hands as I tried to calm the fuck down. I wanted to punch someone. I had never once regretted my obligations to the club coming before everything else, but I had never felt like I did about Stephanie before either.

"I get it, bro. Totally. I told you, she's like my little sister. Let's talk to Snow and see if he has any ideas or thoughts, okay? If he says we have the go-ahead, I'll do what you need. Anything." I stood and reached out, clasping his hand as I gave him a rough hug and pat on the back.

"Thanks, man. Now put some fucking clothes on. Shit, I think your dick just touched me."

I walked out of the room laughing and looking forward to at least seeing Stephanie at lunch. I went to take a shower while I waited for Snow to show up at the clubhouse.

Stephanie

Remi and I were early, and she was busy coloring on the paper placemat when Reaper walked in, causing the little bell at the top of the door to jingle. I saw him scan the room until his gaze landed on us at the booth in the corner. His hair still looked wet, like he had just stepped out of the shower. The thought of him naked with hot water streaming down his body had my cheeks flushing and my girly parts tingling.

Bad, bad, *bad* girl…

I wasn't sure how he was going to take my news, but I hoped he would be happy for me and supportive. I smiled up at him as he stopped at the edge of the table and leaned down to kiss first me and then Remi.

"My two favorite girls." He slid into the booth across from me and reached for my hand, raising it to his lips. God, this man was more than I could stand sometimes. He sure had a sweet side, despite the shit he'd been through.

"So, I have some news to discuss with you, and I'm not sure how you're going to feel about it all." I felt nervous. What if he didn't want us up his ass all the time? Would we cramp his style? He looked at me with some trepidation in his eyes.

"Uh, okay. I'm listening." His face was an expressionless mask.

"So… I have an opportunity." I cleared my throat and blurted the rest of my news out before I lost my nerve. "I'm going to buy the Oasis. I'm moving home." As I sat trying to gauge his reaction, my heart felt lodged in my throat, and my teeth worried my bottom lip. Would he really want us around?

"Are you fucking kidding me? Don't fuck with me, Stephanie. I mean it, I don't think my sanity could handle it if you told me this was a joke." His face remained impassive, but surely his response meant he was okay with this.

"I'm serious. Are you mad? I don't want Remi and I to cramp your style or have you thinking I'm trying to be up your ass."

"Jesus, Stephanie. No way! Shit, do you have any idea how happy this makes me? Being able to see the two of you every day if I want? Damn, baby, I'm over the moon right now." It made me get all gushy inside when he called me baby. His face was lit up with the sexy smile that I had come to love, replete with dimples. My heart thudded in relief and I smiled back at him.

"There are a few things that I need to talk to you about though… I need to go into work tomorrow so I can turn in my two-week notice, and I need to pack. My parents want me to leave Remi here with them. For several reasons, I agree. While I'll really miss having her with me—I mean, I've never been away from her—I think it would give you an opportunity to spend quality time with her. What do you think?" I questioned. We were never going to get those years back, but I really felt it was important for him to be able to have some one-on-one time with her.

"Hell yeah, I would love to be able to spend time with her, but can't you just call them and tell them you're not coming back? If so, I can see if I can leave for a couple of days to help you pack and bring your stuff home. I don't like the thought of you going back alone with that stupid fuck still hanging around." He looked frustrated and his fingers tapped rapidly on the table. Truth be told, I didn't even really know him, but it felt good to have someone who wanted to protect me.

"Reaper, I don't think I'll need to worry about Michael after the 'come to Jesus meeting' you had between your fist and his face." I was pretty sure Michael wouldn't be bothering me anymore. Granted, I wasn't looking forward to the thought of possibly running into him in the halls, but I didn't think he was a worry now. "I'll be back the weekend after next."

"I don't fucking like it. I want you to check in with me every time you leave your place and every time you get home and have your door locked. I'm not trying to control you, baby, but I'm really worried about you going alone. It also might be a good idea to have Hacker set up his tracking system on your phone." He still didn't look happy, and I appreciated his concern, but for a second, I felt my hackles rise when I felt he was dictating checking in with him. The thought of having a tracker on my phone almost sent me into panic-mode. After I searched through my phone and found the app Michael had buried in a folder, I was sick, but when I tried to put myself in Colton's place, I understood his concerns.

We made the decision to drop the subject for the time being and enjoy our lunch. Remi had been absorbed in her coloring, but when I asked her if she wanted chicken or grilled cheese, she seemed to realize "Daddy" was here and begged to go sit by him. The rest of lunch consisted of Remi trying to "share" her food with Daddy and stealing his fries with a giggle every time he acted surprised that she had taken another one. Watching them interact warmed my heart. The physical similarities were uncanny really. I could imagine what Colton had looked like as a small boy.

"So why Remi, anyway?" he surprised me by asking suddenly. At the sound of her name, Remi looked up at him and smiled with her face stuffed full of fries. We both laughed at her comical expression.

"You mean, why did I choose the name Remi?" He nodded when I asked. "Well, it's kind of silly, I guess, but her daddy was 'Colton' and it was like a Colt pistol… so her name is Remington Amelia. Remi for short. Remington because it was another brand of firearm. Am I sounding crazy?" I began to blush and fidget. At the time, it made total sense to me. Now, maybe it seemed a little odd.

He was quiet for several minutes. I looked up to see his reaction to my crazy rationale. He appeared slightly taken aback.

"So you basically named her after me," he said in a quiet voice.

"Well, yeah. I didn't have your last name, or I would have given it to her, even though I couldn't find you. So that was the most creative thing I could think of. It sounds a little weird, but it made sense at the time, and I liked the name." I twisted my fork in my hand nervously. I hoped he didn't think it was stupid.

"Thank you, baby. Every time we talk, I find more and more things you do that blow me away. You really are an amazing woman. I don't deserve either of you, you know? I'm really a fucking mess inside. I'm not the same guy you met back then, and I probably wasn't completely sane back then. I've kil—I've done things," he whispered so Remi wouldn't hear, "and I would do it again to keep my brothers, sisters, and my country safe. But you have made me selfish. I want you and Remi in my life; I just don't know how it'll all work out." To hear him voice aloud the fact that he had ended people's lives was a bit of a shock, despite knowing he had deployed as a sniper. I could also tell by his expression that he truly believed that he didn't deserve us. I pushed my plate to the side and grasped his hands firmly in mine.

"Stop. You do deserve her. Everyone deserves to be loved and cared about. Reaper, you can act all hard and tough, but you really are a good man. Don't sell yourself short. She adores you, and she just met you. I've been stuck on you for years because of how good you were to me that night, and again now. You could have told us to get lost, but you've embraced her like you've been there since day one. Now, change of subject but speaking of names… what's up with 'Reaper' anyway? Why do they call you that?" His face went flat momentarily at my question before he met my eyes and tried to play it off as nonchalantly as he could. I was beginning to wonder if I had stepped out of line with my question.

"It was Hollywood—Mason—he had told the guys in the MC that I was a sniper. So for a little while, they called me One Shot for… uh well, then they switched to Reaper when I began to officially prospect." He looked down at the table and my hands resting on his. "Anyway, it stuck."

"It's kind of sexy…." I wiggled my eyebrows in an exaggerated attempt to lift the mood and neutralize the somberness weighing heavy at the table.

He smirked and laughed as he shook his head at my ridiculous attempt at humor. God, I loved this man's smile and the deep sound of his laughter. If I had my way, he would smile and laugh 24/7.

It was time for me to head back to the house and prepare for my trip back to Des Moines, but I was loathe to leave Remi and him behind. I told myself it was only two weeks; I could do this. I did break down and agree to let Erik set my phone up. I told him I would meet him at the MC's clubhouse on my way out of town to pick it up.

Chapter
THIRTY-TWO

Reaper

Hacker had the phone ready for me in record time. Snow had agreed to the resources used for the phone after I told him about Stephanie and Remi and where I hoped things were going. Hacker was fucking good at his job, and it amazed me how a guy who had been such a jock in high school could be such a brainiac computer nerd. The guy was truly indispensable with all the techno shit he did for the MC. If he couldn't find the software or hardware for something we needed, he fucking created the shit. The man was a fucking genius, and I loved him. Next to Hollywood, he was probably my best friend. Part of it was that he had a rough deployment when he was in the Marines and so he, Hollywood, and I just got each other.

Joker knocked on the open doorframe to tell us there was a blonde chick named Steph, who had come into the garage office portion of the clubhouse, claiming to be here for me. I couldn't hold back my grin. Jesus, I was so fucked. I couldn't even hear her name without smiling like a fucking idiot. By the way Hacker was laughing at me, I could only imagine he saw it too.

"Fuck you," I said to him with the smile still plastered on my face, and I followed Joker out to greet Steph and bring her back to Hacker. There was a rule in the MC that no bitches or old ladies were allowed in the clubhouse without the escort of a patched member. The only exception was if the member had to conduct business or was otherwise called away, a prospect could be placed as a guard, of sort, if she wasn't escorted by her old man.

Club whores and the sluts, or "party girls," who specifically came to the parties to brag about fucking a biker were the only exception, but these women all understood they were making themselves available to any member that took an interest. We had a strict rule that the specifics of the acts be consensual though. We didn't condone rape, specific non-consensual sex acts, or underage girls. Period. No exceptions. Ever.

I arrived to the office at the front of the garage to see Stephanie looking around at the framed pictures of classic bikes, cars, and trucks we had either restored or customized. I felt a burst of pride knowing several of the pictures were personal pet projects of mine that I had a hand in. My favorite was a '67 Camaro we had restored for some rich fucker down in Florida. It was a deep red with wide white racing stripes up the hood, which sloped along the hood scoop. Damn, that was a sexy-ass car. Not as sexy as the blonde standing there admiring the pictures though. Yeah, my fucking smile just got downright lecherous at the thoughts of everything I wanted to do to her in that moment.

When I slid my hands slowly around her hips, drawing her back into my stiffening cock, that I was *not* trying to hide from her for the record, she placed her hands on mine and looked over her shoulder at me. Those eyes. Fuck, they slayed me every time. I couldn't resist biting down at the juncture of her neck and shoulder. When she squealed and spun away laughing, I had to force myself not to throw her over my shoulder caveman-style and haul her back to my room.

"Come on, baby, let's go see what Hacker has for you." I took her hand, leading her past the guys working on various bikes and cars and through the door at the end of the shop, which entered into the clubhouse. "Stay with me and hold my hand. Sorry if you see anything that's too shocking, but it's midday so the guys should mostly be busy working unless they're taking a late 'lunch.' Okay?"

She nodded and held tight to my hand, eyes wide. I laughed at her innocent, uncertain expression as we headed into the gloom of the clubhouse bar. Someone had some old Nirvana song playing in the background, and I suspected it was Cammie. She loved the 90's grunge rock. The smell of stale cigarette smoke, cheap perfume, and sex lingered as we walked through the main area and wove through tables scattered around the pool table at the center of the room. I knew Stephanie was trying not to gawk or look around too much, but I also knew it was hard not to notice Dice sitting in the corner with his hand resting on a brunette's head as she had her head bobbing between his legs. Like I said, late "lunch" and dessert. I laughed to myself. I never did understand the guys wanting to do that shit out in the open, but to each their fucking own.

Just as we were getting ready to head past the bar and into the hall, I saw Cammie give me a warning look and tip her head toward the hall. Too late, I saw a bleached platinum blonde in a short red T-shirt that must have been three sizes too small, and cutoff jean shorts so short they left half her ass hanging out head straight out of the hall and flat up against me, running her bright red nails along my chest. *Well, fuck.*

I used my free hand to stop the progression of Gretchen's hand as she began to trail it lower and pushed her back out of my personal space. I felt Stephanie tense next to me, and I didn't blame her ass one bit. I supposed it didn't look too fucking great on my part, even though I knew Gretchen was just trying to stir the shit. Fucking bitch. She was really beginning to piss me the fuck off.

"Hey baby," she cooed, and I saw her eyes flick briefly over to Stephanie by my side, "I've been waiting for you. What took you so long?"

Oh fuck no, she didn't. I felt Stephanie try to pull out of my grip, but I held tight, pulling her up against me and wrapping my arm around her.

"That's funny, Gretchen, because I've been here working with Hacker and just went up to get Stephanie after she arrived." I saw her eyes narrow and her lip curl slightly. "I'm sure you have someone, uh, I mean *something* to do. Bye."

I pulled Stephanie along with me as I brushed past Gretchen, pushing her out of the way with my shoulder when she refused to budge to let us pass by her. I was going to have to set that bitch straight so she finally got it or she could pack her shit and hit the fucking road. I wasn't going to put up with her bullshit anymore. I didn't bother introducing the two of them because that slut, Gretchen, wasn't even close to being on the same class and level as Stephanie.

"Who the hell was that?" Stephanie demanded as she dug in her heels and crossed her arms over her chest as we reached Hacker's door. She stood, tapping one foot, glaring at me with one brow raised. Fuck, I didn't want to deal with this shit now. Gretchen wasn't important, and I didn't want to waste a second with Stephanie before she had to leave explaining exactly how unimportant that whore was. Dammit.

"Are you sleeping with her, Reaper? Please tell me you didn't bring me here where you keep your floozies. I know what we have is tenuous at this point, but I would really hope you wouldn't be fucking someone else while you've been with me! Please. Tell me I'm wrong, Reaper." She looked to be getting redder in the face with each passing second.

"No! Hell no, baby! I haven't touched a single fucking soul since the night of Mama's birthday bash when we hooked up. Please give me some credit. Jesus. You know I wasn't celibate before we found each other again, but there hasn't been anyone but you since then, for fuck's sake. That bitch doesn't seem to know her place here lately, but I'm going to make sure it's crystal clear for her. That I can promise you. I don't want anyone but you, baby." My hand cupped the side of her face and my thumb brushed along her bottom lip. I needed her to understand that she was it for me. She would be it for me forever.

She looked slightly mollified as I knocked on Hacker's door. Hacker answered and enveloped her in a big bear hug. The possessive fucker in me felt a moment's jealousy, but the rational side knew they were just friends and Hacker's feelings for her were strictly brotherly.

I sat in his recliner as Hacker explained the tracking program to her and the safety features he embedded in it. It was a bit of a relief when she took it all in stride, and I loved that she had the ability to enter a three digit code that set a panic beacon off to his computer if something happened, which would forward to his phone if he wasn't at the computer. It was the next best thing to me being able to protect her.

"Sam and Sean are coming down next Thursday night to help me load everything up so we can head back no later than Sunday morning. So I'll be down there alone for less than two weeks. Not to mention, I have Pam and her husband down the hall and my friends at work. I'll do my best not to be alone outside my apartment. Okay? And if I have to, I'll keep my phone in my damn bra so it's always on me. Does that make you feel better, Reaper?" Something in my expression must have told her that it didn't ease my worry, because she added, "Trust me, babe, I want to come back to you and Remi just as bad as you want me safe." I knew she was hoping to reassure me, but until she was back here permanently where I could protect her, it wasn't really working. She sat in my lap and feathered her fingers through my hair. Damn, that felt good.

I couldn't discuss club business with her, but if everything went well, I would be in Des Moines and the club could even escort her back if she was ready to leave by Saturday night. I made a mental note to talk to her brother to ensure that was possible, but I didn't mention it to her because I wasn't sure what the threshold of her tolerance was in regards to my interference in her personal life. Our relationship was new and still fragile.

"Yeah, okay. But I'd still feel better if I was with you." I held her close, feeling the silky strands of her curls tickling my nose. She smelled so good, like sunshine and flowers, and felt even better held close to me. I just wanted her safe. She was the mother of my child.

When it came to her safety? I wasn't fucking taking chances…

Stephanie

I had to admit, having knowledge of a tracking device on my phone was different than one being applied to it without my knowledge. I felt some level of relief after Erik—I still had a really hard time calling him Hacker—showed me the safety features he had created for me. I felt certain there would be no issues with Michael, and I knew I could count on my friends, and Pam, to be my safety net while I was there. Speaking of Pam, I would really miss her, and I knew she would miss Remi, but she would understand after I explained everything to her.

As we left Hacker's room and his multitude of computer screens and laptops, Reaper leaned against a door, two up from Hacker's, and pulled me close to him. He reached behind his back, opening the door and backing into the room with me. As soon as the door was closed, he pressed me against it, holding my hands over my head and placing his lips against mine in a wild and desperate kiss. Our tongues battled for dominance as our teeth nipped each other's lips and our tongues followed to soothe the bruised flesh. He broke away to trail kisses and bites down the side of my neck, pulling my tank top strap over my shoulder with his teeth and running his tongue along the top of my bra, pushing under the edge, reaching for more and more of my breast.

I was panting like a wild animal as I tried to move my hands down to touch him, but he held them tighter whispering "no" against my chest, his breath tickling the tops of my breasts. I moaned and writhed against his erection, as it pressed against his jeans, in an animalistic attempt to gain freedom and get him closer to me. I wanted him with a frantic desperation, needing him deep inside me.

Right. Now.

He let go of my hands to grab my ass, lifting me so I could wrap my legs around his waist, pressing my wet core against his cock. The friction of the double layer of the seams of the denim between us bordered on painful pleasure as it pressed against my clit with each thrust. I tried to hold back my release, but Reaper seemed to sense this and gripped my ass tightly, grinding into my mound until I was sure my wetness had seeped through and he knew how incredibly turned on I was.

"Don't hold back on me, baby," he whispered against my lips. "Give it to me. Come for me." He kissed me deeply, swallowing my moans and screams as I came at his whispered words. Every orgasm with this man left me feeling shattered, my body speaking to his without words. As my nerves reconstructed after the initial explosion, I drifted back to earth, culminating in the pulsing centered between my legs.

I gasped against his lips, "I need you, Reaper. Now. Please." I felt agitated and needy. I wanted him to lay me on the bed and fuck me like crazy. I prayed he would give me what I wanted and not make me wait.

"Colton. Use my real name when we're alone. God, I desperately want to be the man you knew before. I'm trying, baby. Now, tell me what you want." He looked intently in my eyes. I grasped the sides of his face, my fingers rasping in the short hairs of his beard, my thumb gently caressing the scar that ran from near his eye, through his beard, to his jaw even though he cringed as I did so. Reaching up, I gently kissed it.

"Colton, I want you to take me. Now. I want to take off your clothes and touch you. I want to worship you and have you worship me. Please. I need this."

He groaned, squeezing his eyes tightly shut as he held me close to him and turned toward the bed. He laid me out on it, climbing over me and straddling me as he slipped off his cut, then grabbed the back of his shirt, jerking it over his head. I couldn't stop my hands from grazing his abs as he revealed them. I traced over his tats and realized there were scars buried carefully within the intricate designs. I lightly ran my fingertips along them as he sat still, barely breathing. Becoming bold, I unbuttoned and unzipped his jeans, freeing the end of his cock. I pressed down on the waistband of his jeans to fully release him. Leaning forward, I allowed my tongue to travel from the base, along the silky skin of his shaft, to the top of his cock where I captured the clear bead of moisture that was gathering at the tip, suckling it off. He inhaled with a hissing breath through clenched teeth. Due to the angle, I couldn't take him in as deep as I wanted, and I felt frustration building.

He pulled back and stood to remove his jeans as I whimpered in protest of his taking away the source of my contentment, then quickly unfastened my shorts and pulled them from my body. He jerked my tank top over my head and unclasped my bra, pulling it off my arms and tossing it to the side. Kneeling, he ran his large, calloused hands up the outside of my thighs, curving over the tops and along the tender, sensitive skin at my inner thighs. I grasped at the blanket, kneading it into a rumpled mess.

His breath was warm against my belly as he skimmed along my skin until he bit down on my clit and then my lips through my panties, sucking on the damp center briefly before pulling them off and dropping them to the floor. He returned to circle my clit with the tip of his tongue, then flattening it as he pressed it firmly, circling again before dipping down into my liquid heat.

I thought I was going to die with the incredibly erotic sensations he triggered. His tongue glided in, out, and around, never stopping, even as I felt the pressure of another orgasm building. My body tensed and quivered as my climax pulsed and burst through me, causing me to scream and thrash as he held me in place, torturing my overly sensitive body with nearly unbearable pleasure. I grasped the longer hair at the top of his head, pulling without thought.

Panting, gasping inhalations escaped me as my breasts heaved with each ragged breath I took. I opened my eyes to him rolling a condom over his thick shaft. As he crawled up the length of my body, I felt his encased erection tease me from my ankle to my thigh before it rested, still and heavy, between my thighs. I reached down to guide him inside me, but he took both my hands and held them to the side of my head with his own, resting the majority of his weight on his elbows. He probed at my wet folds, teasing me until I was squirming and clutching at his legs with my own.

I pressed my heels into his tight ass, trying to bring him home, but he still resisted, smiling a shit-eating grin at me because he knew the agony he was causing. My body felt strung taught, and I wanted to feel him sheathed within me so bad I growled in frustration. Yes, I fricking *growled*. I felt rabid and animalistic in that moment and completely out of control.

"Tell me exactly what you want, baby. Tell me what you want me to do to you and how you want me to do it. I need to hear the words or I won't go any further." I was going to strangle him after this was over. I swore I was. He was making me crazy. Certifiably insane. I felt like a raving sex addict fiending for my next fix. Was it possible to have an addiction to someone's cock and the sex that accompanied it? Because if so, I was hooked and I wasn't interested in rehab.

"I want you. Now. I want you inside me. I want you to fuck me. Hard. Deep. Bury yourself deep in my pussy over and over until you fill me with your cum. Make me feel you inside me for the next two weeks." Two could play at this game. *How do you like those bad apples, Mr. Sex-on-a-stick?*

Evidently, he wasn't quite expecting that response because his eyes flashed wide before he closed them tight and plunged so deep and fast into me I felt his balls hit my ass. He reached down, grasping my legs and raising them over his shoulders to provide a better angle, and he lurched into me in a mad but steady rhythm. His balls slapped against me and I heard my wetness and the sound of skin against skin with every stroke into me. Who would have thought those sounds could be the strongest aphrodisiac? I was in sensory overload, and as I felt another orgasm building, I knew this one would be more intense than ever before.

When it hit me, it was like blinding light and pure silence as I clenched and tightened around him, every muscle in my body responding to the overwhelming pleasure he had just unleashed upon my soul. It hit me like a crashing wave, knocking me senseless. As sight and sound slowly returned and I was reduced to a satiated puddle, I felt his pace quicken and his strokes shorten as his breathing became more ragged and labored.

His hair and skin were soaked in sweat, and knowing how he had reached this state gave me a sense of elated power. Knowing I could cause his loss of control like that allowed me the boldness to free my hands from his to grab his hips in an attempt to guide his strokes. As my calves tightened around his neck and shoulders, my inner muscles tightened around his cock in anticipation. I saw him lose the battle with the last shred of his control as he threw back his head, plunged deeply one last time, and yelled out in a primitive roar. I felt the explosion and throbbing of his cock as it filled the condom within me, the heat of his cum reaching through the thin barrier to warm me from the inside.

"Fuck. Fuck. Oh my God. Shit. Fuck." He collapsed on me in a sweating, heaving heap, kissing my breasts, my neck, my shoulder, anywhere his lips could reach before he fell to the side, pulling me with him. He held me tight in his arms with his chin resting on the top of my head, my ear pressed to his racing heart and our legs a tangled web of limbs.

"Jesus Christ, Stephanie. Damn. That was incredible, and I can honestly say I have never felt anything like it in my fucking life. I don't know what you do to me, or what magic your body performs on me, but I'll take it every chance I can. Fucking hell." He was out of breath, and I felt satisfied and blissful in that brief moment in time, like nothing in the world could harm me or ruin this feeling.

We must have dozed off in our exhaustion before I woke to his startled jerk. He looked around with wild eyes briefly, before they settled on me, and I watched them slowly clear to focus on me. My hands stroked his chest and I kissed his shoulder. He nudged my face up and kissed me reverently on my swollen and bruised lips.

My forehead rested against his, and I knew I couldn't postpone leaving any longer. As it was, it would be late by the time I arrived at my apartment. I wouldn't have traded a minute of this time together, though, and you wouldn't hear a peep of a complaint out of me.

"I don't want to, but I need to get on the road," I finally whispered. His response was to hold me tighter, and I knew he didn't want to let me go either. He must have finally obtained the resolution he needed to release me, as I felt his arms loosen and he lay on his back staring at the ceiling.

"Do you care if I use your shower?" I asked, spying a bathroom ahead of me. He waved a hand as if saying "be my guest" but didn't meet my eyes. I sat up and gathered my clothes. I knew he was trying to hold it together as hard as I was. So I gave him his moment as I closed the bathroom door and flipped on the hot water.

Chapter THIRTY-THREE

Reaper

LETTING HER GO THIS TIME NEARLY FUCKING KILLED ME. I WISHED I had told her how I felt before she left, but I just held her and kissed her, keeping my words sealed inside me like the damn coward I was. Yes, I had told her I loved her before, but I hadn't asked her to stay or told her I needed her to stay. I just knew, if I opened my mouth, I would beg her on my knees not to leave me, and the tears that burned the backs of my eyes would escape, branding me a weak, fucking sappy-ass fool. Dammit, I should have put my foot down and had someone else pack her stuff and bring it up.

Instead, I stood there and watched her drive off in silence.

I needed to get a fucking grip. I promised her I would go see my baby girl. She was sure it would be difficult for Remi without her momma, and she made me promise to go over to her and take her with me to spend time together. I would do anything for my girls. That thought had me smiling despite the ache of loneliness I felt at knowing she was traveling farther and farther from me with each passing second. I fought off the feeling of the panic attack trying to sneak into the edges of my consciousness. Taking deep breaths, I pictured the look on her face as she reached her last orgasm. That look, and doing everything to accomplish it every time I was with her, became my goal and grounding rod.

I told myself repeatedly that I wasn't alone anymore. She would be back, and I had my brothers… I had my daughter. I felt the waves of panic recede like the tide going out.

Hollywood walked up behind me, causing me to jump slightly before I hid it behind rubbing my hands over my face and through my hair.

"Hey, man, you okay?" he asked me in a low tone.

"Yeah, bro, I'm good. I'm just really worried about her, and it's just giving me a really bad feeling. It's probably nothing, but I can't shake it." I shook my head and stuffed my hands in my pockets.

"Your instincts are pretty finely tuned, bro, but I think it's probably just the thought of her being so far away and that dickhole being out there. Things will be fine and these next couple of weeks will go by faster than you think. Hacker hooked up her phone, right?" I nodded. "All right then, don't worry, man. She knows what to do if anything goes to shit. Oh, and by the way, I didn't know you could put on such a show." He gave a wicked grin and laughed as he took off running before I could catch him and beat his smart ass. Little fucker. In truth, I really didn't give a rat's ass if every brother heard me fucking her. Good, I thought. Let them all know I was claiming her and they could keep their hands and eyes off her. I shook my head and began laughing myself.

I grinned as I thought, *I need to go shopping; my baby girl needs a car seat.*

Chapter
THIRTY-FOUR

Stephanie

THE TRIP BACK WAS WAY TOO LONG AND BORING AS HELL, resulting in too much time to think. I began to question the sanity of leaving my bugga-boo behind and leaving my job and apartment all to chase the dream of owning my own place. I knew the Oasis had the history of being a steady business, but was I really cut out to be a bar owner, and would the improvements I had in mind chase away customers who were loyal to Mama Jean? Would they be resistant to change? I would lose my parents' investment. It was a big stressor, weighing heavy on my shoulders.

My dad and brothers had offered to help with the construction portion of the remodeling I had in mind, but I would still have to use a lot of my savings from the past few years to buy the materials.

It would nearly wipe me out. It would mean staying with my parents a little longer than I had hoped before we could start to look for our own place, but I figured we could live with that. Not to mention, my mom would be over the moon at having her granddaughter under the same roof. But was I ultimately doing what was best for Remi? Because that was what really mattered in the long run.

Going home had made me think a lot about Remi's future. Sure, she was young now, and I could keep her pretty safe and sheltered with Pam watching her, but what about when she started going to school? It was a big city, and the schools were big as well. What happened if she became a number and got lost in the crowd, falling behind in her learning? What happened if she didn't have her chance to shine because her teachers were too busy trying to maintain a classroom with too many children, spreading their time with each student so very thin?

The thought of raising Remi in the same small town that I had been, felt comforting. It was nearly unheard of for crime to be in the news. Of course, a lot of people felt that was because the MC scared a lot of the troublemakers away. They kept their seedier businesses, like their strip club, out of town, leaving the garage and the lumberyard as their businesses in town. The lumberyard made a killing because they were the sole supplier to all the construction companies and contractors in the area. In fact, that would be where a lot of the materials I needed for the remodel would come from, with the exception of restaurant and bar-specific equipment that I would need to order from a special supplier.

And Colton. Colton was on my mind about every other second. That had to have been the most mind-blowing sex I had ever experienced. Jesus Martha. Talk about hot. I wasn't sure what made that time better than all the rest, but it seemed like each time was better than the last with us. Which got me wondering... will there be another time? He had told me he loved me, but it was only that one time. And he was really quiet when I left. I wasn't sure how to take that.

I called Pam to let her know where I was and approximately when I would be home. Dang, I sure would miss our visits when I stopped by to pick up Remi after work. She said she hadn't seen Michael all weekend. Of course she hadn't, probably because he was too busy stalking me back home. I was being careful on the trip and trying to be observant of headlights that seemed to follow me. So far, anytime I slowed down if I got nervous, the vehicles all just went around me. Thank God. I really didn't believe he would mess with me again, but the experience had definitely made me more aware of my surroundings—something I should have done before. Hindsight really is 20/20.

I was getting pretty sleepy by the time I pulled into the parking garage back at my apartment, and I was actually looking forward to crawling in my bed—well, sofa—and getting some sleep before work tomorrow. Pam called as I was pulling my SUV in and parking. She was checking to see where I was because she was worried about me driving back so late and was relieved to hear I made it okay.

We continued to talk as I went upstairs after collecting my new key from my mailbox. I hung up with Pam, promising to go over to visit her after work tomorrow, and secured all of the locks on my door. Dropping my bag just inside the door, I hung up my keys and went to the bathroom. After I brushed my teeth and peed, I shuffled out to the living room, set the alarm on my phone, and crashed on the couch.

In the morning, I didn't remember even falling asleep. I did, however, remember my dreams were once again plagued by a blue-eyed sex god, but this time they were so much more vivid and realistic...

Chapter THIRTY-FIVE

Reaper

THIS WAS MY SIXTH NIGHT HAVING DINNER WITH THE RAVEN-haired beauty sitting next to me. Sixth. Almost an entire week. I hadn't missed a single day with her. After all, I had over two years of her life to make up for. I wasn't missing another second that I didn't have to. Stephanie's parents had been great. They had her ready and waiting at 5:30 p.m. every day after I got off work. I would pick her up, and it would just be the two of us. Of course, she had asked where her mommy was about a hundred times, and that broke my fucking heart.

Tonight she had a little pink princess backpack on her back when I picked her up. She had stood at the top of the steps to the porch holding her grandpa's hand, jumping up and down in excitement as I pulled up in my truck, complete with her hot pink and black car seat strapped in the back seat. I could not believe how happy this little girl made me. It was like her sunshine lit up all the fucking darkness in my head. When I was with her, I felt bright, happy, free... saved.

Tonight she was spending the night with me for the first time. I had finally made the decision to buy my own place. I was able to take quick possession because the house has been empty for months after the elderly owner had moved to Arizona. His kids didn't want it and it had just been sitting there collecting dust. I had spent every lunch this week mowing the grass down, cleaning up inside, and picking up the bare necessities for furniture. I had become a right fucking Suzy Homemaker. Who would have thought? The guys gave me shit every day, and I just laughed. What the fuck could I say? They were right and I didn't give a flying fuck. My life felt nearly perfect for the first time in years. It was like this little girl of mine had breathed new life into me. Now if I could just convince her momma to join us...

I helped Remi cut up her food and then handed her the fork, keeping the knife over by my side of the table. I was learning all the little things that parents did to keep their children safe, and it felt fucking amazing. She smiled at me as she sat on her knees and popped a bite in her mouth. She had insisted she didn't need a booster seat 'cause she was a "big girl," and hell if I was gonna tell my little princess she wasn't. Shit, this little girl of mine already had me wrapped around her tiny finger, and she didn't have a fucking clue. I laughed to myself.

My mind wandered off to her momma again. I had chosen the house on the edge of town with her in mind, but I hadn't told anyone that. It was on the road out of town that ran down to the town square where the Oasis was located. It was also a little bit country, sitting on fifteen acres, so Stephanie would feel much like she had growing up. It would also allow Remi to have room to stretch her legs. I already had the guys lined up for tomorrow to help me install a fence along the perimeter and a solar-powered automatic gate across the driveway. I wasn't taking chances with my little princess getting out on the small highway.

It felt good to finally put the money I had earned and stashed away for years to good use. I got a great deal on the house, and I planned on updating it while preserving some of the old farmhouse character. I was hoping Stephanie would help me make some of the choices for materials and colors. I was nervous as shit to ask her, but I really was hoping we could make a go of trying to be a family. I didn't know where, exactly, our relationship would end up. What I did know was the sex was fucking incredible and I enjoyed being with her. She was sexy, smart, ambitious, loving, and a great mother. I could certainly do worse.

Remi and I finished our meals, and I paid the waitress. Funny how I noticed she was trying to flirt with me and coo at Remi, but my dick didn't seem to give a shit, not even when she bent down to pass Remi's plate over, giving me a clear and unobstructed view of her tits spilling out of her top. Hey, I didn't say I never noticed. A man appreciates a nice-looking set of tits like a hot bike or a smoking car, but it doesn't mean we want to own them all.

I gathered Remi up and loaded her in the truck, buckling her car seat like a pro now. Who would have thought Colton Alcott would get the hang of this dad stuff so easy? Not just get the hang of it, but love the hell out of it.

"You ready to go see Daddy's new house, baby girl?" I wasn't sure how much she understood of what I said, but she sure seemed to understand a lot. My girl was one helluva smart cookie.

"House!" Remi slapped her hands on the armrests of her car seat. I smiled and kissed her cheek.

As I started up my truck, Sixx AM's "Life is Beautiful" blasted through the speakers. I looked in the rearview mirror at my daughter bopping her head to the music. Yes, yes, it most certainly was... and getting better every day.

Chapter
THIRTY-SIX

Stephanie

MUCH TO EVERYONE AT THE RESTAURANT'S SURPRISE AND disappointment, I had turned in my notice. It was a sad moment for me as well, but I knew there were amazing things waiting on my horizon. I had been packing like a fiend all week too. Remi's room was mostly packed—I hadn't realized how much that little girl had! She had more clothes than I did! Sheesh!—and I was trying to go through her baby stuff to donate the items she had outgrown.

All of the stuff in the kitchen was packed. Well, all the stuff I wouldn't use over the next week, anyway. I had left out a single place setting for myself, a couple of pans, a bowl, and a cup. There wasn't much in the living room, and my brothers would help me with the big stuff like my couch and TV stand. I hadn't really acquired a lot of furniture over the last few years, which would help make the move a little easier.

I sat down to watch a movie with a bowl of popcorn. It was Friday night and I was taking a break from packing to just relax and chill. My phone rang like clockwork at 8:30 p.m. Reaper would make a point to have Remi call me after he had her dropped off at my parents and she was ready for bed. I smiled as I picked it up and answered.

"Hi Mommy! Wemi go to bed. At Daddy's house! Miss you, Mommy. Daddy talk. Nigh-night!" Those were the main points I caught of her conversation which was interspersed with nonsensical toddler babble. It was hard not to laugh when she was trying so hard to sound big. I heard a rustling and pattering feet along with a muffled "I'll be there to tuck you in shortly, princess" before his deep, sexy voice came on the phone.

"Hey, baby. Everything okay with you? I guess you heard Remi is staying with me tonight? I really hope you don't mind. I probably should have discussed it with you first. I didn't really think about that until I had already spoken to your parents and made the plans." He was rambling about as much as his daughter had, and I was pretty sure he was worried about my response. I wasn't really sure how I felt. I hoped everyone would behave tonight, because I didn't want my daughter exposed to the sort of things I saw on Sunday.

"Ummm, yeah. Are you sure it's a good idea to have her there though? I don't want that Gretchen bitch near her." My hackles were rising. I didn't even know that wench, but I sure as hell didn't like the way she had tried to start trouble between us. I especially didn't want to think about what he may have done with her before. That made me a little nauseous.

"Well, about that… We're not at the clubhouse."

"You're not? Where are you then? Did you get a hotel?" Please, God, let him have her somewhere safe. Not that I didn't trust him with her, but I knew he wasn't used to making child-centered choices yet.

"No… I actually wanted it to be a surprise to you, but…" I heard a shuffling as he moved the phone around. "Well, I bought a house. I was hoping you would give me some feminine pointers on some of the decorating and remodeling. I wasn't going to say anything until you came back. I guess I didn't plan on Big-Mouth-Magee spilling the beans." He gave a nervous laugh. "Are you mad? It's clean, I promise."

"I'm a little shocked, I guess. But, no, I'm not mad at all. I just didn't expect you to leave the guys at the clubhouse. I thought you liked being close to them." Absently, I flicked pieces of popcorn around the bowl. I missed Remi something fierce. It had pretty much been her and me against the world for the last couple of years, so I was a little jealous on top of missing her. I was also really missing her daddy, but I didn't know if he wanted to hear that. I heard Remi holler "Daddy!" in the background.

"Baby, can I call you back? I want to talk to you, but our princess is waiting for me. I won't be long."

I agreed and ended the call. My head was spinning. Wow. He *bought a house?* Whoa. I was impressed and surprised. He really was taking his new daddy role seriously. I began to imagine what sort of house he would choose as I waited for him to call back. Probably something close to the shop and clubhouse in case he was needed. It would definitely need a garage big enough for his bike, and probably his truck. I hadn't realized I had eaten the entire bowl of popcorn until I noticed I was pushing seeds around trying to find more popcorn. I got up and placed the bowl in the sink and refilled my water. I had just sat on the couch when my phone started to ring again.

"Hey you! That was quick," I said without looking at the phone. The answer was silence. "Hello? Hellooooooo?" I looked at my phone, thinking he must have a bad signal and lost the call. *Unknown caller.* Weird. I rarely got those calls anymore. "Hello?" Nothing. So I hung up. Must have been a wrong number. I thought I heard my doorknob rattle then, but it must have been my imagination or someone bumped it as they carried stuff down the hall, because I never heard anything else after that.

It rang again and this time *Colton Sex God* popped up on my caller ID. I chuckled as I blushed, remembering entering him into my contacts like that after the birthday bash. I hadn't thought to change it, but I probably should before he saw it. Talk about embarrassing. Lordy!

"Hello there, good looking," I said in a sultry phone-sex-line voice, teasing him. I heard him chuckle and then groan softly.

"Shit, baby, don't do that to me. We're too far away for that shit, and I think my dick heard you. Thanks a lot."

"You're so crude," I giggled, "and I like it." I wiggled my eyebrows as if he could see me. *Man, I'm such a dork.* If he knew how many times I had touched myself imagining it was him, he would have a heyday with that. I felt my face flame with embarrassment and was glad he couldn't see me.

"Baby, you haven't seen crude. Facetime me and I'll show you how crude I can be." I could hear the lasciviousness and the smile in his voice. I also knew I looked like total crap right now and there was no way I was letting him see that!

"Uhhhhh, yeah, I don't know if that would be a good idea. I look like poop on a stick! And what if Remi woke up and caught you? Hmmmmmm, *Daddy?* How would that look, you naughty boy?" I teased him, hoping it would be enough to get him to drop the Facetime thoughts. He laughed.

"I love hearing you say that. I also love hearing you call me 'Daddy.'" He laughed. "And okay, I'll behave. But let me Facetime you. I need to see you. I don't care what you look like, baby." He was not going to let this drop, so I reluctantly agreed.

Seeing his gorgeous face pop onto my phone screen made my heart lurch. This man did something to me with that smile and those dimples. I wanted to reach through and mess up his dark hair and land kisses all over his face. I wanted to run my hands through the scruff along his jawline and across his cheeks. God, I knew I was smiling like a goof.

"There's my gorgeous girl," he said. "Man, I have missed you. Don't get me wrong, I love having this time with Remi, and your family has been great about it, but I kinda like having your ass around too." He winked and I laughed.

"We aren't even really dating. We're just co-parenting and getting to know each other. How can you miss me?" I laughed and tried to capture some of the stray hairs that insisted on escaping my messy bun, wishing I had put a little makeup on today. "Besides, I look awful, you don't need to fib to make me feel better."

His face turned serious, and I thought I had said something to piss him off.

"Is that all you see us as? Really? I mean, granted, I don't know exactly what the future holds for us, but we obviously have more than co-parenting going on. We have an amazing sexual chemistry, and we seem to get along well. How about if we reserve judgement for now? We'll let things lie until you get back and then see where things take us. And you are absolutely fucking sexy right now, so I don't need to 'fib' to make you feel good." His grin returned, and I felt my panties melt. Jesus Nelly, that damn smile of his was a killer.

"Okay, I think that is doable… So, how is Remi doing with you? You should Facetime me with her in the morning before you take her home. God, I miss her."

"She misses her momma too. She asks me about you every day. Damn, Stephanie, she is so fucking smart. She amazes me daily. You have done an incredible job with her. She is so good and polite. Everywhere I take her people compliment me on her behavior and manners. It makes me proud because she's mine, but I feel guilty because I can't really take any of the fucking credit for it. I kick myself all the fucking time for throwing out that damn piece of paper. Things could have been so different." He ran his hand over his face in frustration. I hated seeing him beating himself up. We couldn't live with constant woulda, coulda, shouldas. It was what it was.

"Hey! We need to stop dwelling on things we can't change. We can only take what we have and move forward. Remi has her daddy in her life now, and I'm so happy about that. I tell myself everything happens for a reason. I don't know why, but maybe this is the way it was supposed to be. I'm just glad you didn't think I got pregnant on purpose or kept her from you intentionally."

"I know you would never do that, Stephanie." He looked at me with a serious expression. "Look, I'm still very fucked up, Steph, but I'm working on it. I've done some fucked up things in my life. Things I'm not going to burden you with, but they still weigh heavy on me."

My finger reached out and caressed the edge of his face on the screen as if he were real. "Baby, it's okay. The past is the past. We can't change any of that. We can only move forward and work to be honest with each other from here on out. Communication is important whether we move forward with a serious relationship between us or we end up simply co-parenting."

He looked down and pulled his lip between his teeth. "About that… The club is working on cleaning shit up, but we still aren't perfect. I need you to understand that Remi comes first, always, but my club is important to me too. They took me in when I was at my absolute lowest. So I know I'm asking a lot, but I need you to accept that there are things that are simply club business that I just can't talk about. It's not about keeping secrets, it's about the trust and rules of the club. No club business is to be discussed with civilians. No exceptions." He took a deep breath. "I just don't want you thinking it's personal, or that I'm hiding things from you, and I want you to know I would *never* do anything to endanger Remi. Speaking of our little princess, she ate all of her lasagna for dinner tonight. But I plead the fifth on the disappearance of her outfit she was wearing at the time." His exaggeratedly innocent expression and the way he acted like he couldn't meet my eyes had me laughing.

"She ate *lasagna*? She usually only eats stinking chicken nuggets! I can't believe you got her to eat lasagna! What did you bribe her with, or what magic are you weaving on her?" I gave him a mocking stern expression with a raised eyebrow before I couldn't hold my smile in.

"I might have told her little girls who eat all their food sometimes get ponies for Christmas…" He looked chagrined as he had the nerve to look all wide-eyed innocence.

"You whaaaaaaaat? Oh dear Lord, we need to work on your parenting style." I couldn't help but laugh as I told him this. I stifled a yawn, as I didn't want to let him go, but it had been a long day, and if I wanted to get out of here when my brothers came next week, I needed to get up early to get the rest of my stuff packed this weekend. I would only keep out the very minimum and necessary items to be packed last minute. I only planned on leaving out my uniforms for work and a couple pairs of sweats and T-shirts for home. Remi's bed still needed to be disassembled too.

"You look tired, baby. I better let you go. Your boss isn't treating you shitty, is he? I can make a quick trip down to kick some asses if I need to. And no sign of or issues from that dipshit, right?" He was so cute, but my job was great with me turning in my notice. They all said they would miss me, but they were happy for me.

"No, nothing from Michael," I laughed. "I told you he wouldn't bother me. And yes, they were fine, really. We're all going out on Wednesday after work, as a little going-away party, sort of. I decided to take a short day on Thursday so I could be home for my brothers when they get here, and then I took off Friday. It was a slow day anyway, and they already have two people hired that are doing great so they really won't need me Friday. But you're right, today was crazy busy and I am a little tired." I hated to let him go. It felt so natural to talk to him about the little random bits of my daily life.

"All right. Sweet dreams, beautiful. And yes, I will Facetime you with our baby girl in the morning. Goodnight." I could tell by his expression he was reluctant to let me go as well. I stifled another yawn and knew I needed to sleep. I really wanted to tell him I loved him, but it made me feel nervous to say it again since he hadn't said it since that first time.

"'Night." We closed down Facetime and I shut the movie off. I had barely watched twenty minutes of it anyway. There was a moment's regret that I didn't ensure he knew how I felt before I let him go, but I told myself we had plenty of time. My eyes grew heavy as soon as I snuggled into my pillow and blanket. That night my dreams were flooded with a little family playing in the yard of their home with a snow-white pony wandering around grazing in the pasture...

Chapter THIRTY-SEVEN

Reaper

W E HAD USED MY PHONE TO FACETIME STEPHANIE, AND REMI was going fucking nuts after talking to her momma. My little princess loved her momma; that was an absolute certainty. I smiled as I shook my head and looked in the rearview mirror at my chattering princess. Every time I brought her back to her grandparents, I hated to let her go, but I needed to head into the clubhouse to check in and take care of a few things. I also needed to make sure there was enough sober motherfuckers to help me with my fence like they said they would.

I dropped Remi off with Stephanie's mom and she talked to me for a little bit about how happy she was that I was able to spend time with Remi. I thought she was hinting a little about finding out what my intentions were with Stephanie, but I played stupid like I didn't catch on and she let it lie. I wasn't sure where things were sitting myself. I also thought it was ironic, considering how skeptical her mom was the first time she met me. She had taken one look at my scruffy two-day beard, tats, chain on my wallet, scuffed motorcycle boots, and I could see she had reservations. She was a little hesitant to let me take Remi that first day, but her husband seemed to approve of me, and I thought he must have talked to her because my reception upon bringing Remi back to them was considerably warmer. Since then, she was my staunchest supporter and was constantly dropping hints about Stephanie and me.

I pulled my truck into the clubhouse parking lot after picking up all my supplies at the lumberyard the club owned. Benefit to that was I got all my supplies at cost, so it didn't dent my budget too bad. I got out, swinging the door shut, and had to wait a minute for my eyes to adjust after heading into the dim interior from the bright sun outside. The sight that greeted me left me wondering how much help I would have today. There were passed-out bodies in the booth benches, on the couches, and some on the floor. Some had half-naked bitches sprawled across them to top it all off. Jesus H. Christ, they must have had one hellova party here last night. I kicked a few boots of those who had said they were going to help today to get their attention and get them moving, if they were still going to help, that was. The fucks.

I threw on a pot of coffee since I was sure they were gonna need it and headed back to see if Hacker or Hollywood were up since they were absent from the piles out in the main clubhouse.

I knocked on Hollywood's door a few times before he shuffled to the door, opening it as he yawned and scratched his chest absently. I saw a red mop of hair fanned across his pillows and a slender arm hanging off the bed behind him. Fucking Hollywood. He was a Lothario with women, and he sure had a thing for redheads.

"Hey, you fuck. You sober? You still on board for helping me with the fence today? Looks like there was one hell of a party last night, and I'm guessing I'll probably lose half of my fencing crew to hangovers." I laughed. I couldn't be mad, 'cause Fridays were our regular night to party. The party girls would line up in hopes to make it in and hook up with a "big bad biker" for the night. Why it was a bragging right to these bitches, I didn't know, but if they made the cut and were admitted, they were hot, willing, and fresh, which made them a nice change from the regular club whores for the guys.

"Yeah, man, I'm there. You know I have your back, bro. I just need to shower and get dressed then kick this crazy bitch out of here. Shit, you know I love women and women love me, but I think this one might be a little fucked in the head." He gestured a thumb over his shoulder at the chick in the bed. "She started crying and talking about how alone she was and how she didn't know what she was going to do since her boyfriend dumped her, blah blah, blah. I didn't even stick my dick in her. I just held her fruity ass and let her sleep off her drunk. I think I'm getting soft or losing my touch. Fucking A." He shook his head in resignation and disgust, and I tried not to laugh at him because I could see he was really beside himself with the situation. I could imagine *that* was quite a change for his horny ass.

"We can drop her off somewhere or call her a cab, bro. Just let me know. I'm gonna go shake Hacker's fucking ass outta bed." He nodded and shut his door as I wandered down the hall toward Hacker's door.

I knocked once and almost fell over when the door flew open right away.

"Hey, bro! What's up? You ready to start this fence shit?" He was already dressed and all wide eyed and bushy tailed. Shit, usually I could barely drag him out of bed in the fucking mornings.

"Yeah, man, that's why I was knocking. Damn, you're up early."

"Yeah, well, I've been working on checking into that asshole that was fucking with Steph. I had a guy that was supposed to call me back this morning, but he hasn't called. I'll have my phone on me, so it's no big fucking deal, I guess. Look at it as a perk. You didn't have to pound on my fucking door again." He busted out laughing.

"Speaking of, what have you found out about the guy so far?"

"Not much. No record. Not even a fucking parking ticket. He did have a bleep that showed up as a sealed case when he was a teen, which is what I'm waiting to hear about. He has three older sisters, a bunch of nieces and nephews. Went to community college for a general studies degree and got a supervisory position at the construction company he worked at through college. Been there since. He transferred with them to Des Moines from the Quad Cities when they expanded. I was a little surprised he would want to leave his family, but hey, maybe they drove him batshit crazy, ya know? Anyway, I have a few favors I called in for some street info too. He leaving her alone?" Hacker could find out if you farted in church last year, so I felt pretty comfortable with the info he dug up.

"Okay, cool, man. No, she said she hasn't heard a word from the dipshit. Let me know what you find out. I'm going to see if these other drunk fuckers are up and moving. You coming?"

"Yeah, let me grab my shades and I'll be out." He turned to go rummaging around through the papers and crap that littered his desk. I headed out to the main room again.

Most of the guys were up and drinking coffee with another pot brewing when I got out there. Vinny was drinking Jack. That was one tough and crazy bastard. He was our VP and was originally from New Jersey. We got along okay, but I wasn't sure if he was all there or not. I wouldn't have been surprised to hear he had some mafia in his blood, but he didn't talk about his past, and we didn't ask.

The prospects, Soap, DJ, and Joker, were straightening out the chairs and cleaning up. Soap looked a little green around the fucking gills, and I had to wonder how much that little shit drank last night. They weren't supposed to drink, but on Friday nights for the last few hours, the guys would look the other way. Joker was laughing and joking, as usual, and giving him and DJ shit for drinking too much of the moonshine his momma sent. Ah, that explained that shit.

"If y'all fuckers are sober enough, we can head out in twenty. With all of us working on this, I know it won't take long, and I appreciate y'all helping me out. I don't want to take a chance with my little girl getting in the road, so y'all are saving my ass. Thanks again." Everyone nodded, and a few of the guys smiled at the mention of my little girl. They were all shocked as shit when I told them I was a father. Shit, so was I for that matter. But they had all welcomed her into the fold. It was still a little mind numbing at times to think I was a dad. I had someone depending on me. Relying on me. And I wasn't alone.

I just prayed I would be a better dad than mine was, and I made a promise to *never* run out on my kid like he did.

Chapter
THIRTY-EIGHT

Stephanie

I DECIDED TO GRAB DINNER OUT SINCE I WAS DOWN TO VERY LITTLE in the apartment in the way of food. I went to the little diner I had suggested to Michael the first night I met him. I still liked the staff and the food was good, so I wasn't going to let my bad experience with him scare me away from the place.

I was really glad I hadn't seen him since returning. It would be awkward, and I was a little nervous, but I wasn't going to admit that to Reaper. He was worried enough as it was.

The waitress greeted me in her typical friendly manner and told me to take a seat wherever I wanted. There were several tables open, so I chose one by the windows where the sun was still shining through, warming me in the cool AC.

I looked around to see if I knew any of the other patrons when I felt someone looking at me. There were families engrossed in laughing conversations, a young couple in what looked to be an intimate conversation, and a few old men chattering at a table in the corner. No familiar faces. No one looking my way. Hmm. I looked out the window, but with the sunlight coming in, it was hard to see out in the parking lot. Must have been my imagination.

I placed my order and noticed a text message from Reaper. I opened it and saw a pretty wrought iron fence separated by brick pillars with a beautiful gate. There was a horse cut in metal highlighted in the center. I laughed when I read the message, "Remi's pony for now. Lol." I zoomed in on the pic because, quite frankly, I was nosey and noticed an older, but pretty well-kept single-story farmhouse. It had a front porch that ran the length of the front of the house. I wondered if there was a matching porch on the back. Shoot, why did I care? It wasn't like it was my house. And Reaper never really said what he wanted for us, just that "we would see where things went," and I wasn't sure if that was a hopeful statement or a blow-off statement.

There was a garage that looked like it was added later with a breezeway connecting the garage to the house porch. There were several large oak trees that looked like they provided great shade in the summer. It looked like a big barn was in the back. Everything appeared in need of paint, but structurally sturdy. Of course, I was judging from a picture, so who knew. Either way, the place looked homey, cozy, and welcoming. I was slightly envious that I couldn't provide that for Remi right now, but if things didn't work out between her father and me, at least she had his place and my parents' place to stretch her legs and be a kid.

After I overindulged in comfort food topped off with fresh apple pie with a crisp, flaky crust, I stepped out into the warm early evening. It was still daylight, but the sun was getting lower in the sky. As I walked to my SUV with the loose bits of asphalt crunching under my feet, I had the feeling of being watched again. I looked around, but still didn't notice anyone. I thought I was getting paranoid because Reaper asked me about Michael last night.

I shook off the feeling and headed home, making a few stops on the way home to get gas, a lottery ticket—because you just never knew—some boxes, and a movie from one of those rental boxes. Sometimes I hated not having cable, but it was a needless luxury, one I was glad I had skipped when I thought about the money I had saved, money that would be going toward the changes I wanted to make at the Oasis.

I stopped by Pam's apartment to see if she wanted to join me for my chick flick I picked, but she answered the door in an above-the-knee sequined dress and heels, putting a set of diamond studs in her ears.

"Hey girl! How's the packing going?" Her smile was bright and infectious.

"Pretty good." I nodded toward my flattened boxes shoved in two other boxes. "Just grabbed some more boxes. I was going to see if you wanted to join me for a movie, but I see you have more exciting plans." I smiled at her and waggled my eyebrows.

"Yeah, I wish," she said with a laugh. "We have an office party for the hub's work tonight. Nothing like schmoozing with a bunch of stuck-up assholes and their banking clients."

"Well, it's your loss. I make some of the best microwave popcorn in the country." I laughed and gave her a hug. Dang, I was going to miss her. We had started as a babysitter/mom relationship, but we had evolved into close friends.

"I can swing by tomorrow afternoon and help you with your packing if you want. Or we can hang out and drink wine…"

I clapped my hands like a small child would, and she laughed and waved as I headed to my apartment.

I dragged my boxes into my apartment, locked the door, and hung up my keys. I headed to the shower to wash off the sweat from lugging the boxes around in the humid air tonight. I set my phone on the counter and started the shower to heat up the water. My clothes got kicked into the growing pile in the hamper. Shit, I needed to do laundry tomorrow. A lot of those clothes would need to be packed up. If worse came to worse, I would shove them in a trash bag and wash them when I got home to my parents' house.

I climbed in the shower, closed my eyes, and tipped my head back into the heated stream. I imagined the water jets were Reaper massaging my scalp. I slid my hands up my torso to cup my breasts, squeezing them gently and pinching my nipples. In my mind, it was Reaper whose hands touched me. As I ran my hands back down my body, one glided over my smooth mound, my finger finding a slick wetness that had nothing to do with the water from the shower. A soft gasp and moan escaped my lips as I pictured Reaper looking up at me as he buried his face between my legs and worked his magic. When I came, it was with his name on my lips.

Drying myself with a plush towel, I felt my core pulse as I dried between my legs. I braced my hands on the edge of the counter, hanging my head as I tried to calm my breathing. My wet hair dripping cold water on my arms became chilly in the AC, and I broke out in goose bumps, shivering. What was I going to do if he didn't want me after all? Let's face it, I was fricking obsessed with him. I was pathetic.

My phone started to ring. The caller ID read *Unknown Caller*. As I walked out of the bathroom, trying to decide if I should answer it, I heard my doorknob rattle again. I answered the call, keeping an eye on my door.

"Hello?" Silence. Are you for real? "Hello? Who is this? If this is a wrong number, please make note of the number you called so you don't keep calling me." No response. This was starting to piss me off. Stupid kids? Surely not Michael. He would just knock on my door and holler at me if he wanted to bother me again.

The call cut off, and I didn't see or hear anything more from my door. I stood wrapped in my towel with my hair dripping on the hardwood flooring for several minutes before I shook it all off and went into the bedroom to put on clean pajama pants and a T-shirt. My phone rang again, and I looked to make sure it wasn't unknown. It was 8:30 p.m. *Reaper.*

"Hey, you," I said with a slight quaver in my voice. I didn't need to let shit shake me up. I was probably letting my overactive imagination make more out of stuff than there really was. Pasting a smile on my face, I tried to keep my tone light. "How was today? I love the fence! Nice job!"

"Thanks, baby. It was a real pain in the ass with a bunch of hungover bikers, but it went better than I expected. So you like it? I didn't want to just put up some crappy chain-link. The pillars were put in a few days ago by some guys moonlighting on their masonry jobs, so I can't take credit for those, but I felt like we did a good job on the rest. I have a key fob for you for the gate when you get here." He sounded so pleased with himself. I knew they had busted their asses. There was no way I was mentioning the stupid phone calls and getting him worked up and worried for nothing.

"Well, it looks great. I'm so pleased you did that to keep Remi safe. You're doing pretty good at this father thing, huh?"

"I'm trying." He laughed. "I know she's probably getting a little spoiled with me, and I apologize in advance. I still cannot get over how fucking happy that little girl makes me. She smiles and pops those dimples on me, and I can't tell her no."

"Ahhhh, now you know how I feel with the two of you!" I laughed too.

"Oh really? Yeah, totally filing that information away for later."

"Whatever! Like you didn't know that already." Every time we spoke he made me laugh so much. I just loved *talking* to him. It seemed as if he was always able to make me feel better when I was lonely or upset, even when he didn't know I was. It may sound cliché or too soon, but I felt like I was falling for him deeper and deeper every time I talked to him. Unfortunately, the fear of getting my heart broken still crept into my mind.

"Hey, your little girl wants to talk to her momma." I heard rustling again and then my precious little girl's voice.

"Momma! Kisses Momma!" It wasn't lost on me that Remi had picked up the more southern term of "momma" for me. Total evidence of hearing her daddy's influence. It warmed my heart.

"Hey, baby! Yes, Momma is here and thank you for the kisses. Only six more sleeps and Momma should be home. I miss you, beautiful!" A conversation with a two-and-a-half-year-old isn't exactly stimulating conversation, but I loved every second of it. The words she knew interspersed with jumbled babble were the sweetest sounds I had ever heard. She finished all she felt was important to tell me and left with a kiss on the mouthpiece of the phone before running off to play before Daddy put her to bed.

"I'm glad you've been able to have her with you overnight this weekend. I hope she hasn't been too wild for you." I worried she would get naughty and have him questioning his sanity at sticking around. It was different for a parent there from birth who was already used to the occasional temper tantrum or naughtiness. I didn't know what it would be like for him stepping in at this stage in the game, and I was worried about him getting overwhelmed.

"Oh, we've had our moments, but I dealt with privates in the Army that were less manageable than her." He chuckled. "I can handle my little princess, but like I said, I make no guarantees on how spoiled she might be by the time you come home. Are you sure you're doing okay? I know you're missing her, and I'm sorry for that, but I hope having her here has helped you with your packing at least."

"Oh, it has. I cannot imagine what it would be like trying to pack with her running around unpacking as fast as I pack and trying to get in her naps and meals. Yes, it has definitely helped. I just really do miss her. Like I said, I've never really been away from her." My heart ached talking about how much I missed my girl. I truly was glad he was able to spend this time with her though.

We talked about my parents, my ideas for the bar, and how many days were left before I would be home. We hung up with a hesitancy that implied we didn't want to let each other go again. It really had my mind wandering in regards to what direction we were heading. He called me "baby," but he was from Tennessee, and I knew they called a lot of people darling, sweetheart, and baby.

A week from today and I would be home—less if my brothers and I could manage to get everything loaded up and out of here quickly. I didn't tell Reaper, though, in case it didn't work out. Lordy, I couldn't wait to see him again.

Chapter
THIRTY-NINE

Reaper

THE LAST FEW DAYS HAD GONE BY IN A BIT OF A BLUR. WE WERE swamped at the garage, and last night I didn't even get to pick Remi up because I worked late. It broke my heart, but I did stop by her grandparents' to see her and tuck her in. That got me really hoping I would be able to convince Stephanie to move in with me. I loved putting Remi to bed every night, and if she and her momma were in their own place, or even at her parents', I would feel like I was intruding on her personal space if I stopped by every night.

I was also fucking bummed as shit that I wouldn't be able to call Stephanie tonight because she was going out for her going-away party. I thought about asking her to call me when she got home, but that seemed pushy. I had the excuse of talking to her every night because of Remi, but Remi would long have been asleep by the time they all ended up calling it a night. I didn't want her to feel like I was keeping fucking tabs on her, but she was the mother of my child and I wanted her safe. That's all it fucking was. Right? I mean, I cared about her, but I could deal if she didn't want a relationship with me. Fuck, I lived twenty-eight years without a serious relationship, I could fucking deal if she didn't want one. It was no big deal. Shit, why did I feel like I was making shitty excuses?

I hopped on my bike and headed over to see my princess, late out of work again. Stephanie's mom had invited me to have dinner with them all when I called and said I was gonna be a little late. Between all the jobs we had going at the shop and preparing for the run this weekend, we were running ragged. I needed to return to the clubhouse for a brief meeting tonight as it was. We were scheduled to leave in a few short days.

I pulled up in the driveway and climbed off the bike. Damn, there must be rain coming. My leg was stiff and sore today.

When I rang the doorbell, I heard little feet pattering toward the door, and I couldn't help but smile. The doorknob rattled as she tried to open the door. Then another set of footsteps approached and someone opened it for her. She stood there holding her grandpa's hand, squealing, "Daddy! Daddy here!"

Stephanie's dad shook my hand as I came in the door, telling me dinner would be ready in a few minutes, and I bent over to scoop my little girl up. The contrast between her ivory skin and the ink on my arms was dramatic. We walked back to the kitchen, and I sat at the table with her after her grandma denied needing help with anything.

"So how is the house coming along, Colton?" Her mom looked over at me from the oven where she was pulling a roast out. I couldn't get Stephanie's parents to call me Reaper, and I quit correcting them. "We drove by and saw the fence and gate. That's amazing! I bet Stephanie is going to love that." Yep, more hints…

"Yes, ma'am, she does. I sent her a picture of it." Her knowing smirk was not lost on me as she tried to turn away without me seeing it. I also heard her *harrumph* at my use of ma'am, but hey, if they weren't going to call me Reaper, two could play at that game. I had told them, despite my somewhat nefarious ways, my momma did raise me to have manners and respect.

"She has her going-away party tonight, right? So will you talk to her after she gets home? I'm so happy to have her home soon." Another fishing episode. I laughed to myself.

"No, ma'am. Remi will be in bed by then, and I only call her to let Remi talk to her before she goes to bed. I'm trying not to push her too much." She looked a little disappointed. *Yeah, Ma, I'm disappointed too.* I had gotten addicted to hearing her voice and sometimes seeing her face with Facetime. Thank fucking God for technology.

Dinner was filled with pleasant conversation. Stephanie's dad talked about the things he had planned for the farm over the next few days, and her mom spoke of the plans for the Oasis Stephanie had told her about. I had to admit, they were great ideas, and I could see she was going to make the Oasis into a great pub where people would love to hang out, eat and drink.

I headed back to the clubhouse after putting Remi to bed, arriving just as everyone was filing into the chapel. That was close. Hacker caught me as we were walking in and whispered he needed to talk to me as soon as we got done. I didn't hear much of the meeting due to wondering what Hacker had to discuss with me. From the expression on his face, it didn't look like it was good news. As soon as Snow called an end to church, we headed out—some to grab drinks at the bar, some to shoot pool, others to play darts, and still some left to go home to their old ladies and families. Me? I found Hacker.

"What's up, bro?"

"Man, come to my room." He headed quickly to his room and shut the door after I entered, then turned to pull up some files on his computer. "I tried to call you earlier, but you didn't answer, and I figured you were with your kid, man. I heard from the contact finally.

That sealed juvenile file? It was for stalking, assaulting, and raping a girl he had dated after she broke up with him. Because they were both minors and his parents paid a big profile lawyer, he did a stint in juvie and everything remained sealed. But there's more."

I didn't like the sound of all this, and I was getting more and more pissed.

"He didn't just leave the Quad Cities because he had a better opportunity. He had been threatening and tried to assault a girl he had been seeing after she broke up with him. She refused to press charges, parents hired the big lawyer again, and he agreed to leave the area and have no contact with the girl again." He looked worried and pissed.

"Motherfucker! Do we know where he is now? Stephanie swears she hasn't seen or heard from him, but his prior MO says he isn't done with her. Fuck. I need to talk to Snow. I need to go to her. Thanks, bro. I appreciate all of this. You have no idea." I headed to the door.

"Hey, Reaper. Can I ask what your intentions are with Stephanie? Not just for my own peace of mind, but for the interest of you and the club. I'm going to ask you straight up what your intentions with her. You gonna make her your old lady, or what? She deserves good things. I don't wanna see you dick her around." His expression showed the depth of his concern.

"Trust me, bro, if I have my way, I'm claiming her. But I need her to be on board with it. And she's my baby girl's mother. I'm hoping Snow will take that into consideration when I talk to him, and let me head out earlier than planned." I left the room, making a beeline for Snow's office, praying like hell his ass was still here.

The light was on as I approached the office, but it was evident Snow was preparing to lock up. He looked up in surprise when I asked if I could have a word, and motioned me to sit. I told him what was going on and his brow furrowed in concern, but he didn't say a word until I was done.

"Reaper, I understand your position, but I really need you on this one. I was planning on sending you and Hollywood ahead to find a good location to set up just so you can be our 'eyes in the sky' if needed. We talked about this tonight at the meeting. Was your head not in the game, son? I don't have anyone else with your particular skill set. I can't spare you. The best I can do is cut you loose as soon as the handoff takes place. I'm sorry, but I have to look out for the safety of the club." He leaned forward in his chair with his fingertips steepled as he raised his brows.

"Look, Hollywood is damn near as good a shot as I am. He could cover this easy." I couldn't leave his office without at least trying again.

"Reaper, you said there haven't been any issues. I'm not gonna send you down there on suppositions. We need you. As soon as we're done, you can be with your girl and take your time coming back. Okay?"

I was fucking pissed. I clenched my jaw to hold my fucking words in. For the first time ever, I was pissed at my club for coming between me and something important to me. My loyalty was to the club, and I wasn't going to go against my Prez, but I was fucking livid.

Not trusting myself to speak, I nodded and stood, walking out of his office. I needed to get in touch with Stephanie. Of course her phone went to voice mail. Fuck. Fuck! *Fuck!* I stormed through the clubhouse, earning raised brows and questioning looks from everyone still hanging around. Hacker and Hollywood rushed out of the door after me just as I turned and punched the side of the building, leaving a dent in the metal and blood on the wall. I could barely feel my hand, but I didn't giving a flying fuck. I wiggled my fingers and clenched my fist. It hurt, but I didn't think anything was fucking broken.

"What the fuck, bro? What happened?" Hollywood placed his hand on my shoulder, and I shook him off in frustration. I still didn't trust myself to speak. As Hacker explained what he knew, I tried to call Stephanie again. No fucking answer. *Come on, Stephanie! Pick up your goddamn phone!*

I told them what Snow told me, and they said they figured that would be his response after what he had discussed in church. I kicked myself for not fucking paying attention tonight. Sonofabitch!

Helplessness was not a feeling I dealt well with, and it pissed me off. Not having control of a situation drove me fucking insane. It made me feel like I was coming unraveled. I needed to cool off so I strode to my bike, and Hollywood followed suit. He was my best friend, and he always had my back. I expected nothing less of him. What the fuck ever. He was welcome to tag along.

I pulled out of the lot like the fucking hounds of hell were hot on my ass. Hollywood was right on my tail. As I rode down the dark night highway with my headlights illuminating the road ahead, I ran through everything in my head. I told myself that she hadn't heard anything from him so far and that was a good thing. I prayed to a God I didn't know if I really believed in that she would get out of there before he made a move. It was all I could do.

Chapter FORTY

Stephanie

W E HEADED DOWN TO A CHIC LITTLE WINE BAR AFTER WE LEFT work and polished off several high-dollar bottles, toasting to my future before we walked down to a small bar to finish the celebration. By the end of the night, we all had to pour ourselves into cabs to get home. I was so glad when the bosses told me I could skip my short day tomorrow, because I *knew* I would be suffering in the morning. God, my brothers were going to be rubbing this in my face. *Ugh! It's okay, I had fun. So poo on them.* Digging through my purse to find my phone and text my brothers so they would know I'd be off tomorrow was a chore with as tipsy as I was. After discovering the elusive phone, I saw two missed calls from Reaper, but shit it was late as hell, and oh my Lord, I was beyond tipsy, I was fucking drunk as hell. Ummmm yeahhhhh, probably not a wise idea to call him back now. I made a mental note to call him, and text my brothers in the morning and tucked my phone snug in my bra. I giggled to myself at the thought that my bigger boobs after having Remi came in handy for something.

Reggie and I shared a cab since we were only a couple blocks apart. I was sure the cab driver was laughing at our drunken exclamations and singing. We were quite a pair, and a singer, I was not.

Reggie hugged me and waved, like the drunken sot he was, as the cab we shared dropped me off in front of my building. I stumbled in and, honestly, had no idea how I got to my door. Jesus, I was getting too old for this crap. I giggled again as I fumbled with my keys and tried to put my key in one of the two keyholes. Since when did I have two keyholes? Did that bastard maintenance man change my door lock too soon? I giggled. After about the fifth stab at it, I finally got it to slide in properly. This caused another fit of giggles that I tried to silence. I kept waiting for one of my neighbors to come out and yell at me for being so loud.

The door swung open, and I lurched drunkenly forward into the entryway. As I tried to swing the door shut, it kept getting stuck and it wouldn't shut. What the hell? Stupid door.

That's when the "stupid door" flew back at me, causing me to lose my balance and fall backward. My purse went flying and I cracked my head on the wall as I fell, causing me to see stars before everything started to go black. The last thing I remembered was hearing a man's voice that sounded so familiar saying, "Now look what you've done."

Chapter
FORTY-ONE

Reaper

T HE BAD FEELING ROLLING IN MY GUTS HADN'T RESOLVED BY THE time I woke up. I tried to call Stephanie again but no answer. Looking at the clock, I figured it was still pretty early and she may not even be up yet. By the time I was able to call her again, and she still didn't answer, I figured she must be at work by now, and she couldn't answer her phone there. *Fuck.*

I called her brothers and they told me they were on their way down and they would have her call me as soon as they got there if she hadn't called me yet. I didn't know if I should tell them about that stupid fucker or not. I wasn't sure how I would explain how I knew all the shit about him or if they would believe me. I finally decided they probably should know. Even if nothing happened, they should at least know not to let the stupid fucker in or talk to his worthless ass.

"Jesus Christ, man! What the fuck? Are you serious?" Sean yelled into the phone. Sam was driving, and I could hear him asking what the fuck was going on. Sean must have tucked the phone under his chin because his relay of the message was muffled. He came back, saying, "Okay, man, we're on our way, like I said, and we'll call you as soon as we get there or talk to her."

"Thanks, man. I'm heading down ASAP, but I don't know when my boss will let me out of here." I hung up the phone and tried Stephanie again, even though I knew it was probably a moot point since she had to be at work by now. I was so fucking frustrated I could spit fucking nails and have them stick in the damn wall. I wanted to fucking punch something or someone, again.

I left the shop and headed to look for Snow. I needed to find out how early I could take off to scope out a location. I was going to make a side trip first, if I could.

Chapter FORTY-TWO

Stephanie

WOKE UP WITH A POUNDING HEADACHE. OH. MY. GOD. I WAS never drinking that much wine again! I was so stiff I could barely move. When I realized my couch felt really hard, I wondered if I had fallen asleep on the floor. I tried to open my sleep-crusted eyes, but they felt so heavy. I went to bring my hands up to rub my eyes and couldn't move them. *What the hell?*

In a panic, my eyes suddenly cleared and I lifted my head to see where the hell I ended up. Did I break my arms when I fell?

That's when I realized I was lying on an old cot with my hands duct taped together and then tied to the top edge of the cot. My ankles were also taped together and tied to the foot of the cot. Holy shit! Holy shit! *Holy shit!* Oh my God! I started to hyperventilate. My face and arms were tingly, and I couldn't catch my breath.

Where the hell was I, and what the heck was going on? Now that I had woke up fully, I remembered falling down in my apartment and hitting my head, but that was all I remembered. Suddenly, the memory of a man's voice rushed back to me. Oh my God, there was a man in my apartment? Yes! I couldn't get the door to shut! He must have been the reason. Oh God, why did I drink so much last night?

I wondered how long I had been out. What time was it? I looked around, trying to see if there were any clues to my location. Every movement made my head feel like it was on the verge of exploding. It looked like an old trailer of some sort. I saw an interior door at the end of the trailer. So there was some kind of other room at the end. An office maybe? I noticed a crappy-looking desk with boxes stacked on it and next to it. A chair with a broken leg sat in the corner toward the foot of the cot with a rolling chair across from me by the desk. There were coats hanging on a row of hooks on the wall, but they had a thick coating of dust on them, so I figured it was pretty safe to assume they hadn't been used in a while. The whole place looked dirty and unused actually.

There was a beat-up looking metal trailer-type door up past the head of the cot and a single visible window that appeared to be boarded up, but I could see sunlight seeping through the sliver-like openings between the boards. The tiny slivers of light felt like search lights to my light-sensitive eyes. So it was daytime anyway. Did I lose an entire day though? Was it Thursday or Friday? Jesus, my brothers must be wondering where the heck I was. Reaper must be pissed because I hadn't answered or called him back. Please God, let someone be looking for me.

Hell, my head hurt.

My heart started to race. Terrified and panicking, I pulled and jerked on the tape around my wrists, but only succeeded in rubbing them raw. What was going to happen to me? I tried to collect my thoughts. I needed to think. I didn't hear anyone in the trailer, but they could be right outside. Oh God, I didn't want to die. My baby needed me still. She was just a baby, God. And her daddy, I just found him again. I love him and he doesn't even know how much. Oh dear God, sweet Jesus, I love him.

Crying, I pulled desperately again at my bound wrists. Why wouldn't it come loose? Dammit, the tape was moving on my wrists, but I couldn't get it off! The fucking tape cut into my wrists, making me bleed. *Shit. Pull it together, Steph. You have to think!* I started to feel like I was hyperventilating again.

Breathe. Breathe, Steph. Slowly. In. Out. Deep breaths. Shit, my boob was spasming. Could hyperventilating or stress make your boobs spasm? No. It stopped. Okay, it was in my head. Hot tears ran unchecked down my face and into my hair as I lay my head down and squeezed my eyes shut. Between my head feeling like it was going to explode and the stiffness in my arms and legs, I couldn't stop crying. I was hurting and scared. *Please God, help me...*

My boob started to spasm again. What the hell was happening to me? My boobs were going to fall off from the stress. Oh dear God, am I having a heart attack? *Wait. Wait a minute. Shit, Steph, you freaking idiot! You stuffed your phone down your bra! Cripes!* I had my phone. He didn't know my phone was in my bra! Great, how did I get at it? I couldn't get my hands loose. I cried more but tried to stay quiet in case whoever took me was outside. I wasn't ready to die, and I just knew I was going to die when they came in.

I needed to pee. Shit, was I going to have to lay here and pee myself? Maybe I did want someone to come in. Maybe they were going to ransom me? No, my family wasn't wealthy. I started crying harder until I was so wore out I fell asleep again.

The door rattling woke me, and my gaze flew toward the door in a panic. Oh shit, please don't let anyone call my phone. They'll hear the vibration. Oh God, please don't let anyone call right now! The door swung open slowly, and I heard someone coming up metal-sounding steps. A man with a ball cap came in and turned his back to me as he began to set things down by the inside of the door. I tried to think of a plan, but there was nothing I could do while I was bound like this. I needed to beg to use the bathroom, then maybe I could access my phone. I needed to activate the app that would signal Erik and the MC; then they would know something was wrong and could track me. Okay, I had a sort-of plan. Now I just needed to figure out how to get to my phone before someone called the damn thing again.

The man turned to me, and I almost swallowed my tongue. Michael. I shouldn't be surprised, but I was. I couldn't believe he would do something like this. I thought he was just possessive or needy. Or maybe a little wacko. I didn't think he would resort to kidnapping. Shit. He looked up and made eye contact with me. Jesus, he looked deranged. Something must have freakin' snapped in him. He barely looked like the same person. Of course, his obviously broken nose and the fading bruises on his face didn't help much. Those must be courtesy of Reaper. Shit, he did a number on him. It almost looked like his eye socket had been crushed and his left eye was drooping.

"I see you're awake, baby. I was wondering if you had hit your head too hard and you weren't going to wake up. That would have been disappointing. I wanted to be able to see your face when I enjoy the favors you denied me but gave to that piece of shit nasty-ass biker. Thanks to him, no woman will ever look at me without disgust in her eyes. After I taste the treasures you gave him, I'm going to make sure you know how I feel. We'll see how bad he wants a piece of your ass after I've made you bleed and destroyed you for other men. Neither him, or any other man, will be attracted to you then." His laugh sounded like a creepy hyena. Oh dear God in heaven. No. I shook my head at him as words failed me. That set off the pounding in my head again, and nausea rushed in. Tears leaked out of my tear-swollen eyes as I settled on his maniacal smile. I needed to get at my phone. Please, God, I just needed to get at my phone. I tried to calm myself. I couldn't let him see me fall apart. *Breathe, Steph.*

"Michael, I don't know what you're talking about. I haven't done anything with any biker. Remi's dad is a biker, yes, but we're just friends. What we had was one night years ago, and that's over and done. Nothing happened between us." I tried to look calm and slightly pleading. I needed him to believe me, despite my heart feeling like it was going to burst due to my heart rate running at about a hundred miles an hour. I prayed the rapid pulse in my neck wasn't a dead giveaway.

"No. No. No. No. No, Steph, baby. I saw you with him. You can't lie to me. He dropped you off at your car. You were on his motorcycle, Steph. I saw you." He spoke to me almost like I was a small child he was scolding. God, he was freaking the crap out of me.

"Yes, he had given me a ride back to my car from my friend's house. That's all. I had ridden with my friend from high school to her house from the little town bar. He was there to see her, and he gave me a ride back. It really wasn't what you're thinking." *Please believe this load of crap, please, please, please.*

"Then what was he doing at your house later? Did you forget he did *this* to me?" He pointed at his deformed face as he screamed.

"Michael." I tried a soothing tone. "He didn't know who you were, and he just saw someone he thought was hurting me. He's protective of all women. It wasn't anything special. He had come by to see Remi because I had told him he could." I needed to get him to calm down long enough for me to use my phone. There had to be a bathroom here somewhere. I really needed to piss now too.

"I really need to go to the bathroom. Is there a bathroom I can use?" It was imperative that I get him to release me and leave me alone briefly. Then I just needed to try to hold my sanity together and keep him from raping me and torturing me. Yeah, piece of cake. Holy shit, I was so screwed. This was not how I ever thought my life would go.

He pulled out a wicked-looking knife from the pile of things he had set inside the door. When he began to walk toward me with it, panic set in again.

Oh God, Reaper, I'm so sorry I didn't give credence to your worries about this crazy asshole.

Sweat broke out between my shoulder blades and across my brow. I was terrified thinking of what he was going to do to me, but I was desperately trying to keep him from seeing how truly shaken I was. My mind screamed at me to fight, scream, or just do something, but I felt paralyzed as I watched him come closer.

He held the knife up under my chin, and the razor-sharp tip touched the sensitive skin under my jaw. My breath was erratic, and I was on the verge of a panicking and tears formed in the corners of my eyes from both the pain and fear. If anyone had ever asked me if you could taste fear before this, I would have looked at them and laughed. Now I could tell you fear did have a taste. Fear was metallic and acidic at the same time. Fear dried your mouth, preventing words from forming on your lips. Fear smelled too. It smelled like ash.

"You better not try anything stupid, Steph. There is nowhere for you to go and no one will hear you if you scream. But I'll have to punish you if you do, because you will have disobeyed me. Don't piss me off, Steph. Don't make me kill you…." He pushed the tip of the blade further in until I felt a warm trickle run down the side of my neck. I whimpered and tried not to cry.

"Please, I won't do anything stupid. I promise," I whispered.

He sliced through the rope tying my wrists to the cot and then the tape at my feet. He left the tape around my wrists and dragged me back to the door by the tape. My wrists burned. He opened the door, flinging me through the doorway. There was nothing in the room except for some old cloth tarps piled in a corner. I looked at him in question, wondering how the heck I was supposed to go to the bathroom.

"Wait here," he ordered as he turned back to the main room, returning with a paint-splattered five-gallon bucket and a roll of toilet paper. He dropped the bucket against the wall and handed me the roll, then stood there looking at me.

"Ummmm, can I have a little privacy? It's not like I can go any-where." I gestured toward the windowless walls. Where the hell did he think I was going to go? I needed him out of the room so I could use my phone, and I sure as shit did not want to have to pee in front of him. How fricking humiliating! Dang it!

"Don't try anything sneaky, Steph. I'm not in the mood."

"I won't." I tried to look meek and submissive.

He gave me a glare and backed out of the room, closing the door. Breathing a sigh of relief, I worked my bound hands to get my phone from my bra. I fumbled as I pulled it out and it slipped from my hand. Thankfully, I caught it to my chest with my forearms. Oh my God, that was close. I pulled down my jeans and perched on the bucket. Jesus, this was uncomfortable. The edge of the bucket pain-fully dug into my ass and legs. As I peed, I opened my phone, turning it completely silent with no vibration. I sent a group message to Erik, Reaper, and my brothers, simply saying: help me locator activated. I wanted to say so much more, but I didn't want to waste precious time or get caught. Then I went to the locator app, clicking on it to send off the signal they told me it would initiate. I noticed my battery life was low, and I prayed they would get the message and the locator notifi-cation before it died. I set the phone on the ground and then shoved it under the tarps with one foot before trying to grab for the toilet paper. The bucket wobbled as I reached, and I almost fell over.

"What's taking you so long?" Michael asked through the door as the doorknob rattled.

"Wait! I'm just trying to wipe. It's difficult with my hands like this." Dickhole. Thankfully, he didn't come in. I was able to wipe and drop the paper in the bucket. Dang, I had to pee a lot. I was so glad I didn't tip the bucket as I got off it. That took some leg muscles, let me tell you! I took a quick glance to make sure my phone was com-pletely covered as I was buttoning my pants. The door burst open and he looked around like he thought I was up to something. Thank goodness I had been able to get my pants done up. It felt like a protective barrier between us. I didn't have much, so I clung to what I had.

He jerked me by my wrists back out to the room and pushed me onto the cot where I landed on my bound wrists, falling forward on my face. I was able to push myself back into a sitting position with my back against the wall. Warily, I watched as he paced in the small space. The knife sat on the edge of the desk, making me wish my hands weren't bound. Of course, I had no idea if I could get to it before he stopped me. Could I actually stab him if it came down to it? I didn't know, but I needed to figure out something in case they didn't find me for a while.

Chapter
FORTY-THREE

Reaper

PULLED IN TO DES MOINES AT AROUND SIX THURSDAY NIGHT. I MET up with Sam and Sean at Stephanie's apartment. After I received their message earlier this afternoon, I could barely contain my anger and fear. Snow let me head out early after I told him what was going on, and I packed a quick bag then hit the road. The whole way down, their words ran like a fucking mantra through my head: "She's gone."

Steph's apartment door was ajar when they arrived. They had cautiously pushed the door open to find her purse with the contents scattered across the floor. The small table inside the doorway was knocked sideways with her mail toppled off and scattered as well. Steph hadn't answered anyone's phone calls or text messages since early last night, and her phone was missing. I prayed she had it on her, and I had Erik trying to track it. She hadn't initiated the locator app, and that made me worried that whoever had her also had her fucking phone.

Shit. Damn it, Steph, where the fuck are you?

Her brothers had already contacted the police, but since we didn't know how long she had actually been gone, they said there was nothing they could do until twenty-four hours had passed. Fucking lazy-ass cops. I fucking knew they could at least *try* to look for the last time her phone was used or something. Assholes. That was okay, Hacker was on it, so fuck them. I was about to call Hacker when a message popped up on my phone.

Stephanie: help me locator activated

Fucking hell! That's my girl, smart, but fuck! Where the hell was she? Was she okay? Fuck. Fuck! *Fuck!* I finished dialing Hacker.

"I got it, man. I'm fucking on it." Hacker's tone was the most serious I had heard him in a while. He said she had initiated the locator, but she must have a bad signal because it was coming and going and he was having a hard time tracking it down to an exact location.

"Give me something, man! Fuck! Just get me to the general location so we can start fucking looking. I can't just sit here!" I knew I was being a real dick with Hacker, and I felt bad, but I was going fucking crazy here. I had no idea if she was even still alive. I was pretty sure that piece of shit had her, but our club had enemies too. What if one of them found out about her? Fuck! Yeah, my fucking vocabulary got really fucking narrow when I was fucking pissed and worried. I ran my hand through the hair on top of my head, scattering it every direction. I could hear Hacker clicking away on his keyboard. Then I heard him swear.

"Shit! Goddammit!"

"What? Hacker, what the fuck?" He was scaring the shit out of me.

"The locator stopped, bro. It fucking stopped. I didn't have a pinpoint location yet!" The frustration and fear was clear in his voice.

"Bro, I am so fucking sorry. I'll let Snow know what's going on." He gave me the closest coordinates he had, and Sam, Sean, and I headed out. I prayed we could find her before anything happened to her. I would never forgive myself if she was fucking hurt.

The coordinates took us to the outskirts of town. There was a lot of construction there. Old buildings and ratty-ass houses being torn down, remodeling of old buildings, new construction. You name it. Shit, she could be in any of these dilapidated buildings. We needed to spread out and look separately to cover more ground. I felt the cold-blooded hunter come out in me. God help the motherfucker who had taken her, because I was going to bring him with me to hell.

Chapter FORTY-FOUR

Stephanie

FELT DIRTY, HUNGRY, AND EXHAUSTED. I HURT AND I KNEW I HAD lost blood from the abrasions on my wrists and the cuts I had on various parts of my body. I hadn't slept all night for fear of Michael coming back and torturing me more. My eyes were nearly swollen shut from crying and from Michael punching me in the face when I screamed the first time he cut me. When he had cut my clothes off, the blade sliced between my breasts, causing me to scream in pain.

Michael had initially cut my shirt off so he didn't have to free my hands. As he jerked my pants off, I fought him by kicking and screaming, and he cuffed me upside my head, making me see stars. After that, he gagged me with a filthy rag and ran tape around my head to hold it in my mouth. My hair was being pulled where it was caught up in the tape, and I battled puking because I was afraid it would kill me with no way to get past the rag.

I had fought to maintain consciousness out of fear for what he may do to me without my knowledge. When he ran his filthy hands up my legs and slid his fingers under the edges of the legs of my panties, I whimpered and cried, trying not to earn another beating. As his fingers brushed against me and slid down to fondle me, I couldn't help it, I screamed through the gag, thrashing and kicking. His fist connected with stomach and ribs. I wasn't sure, but I thought he may have broken one of my ribs. It hurt so much to breathe.

Little did I know that would only be the beginning.

He tied my hands above my head, still bound together. My elbows Masont above my head and my fingertips brushed the ground. Then he tied my feet so my legs were spread and each knee was off the sides of the cot with my heels touching the floor.

Using the knife, he made superficial cuts along my left thigh, working up toward my abdomen. I couldn't stop crying. The pain and terror I felt was indescribable. When he was done slicing up my leg, he moved on to my breast, stabbing me—not too deep, just enough to scare the shit out of me because I really thought he was going to kill me. He laughed at my muffled pleading.

When he began stripping out of his clothes, I frantically shook my head no as my sobs increased. His member hung flaccid between his legs as he climbed on the cot with me, half lying on top of me. He told me I was going to have to suck on him to make him hard, that I was so pathetic he couldn't even get hard looking at me. Spittle sprayed my face as he laughed and rubbed his body on mine, smearing my blood all over himself and me. Then he leaned down like he was going to kiss me, but instead licked the side of my face. He fucking *licked* my face. I gagged again, choking on my sobs. God, forgive me, but I wished he would just kill me, because I had given up on anyone finding me.

Brutally, he squeezed and twisted my breasts, bruising the tender tissue before biting them. The crazy asshole fucking bit me. I had no idea if he broke the skin or not, but the pain made me stiffen and arch off the cot, screaming through the gag.

"Yes, oh yes, baby, rub up against me. I love that." His moist breath ran across the side of my head as he whispered in my ear. I jerked my head, turning away from him. That's when he grabbed me by the hair, twisting my head back to face him. He held the knife to my face and licked across the tape over my mouth. Sick fuck. God, I hated him. I prayed and prayed for some form of salvation.

He cut through the tape in front of my ear, and I knew he cut my face because I felt the warm liquid trickle down to the bottom of my ear and neck, but I couldn't do anything to stop him. He ripped off the tape, pulling my skin painfully and ripping out some of my hair. I winced and yelped in pain, which just earned me another backhand across my face.

"Shut up! I told you, you don't make any noise unless I tell you to!" When he grabbed hold of his flaccid member and tried to shove it in my face, I shook my head, trying to avoid what I knew was inevitable. He grabbed me viciously by my jaw, holding my head still. "Don't even think about biting me, Steph, or I'll cut your throat now and be done with you."

I cried silent tears, which ran down the sides of my head, pooling in my ears before running into my matted, filthy hair. He proceeded to shove his nasty, soft penis in my mouth with one hand as he held my mouth open with the other. I refused to give him the satisfaction of actually sucking on him. He was insane if he thought I would. Then he stooped to a new low I couldn't believe anyone would by threatening my daughter. My sweet, innocent Remi. I did it because I didn't want his deprivation anywhere near her. I was ashamed of my actions, but what choice did I have? I couldn't let him have anything to do with my baby girl. For the millionth time, I was thankful I had found Reaper and she would at least have her daddy now. He would protect her. He wouldn't let this sick bastard near her.

Michael continued grunting and gagging me until he pulled out and came in my hair. I just laid there staring at the ceiling. I felt myself drifting further and further into my mind to escape my reality. He then patted my cheek like a small child, telling me what a good girl I had been. I couldn't believe it when he got up, dressed, and went to the door.

"I'll see you in the morning, Steph. I can't wait to feel you tomorrow. Tomorrow, I'll have *all* of you. Then maybe I'll deliver you to your precious biker. We'll see how much he wants you after you are used up. Or maybe I'll keep you around for a while, plant my baby in that belly first and make him watch it grow in you. I haven't decided."

I didn't look at him as he shut the door. I heard what sounded like a padlock being utilized outside the door, but I just continued to stare at the ceiling until sobs escaped from between my lips. I didn't know how much more I could take....

Chapter
FORTY-FIVE

Reaper

COULDN'T BELIEVE WE DIDN'T SEE ANYTHING ALL NIGHT. SAM, Sean, and I had combed all through this shithole area. I didn't see any sign of that asshole, his truck, or Stephanie. Motherfucker! Where the hell was she? My heart ached when I briefly wondered if that piece of shit may have already killed her. *No!* No fucking way! I would have fucking known. I would have felt the loss, I just knew it. She was my angel. She had kept me going through situations I didn't think I would live through. I couldn't imagine that I wouldn't *feel* if she was gone.

Sam and Sean headed back to Stephanie's apartment to recoup and try to call the cops again. I had zero faith in the fucking cops. Those bastards didn't give a fucking rat's ass about her. They had pretty much hinted that maybe she had run off with a guy. *Are you fucking kidding me? Really? Stupid fucks.*

I knew she was still alive, and she was here somewhere. She would never run off and leave Remi behind. I sat on the ground in an alley, leaning against a brick building listening to the rats scurrying behind the dumpster and boxes next to me. Running my hands roughly along my face, I tried to focus. Fuck, I should have gone with them and tried to get some sleep, but it didn't seem fair to sleep when my angel was out there. I had dozed off briefly against this wall after the guys left in the wee hours of the fucking morning. Damn, I was fucking stiff. I stood and took a piss over by the dumpster.

After climbing on my bike, I flipped the switch and prepared to ride around the area again. That's when I heard a vehicle coming. I wasn't sure if it was the guys coming back, so I rolled my bike toward the edge of the alley. An old, rusted Chevy truck in the most disgusting shade of mustard yellow was coming up the road. Shit, that wasn't either of their fucking trucks. I was on the verge of starting my bike as the truck rolled slowly by. If I had been looking down at my bike to put it in neutral at that time, I would have missed the driver. Fucking A! It was him! I shot off a text to the guys, Hacker, and Hollywood to let them all know I found him and I was going to follow him. I had to be careful and stay back far enough that he wouldn't see me.

I watched as he turned down a street about three blocks up and slowly crept out into the road, keeping my eye on the street he turned on. When I got to the street, it was just in time to see him turning again. I continued to follow and saw him enter into a fenced construction site. I got as close as I could and parked my bike in the nearest alley. After making sure he wasn't coming back out, I crept over to the fence, noting he had chained the gate. There were several construction-type trailers parked in the fenced area, and I assumed it must be a storage site for one of the construction companies. I knew it wasn't the one he worked for because Hacker had found every site they were working and owned. We had already checked all that shit out when we couldn't find anything around here last night. Then we returned here to look again before the guys headed back to the apartment. We had driven by this area several times but never saw any vehicles or signs of life and had written it off. Fuck, he must have left by the time we came by here.

I was able to pull back a section of the fence in the corner where the attachments had broken. It looked like someone had hit it with a car. Lucky for me anyway. I crawled and slid through the opening, tearing my shirt where the rough edges of the fence caught it, looking for where the shitty truck went. Leaning against one trailer to carefully look around the corner before stepping from behind it, I slowly made my way through the lot. The truck was parked toward the middle up against one of the trailers.

Motherfucker, I have you, now.

Leaning carefully against the trailer so I didn't make noise, I placed my ear to the side of it to see if I could hear anything inside. At first, I didn't hear anything. Then I heard a muffled male voice talking. I didn't hear another voice, so it didn't seem like he had any accomplices with him, but I listened a little longer to be sure. Nothing. On the other hand, I didn't hear any female voices, either. Shit.

That was when I heard a scream.

Okay, fuck the stealth shit. I needed to get in there *now*. I only saw the one window as I made my way around the trailer, and it was boarded up. There was a shitty-ass set of metal stairs going up to the beat-up door. Of course, the fucking door opened to the outside. Fuck. So much for kicking it in and having the element of surprise. I prayed it wasn't locked. There was an open hasp with a lock hanging from one side, but that didn't mean he hadn't locked the fucking handle. I pulled out my pistol from the holster at the back of my pants, ensuring I had a bullet chambered. I wasn't as comfortable with my pistol as I was with my sniper rifle, but I was a fucking good shot just the same.

Grabbing the handle slowly, so it didn't fucking rattle, I stood to the opening side and slung it open as I launched up the stairs and in the door. The sight that greeted me made my blood run cold.

He was holding her panties in one hand and a fucking Ka-Bar knife in the other. I barely registered all the blood covering her body. I didn't even have time to check her before he looked up at me. His eyes were glassy and had a crazed look. I had seen that look in the eyes of people who had snapped in combat and knew there was little hope of reasoning with him, which was fine by me because I would be happy to put a bullet between his eyes.

"Get away from her. Back the fuck up now, you piece of shit." My voice came out low and gravely. I stuffed my fear and worry for Stephanie to the back of my mind, falling into the detached and trained killer that still lurked within me. I knew he wasn't leaving here alive, but I needed to get him away from Stephanie. What happened next occurred in the blink of an eye. Training and instinctive reaction was all I had when I watched him smile at me in an evil, sadistic way.

"You're too late to be her hero. She is damaged goods now. You're just too late. Much too fucking late." I watched him in what seemed like slow motion as he raised the knife above her lifeless-looking body. As he started the downward plunge, I pulled my trigger smoothly, watching as a shocked expression interrupted his maniacal cackle and blood seeped out of the hole that was now in the middle of his forehead. He toppled forward, and I watched in sick horror as the knife continued its descent into Stephanie's abdomen. She screamed as the knife entering her body shook her from her pain-and-trauma-induced haze.

Kicking his lifeless body to the side, I knelt to her side and pulled out my phone, dialing 911. Shit, I was thankful I had taken my cut off last night. That was publicity the club did *not* need. I explained to the operator what had happened, where we were, and that they needed to hurry. I left my phone on speaker and dropped it to the floor as I focused my attention to my baby, trying not to lose my shit when I saw the knife sticking out of her side and all the bruising and blood covering her body. The smell of the blood nearly made me lose my guts as it brought back another time where I was helpless to save someone who counted on me. I didn't dare take the knife out since I didn't know what it had hit or what I may let loose by pulling it out.

"Stephanie, baby, can you hear me? I'm here. You're going to be okay, baby. I'll take care of you. God, I'm so fucking sorry I didn't get here sooner." Her eyes stared at me but were so glazed with pain, I wasn't sure if she heard or recognized me. I pulled my own knife out and cut through the ropes tying her arms and legs to the sides of the filthy cot she lay on. My hands shook as I took off my long-sleeve denim shirt and laid it over her nude body to provide her a semblance of modesty. I gently brushed her matted hair back from her face. What was once bright and golden, like pure spun gold in the sunlight, now barely resembled straw. Her eyes were swollen and the usual bright blue, what was visible anyway, was dull and glazed. My lips gently brushed across her parched and cracked lips.

"Colton?" Her voice was a dry whisper. She looked confused and unable to focus. Then she closed her eyes halfway, and she was gone. I couldn't see her breathing. Oh Fuck. *No!* Fucking God, Jesus, no.

"Noooooooooooooo!" The voice screaming in agony and denial barely registered as my own as I realized there were sirens outside and someone was trying to pull me away from the only woman I had ever loved....

Stephanie

When you die, your soul doesn't understand or believe you've died. I know this now.

I stood calmly beside Colton as he clung to the bloody and beaten young woman in front of him. I didn't understand what was going on. What had happened to her? Why was he so heartbroken? Did he love her? I had no hope with him if that was the case. His exclamation of love to me the one time must have just been in the heat of the moment. He had the look of someone who was consumed with grief over her state.

When the paramedics rushed into the trailer, I stepped back to get out of their way. He was gently but deftly moved back from the body by paramedics as they were assessing the male body on the floor as well. I heard them say the man was gone and the female wasn't breathing, but she may have an irregular and faint heartbeat. I watched as they worked on her. I knelt by Colton and kissed his head as he held his face in his hands and sobbed on his knees. He was so upset, he didn't even register I was there.

I watched as they loaded the woman on a stretcher, trying to keep her covered. The poor thing wasn't even dressed. And there was so much blood. They called into the handsets of their radios to the hospital to tell them they were on their way and that she would need the surgeon. That's when one of them yelled they were losing her as they rushed to load her in the ambulance.

A policeman was talking to Colton outside now, but he still wouldn't talk to me. I heard him sob my name. It started getting so bright out, I could barely see him anymore. When I yelled to him, he didn't even look at me. I tried to get one of the policeman's attention, but no one would listen to me.

"Someone listen to me! What is going on?" I screamed.

The light was so bright, it swallowed me. Everywhere around me was light. Then I heard murmuring and a wave of calm and comfort swept over me. The disjointed voices said it wasn't my time and I "still have things to do."

That's when it hit me that I was the broken and bloody woman. I had died. When that realization dawned, everything started to go black.

"No! Wait! Where am I? What is happening?" No one answered

me as the blackness engulfed me.

My eyes opened with so much effort, I felt like my eyelids were weighted. My eyes burned, and when I tried to look around to see where I was, I gasped in pain. I hurt everywhere.

"Shhhhhhhh. It's okay, Mrs. Quinn. I'm right here. My name is Kristina. I'm your nurse." She pointed to a small white board that listed her as my nurse for the day. "Your husband will be so happy to see you're finally awake. I just hate to wake him since he hasn't slept since they brought you to us after your surgery." That's when I noticed a young nurse, with a brunette ponytail hanging down her back, changing out a bag of fluids by my bedside. "I'll be right back," she said as she rushed out of the room. She returned quickly with a cup of ice and a spoon.

"What happened? How long have I been here?" My voice croaked and my mouth was so incredibly dry, I felt like I had been eating cotton balls. The nurse turned to me with kind eyes and spooned a few small pieces of ice up and offered it to me.

I allowed the cold chips to melt across my tongue. Nothing had tasted so amazing, and I closed my eyes in momentary bliss.

"I don't, uhhh… have a husband?" I questioned the nurse as I looked over at the dark head resting on the side of my bed. The man had my hand held in his and his soft breath puffed across our clasped hands as he slept.

"It's okay, you may have gaps in your memory for a little while. You went through a very traumatic experience. Your husband has been fiercely protective and worried about you. He hasn't left your side once." She smiled warmly, and it reached her light hazel eyes. "I can only pray I find such love and devotion one day." She placed a small box in my hand connected to the bed by a cord, telling me to press the red button if I needed anything and that she was going to let the doctor know I was awake so they could start pain meds I had control over.

Huh?

I reached my right hand over to brush back the long, dark hair that had fallen over the man's face. Even that little movement made me gasp with the pain and effort. Jesus. Yeah, pain meds would be nice, 'cause whatever they may have given me felt like it must have worn off hours ago.

At my touch, sky blue eyes popped open, momentarily disoriented. He raised his head in surprise, his mouth slightly open. His other hand shot out and touched my face in a tender caress.

"Stephanie? You're awake! Oh God, baby, you're fucking awake!"

Colton... it was Colton. Here with me in a hospital. What the hell was going on?

"Colton? What happened? Why are you here? For that matter, why am I here?" I knew I hurt everywhere, but I was so confused. I didn't understand why I was in the hospital and why he was here. Truth be told, there was no one I would rather have as my first sight in the morning, but I didn't understand what was going on.

"The nurse said you're my... husband? Colton. What is going on? What happened? Why are we here?" I needed answers because I was starting to seriously freak out.

"Baby, it's okay. Don't get upset. You're making your heart rate shoot through the fucking ceiling, and you'll have everyone running in here again." He pushed his hair back with one hand, refusing to let go of my hand. "I lied. It was the only way they would let me in here with you at first and the only way they would tell me anything. Your parents backed me so they wouldn't kick me out."

"My parents are here? And again? What do you mean again?"

"Jesus, baby, you've had us so fucking worried. You crashed right after they brought you here after you came out of surgery. They said they were afraid, between the damage done to your body and the shock to it from surgery, you may not make it. They tried to kick me out because I lost my shit then. I told them you were *not* going to die and leave me." I watched as his eyes filled with tears before he looked away and tried to wipe them away before they fell. "You've been in a medically induced coma for four days, baby. They brought you out of it this morning, but you hadn't woke up yet. Your parents are here with Remi. They've been taking turns with her at your apartment because none of us wanted her to see you like this. Your mom just went down to the cafeteria for some coffee."

He had stayed with me here for *four days*? My heart began to flutter in hope. Did he still care about me then? Oh please, God, I loved this man. Please let him feel the same way about me. I didn't know why I was here, but I needed to tell him how I felt. I couldn't take a chance that I may die without him ever knowing. But just then, the nurse came in and gave me something in my IV for pain until they could get whatever she said hooked up. I felt so tired and my head was still killing me. My smile was weak as I squeezed his hand.

"Rest, baby. We can talk later." He kissed my hand clasped in his as my eyelids became too heavy to hold open anymore. *I love you*, I thought to myself.

Chapter
FORTY-SIX

Reaper

THANK FUCKING CHRIST! JESUS, MY BABY WAS AWAKE. I HAD DAMN near given up hope on her waking up ever again, but my stubborn heart refused to believe she would leave Remi and me behind. I prayed to a God I still wasn't sure existed that she would make it through all this. She obviously didn't remember what had happened. The doctors and nurses had said she may not. They explained that sometimes the mind closed off traumatic events and the memories sometimes returned, sometimes didn't. After seeing the state she was in when I found her, I fucking hoped she didn't remember. Jesus Fucking Christ, my heart would never be the same after that.

I had no idea what all had happened, but she had been covered in blood and I saw cuts and bruises all over her body when I found her.

The nurses had helped me wash her as best we could yesterday, and I washed her hair over a basin, finger combing all the tangles from her hair as she remained unconscious. The nurse said she may hear me even though she was heavily sedated so I had sat and held her hand, talking to her about Remi and trivial nonsense, anything just to hear myself talk. The silence in the room was nearly unbearable.

My anger exploded and I had refused to believe them when they said she may not make it. Fuck them. I knew my girl, and she was tough. She had gone through a fucking pregnancy and delivery by herself as a single mom and had been raising our little girl all by herself, not knowing where the fuck I was. She was tenacious and loving with an amazing heart. She loved our little girl, and I fucking knew, if anything, she wouldn't leave her.

Yeah, I lied to the staff when I told them I was her husband, and I had zero fucking remorse for that shit. In fact, it felt so fucking right when I said it. I wanted this woman for my own. She didn't know it, and I didn't know if she would agree just yet, but fuck if she wasn't mine. *Mine.*

The relief I felt was profound when the doctor told me she had made it through surgery and that, despite the condition in which she was found, there were no signs of her being raped. Maybe not in the classic sense, but the rest he told me had me seeing red. She had been tortured. Cut, stabbed, and beaten, all before the final stabbing I witnessed. He told me there was evidence of semen in her hair that had been collected and sent to the lab, but with the suspect dead, it was just a technicality. It would at least rule out the involvement of others.

If I hadn't already killed him, I would have tortured his ass and *then* killed him. That piece of shit motherfucker. The rest of what they told me had stunned me, and I was a little nervous to tell her. I didn't know how it had happened, but it did and I prayed she wasn't going to flip her shit when she found out. I knew I would have to tell her.

The guys had made the drop off without me, and I felt like shit for letting them down, but I couldn't leave her. Snow had understood, and they had all come by the hospital this morning to see if there were any changes before they headed back. Hollywood and Hacker had stayed with me, bringing me food I had little appetite for and trying to get me to let them take over so I could get some sleep and shower. I couldn't fucking leave her. Never again, if I could fucking help it.

Speak of the devil... They both came barreling through the door trying to squeeze through at the same time. I glared at them for being so fucking noisy. The cute brunette nurse came rushing over with a don't-fuck-with-me look on her face as she confronted them both, telling them if they disturbed her patient, their "sister," which the nurse looked like she sure as shit doubted was the truth, they would be without their visitation for the rest of her stay. The two big bad bikers had the balls to look sheepish. I almost laughed. I watched the two of them gawking at her ass in her scrub pants as she walked back out to the nurses' station. Shaking my head, I smirked at the two of them.

"She woke up," I said in a soft tone, trying not to wake her as she rested peacefully. "If you two assholes are done staring at her nurse's ass, I'll take y'all up on your offer to sit with her and use her shower. I feel like I'm nasty as fuck, and I smell like a bag of smashed assholes." When Hacker took my seat next to her at the side of the bed, I shot a quick text off to her mom, dad, and brothers, letting them know she had awaken briefly and was resting again. They had both already been by once today, and had returned to the apartment to help their dad with Remi and to get some sleep.

The hot water in the shower felt fucking amazing on my back, which was sore as shit from sitting in that uncomfortable-ass chair for four damn days. My leg wasn't feeling much better, and I knew I was going to suffer with it for a while for sitting so long and letting it get stiff. Fucking A, but I would do it all over again for Stephanie.

I quickly finished showering and dried off with the tiny fucking hospital towel. Jesus, as much money as hospital's charged, you would think they could get better towels. I wiped the condensation off the mirror with my forearm and looked at my reflection. I had dark circles under my eyes. Fuck, I hadn't really slept in days though, so go figure. I needed to trim my beard; it was getting a little long and was starting to itch like hell. I may rebel against shaving, but I didn't like having a big old bushy beard either. Shit, I needed to shave down the sides and back of my head too. I slicked back the hair on the top and dressed in the only change of clothes I had shoved in my saddlebags before I left home.

Stephanie had her eyes open and was talking to her mom and Hacker when I walked out of the bathroom. The sight of his hand holding hers had me gritting my teeth. I had turned into a jealous, greedy fuck when it came to Stephanie.

"Quit trying to steal my woman, you fuck." I tried to make it sound teasing, but fuck if I wasn't a selfish bastard when it came to her affections.

"Man, what the fuck ever! Like my little Stephie would want anything to do with your ugly ass anyway." Hacker laughed at my scowl. "Easy. Down, boy, she's like my baby sister, dickhead."

"Language, boys!" her mom chastised us from her seat at Stephanie's bedside. Hacker winked at Steph but vacated the spare chair next to the bed so I could sit by her again. I noticed Hollywood was not in the room and asked where the hell he ran off to.

"He's chasing Steph's poor nurse around the hospital." He laughed. "She went on break, and he insisted on escorting her down to the cafeteria. Horny little fuck. That girl isn't going to want a damn thing to do with his ass, but hell if he can figure that out."

"My mom is right, you guys have terrible language, you know. I don't know if I should let my little girl hang out around you. You may teach her bad habits." It was good to hear Stephanie teasing and joking, even if she did sound raspy and weak.

"Hey, my little princess doesn't have any bad habits, and she is above picking any up," I said with mock growly disdain. Everyone laughed at that, and I couldn't keep a smile from breaking out on my face.

"There're those dimples I love." Stephanie reached out and touched my face as I sat in the chair Hacker had vacated. I grabbed her hand, holding it to my face. Her smile faltered for a second before her face flamed and she gave a nervous laugh.

"Okayyyyyyy, then. I'm gonna go see if I can rescue that cute nurse from Hollywood's dumb ass. I'll leave you two for now. See ya!" Hacker quickly exited the room. I was surprised he didn't stick around to give me more shit.

"Stephanie, do you remember anything about what happened?" I was hesitant to ask her, but I needed to know where she was with all this.

"I remember going out for my going-away party and getting home and the door not wanting to shut. I remember falling over and hitting my head, but that doesn't explain why I hurt all over and all these bandages. And you said I had surgery. Colton, what the heck happened?" She bit her lower lip, looking worried and confused.

I didn't know what all I should tell her. The doctor said I shouldn't push her to remember and to be careful with what I told her if she seemed to be getting upset. I decided to gloss over the events until she could remember on her own.

"Michael took you, Stephanie. He kept you tied up in an old construction trailer. He… uh… he hurt you, baby, and I'm so sorry for that. I should have been here. I should have protected you. I feel like I let you down." My shame for failing her weighed heavy on me. On top of everything that had happened, she had died twice, and that gutted me.

She was quiet for quite some time before she spoke again.

"He took me? And he hurt me? God, did he… did he…?" Tears welled in her eyes, and she had a hard time finishing her question. I watched her twist the blanket in her fingers. I had to have mercy on her and save her from having to ask it.

"The doctor's said there were no signs of rape, in that way, but we aren't sure exactly what he did to you other than beat you up pretty bad, cut you... and he stabbed you." I had a hard time meeting her eyes as I told her of the assault she suffered. This was killing me. I wished I didn't have to tell her.

"I want a mirror."

"Uhhh, I don't think there is one in here." I hesitated. I knew she wouldn't want to see her face right now. It was swollen on one side, she had two black eyes that were still slightly swollen, bruises all over, and she had a cut along the side of her face in front of her ear.

"Get me a mirror, Reaper!" She was angry, her use of my road name a sure sign. I went rifling through the small bag her mother had brought and found a small compact in her toiletries bag. Reluctantly, I handed it to her.

"The doctors said it will all heal. It'll just take some time and the scar will fade. That I know from experience." I tried to tell her quickly before she saw her reflection. I knew how devastating scars on your face could feel, and I hated that she was going to feel that way.

"Oh my God, Reaper... I was so stupid. I should have listened to you when you were worried about him. I feel so disgusting. Filthy. I wouldn't blame you for hating me. The things he must have done. I'm ruined now. You don't deserve that." Tears leaked from the corners of her eyes, and she dropped the mirror to her lap as she averted her face from me. "Please leave. I don't want you to look at me. Good God, I'm hideous."

"*No!* Don't you do this to yourself! This was *not* your fault. You are beautiful to me, and I do *not* hate you, nor could I hate you for something some stupid-ass fucker did to you!" She was pissing me off. She was fucking beautiful, and I hated that she was feeling like this because of that asshole.

"Go!" she screamed. Of course that got the nurse running in here in a blur of turquoise scrubs with Hollywood and Hacker on her heels.

"Sir, I'm going to have to ask you to leave if you're going to upset your wife. She needs to stay calm so she doesn't tear any of her sutures." The nurse was trying so hard to look like a badass. She was cute. Yeah, no fucking nurse was going to kick me out of my girl's room.

"I want him to leave," I heard Stephanie say in a muffled voice. She had her hands over her face as she lay in her bed crying. Her mom looked at us with sympathy as she tried to console her baby girl.

"Sir, I need you to leave for a while. Just give her some time to calm down and rest," the nurse said quietly as she stepped between me and Stephanie. Hollywood and Hacker came closer, and Hollywood placed his arm around my shoulder.

"Come on, bro, let's go grab a bite to eat and let your girl chill. We can check on her in a bit. She'll probably be better then. Okay?" He was trying to talk quietly so Stephanie couldn't hear him and argue with him, I knew. I shook off his arm and turned to the bed.

"I'll be back, baby. Fucking wild horses couldn't keep me away from you. You are beautiful. Always." I took a fortifying breath. "You. Are. Mine. Please, don't make me stay away." My voice fucking cracked as I begged her not to shut me out, and my heart was breaking for her and for the rift I felt building between us. When she didn't answer, I stuffed my hands in my pockets and stalked out of the room. I needed some wind therapy. Fuck.

Chapter
FORTY-SEVEN

Stephanie

OH MY GOD. I LOOKED LIKE TOTAL HELL. HOW COULD I LOOK LIKE this and not remember what had happened to me? How could Reaper look at me and not think I was disgusting? The nurse was checking the machines hooked up to me. I looked at her and hesitated before asking her, but I needed to know. Desperately, I fought back more tears as I spoke.

"Kristina? Can you please tell me what happened to me? I need to know exactly what's wrong. I can't remember any of it." I was so confused, and no matter how hard I tried, I couldn't remember anything that happened. That made me angry and frustrated. My head was pounding by then.

She looked at me then at the floor before she took a deep breath and slowly let it out. Grabbing the chair, she sat down beside me. She made me feel better by doing that. Somehow I didn't feel like she was looking down her nose at me then.

"You went into hypovolemic shock from blood loss and dehydration, suffered abrasions to both wrists and ankles, your cheekbone is fractured, and you have several severely bruised ribs and suffered from a collapsed lung on arrival. You have multiple lacerations to the side of your face, abdomen, and legs, and significant stab wounds to your left breast and abdomen. You also had been… umm… bitten several times." I watched her face blanche as she tried to maintain a professional demeanor. "The stab wound to your abdomen was what required surgery. Because you had lost so much blood, you received two pints of blood. Thankfully, and fortunately for your recovery, it didn't severely damage any major organs. It did nick your intestines, but the integrity of the intestinal wall was preserved. In other words, it didn't go through the intestine. The doctors decided to keep you in a medically induced coma due to the trauma to your head, with a slight brain bleed noted, combined with your cardiac arrest after surgery. You have a fairly long road to recovery, but not as long as it could have been. Oh, but don't worry, the baby is fine. You were lucky you were so early in your pregnancy, or it could have been much worse." She finished with a smile.

I knew I was staring at her like she had just sprouted a third eye. I couldn't close my mouth and I couldn't find words.

"Excuse me?" Surely I heard her wrong because I was so shocked by all the things that had happened to me, despite my having no memory of it. Perhaps she had looked at someone else's chart. "I am *not* pregnant. You must have the wrong information. I have *not* had unprotected sex, and that was only maybe a few of weeks ago! There is clearly a mistake." I know I had *not* had sex with Reaper without a condom. I was sure we didn't. No way.

"Well, Mrs. Quinn, umm, the hormones don't lie, but if you want I can have the doctor check again. Of course, the results were blood results, which are usually extremely accurate, but it's up to you." She looked a little nervous now, and I felt bad for her. She had no way of knowing. She thought Reaper was my husband after all. Shit. Oh my God, did they tell him? They thought he was my husband! They would have thought he knew. I groaned and covered my face with my hands.

"Are you hurting again? You haven't used your PCA yet. All you have to do is push the button. If it is time for you to have medication, it will allow the machine to give it to you. Don't worry about over-dosing, the machine is designed to prevent that from happening. Just don't let anyone else press the button for you." Kristina was sweet, and I felt horrible for being bitchy to her.

"No, I'm okay. I didn't know I was pregnant. God, I don't know what to do. It would have to be Colton's, right?" My brain wouldn't function and my brain felt like mush. "What if it's not Colton's? Is that possible?" I closed my eyes, but the tears still escaped. My mom held a cool washcloth to my head and whispered words of comfort much like she did when I was little. I lay still against my pillow. "When can I take a shower? I feel gross." I was shaking, and I just wanted control over something in my life right now.

"I'll check with the doctor and let you know." She stood, rested her hand on mine and gave me an encouraging smile before leaving the room. Was my life ever going to be in my control?

Reaper

Hacker and Hollywood had wordlessly followed me out of the hospital and down the highway at 80 mph as I chased my demons. I couldn't believe she could think she wasn't beautiful to me anymore. She was fucking gorgeous. I didn't care about what she looked like right now. I fucking loved her inside and out. I didn't care if she had five eyes and no nose, I would still love her. Okay, that was a little extreme, but you get what I fucking mean. Shit. I fucking loved her. When the fuck did that actually happen? When I first saw her again, I told her I loved her, but I didn't know just how deeply at that time. It became a painful reality when I thought she was dead to me forever, but I honestly believed I'd loved her from the first moment I saw her. She had been my saving grace, my angel, while I was deployed and throughout my hellish recovery. I carried her in the back of my mind this whole time.

When I found out she had given birth to my child? Shit. First I was angry thinking she had purposefully kept my baby from me. It was stupid, but I wasn't thinking clearly. Who would when they just found out they had been a dad for over two fucking years without knowing? That was quite a shocker. I was an only child, and I had lost my mom my senior year of high school and never knew my dad. Family was a rare and precious commodity to me. Deep down, I knew she wouldn't do that. She was too good a person, but I was fucking angry and hateful.

She truly touched and unfurled a part of my soul I thought had shriveled up and died in Afghanistan. She made me feel like I had a purpose in life again. What was I going to do if she fucking turned her back on me because she couldn't get past this? I knew the dark place I was in after leaving the Army. I couldn't even imagine her being in that hellish place. I needed to fucking *be there* for her, but if she shut me the fuck out, how did I make her let me in?

We returned to Stephanie's apartment late that night. Hollywood and Hacker split off to go have some drinks and then head to their hotel. I felt bad that I missed Remi before she went to bed, but I didn't want her to see me this way any more than I wanted her to see her momma like she was right now. I spoke with Stephanie's parents briefly, bringing her dad up to speed on what was going on before he headed up to the hospital. Her mom placed her hand on my face and told me to be patient with her and things would work out. She started to say something and then appeared to change her mind. She looked as drained as I felt from being at the hospital most of the day. Feeling completely exhausted, I went to Remi's room to crash on the floor by her bed where I could listen to her soft, sweet, innocent breaths as I drifted into a restless sleep.

"Daddy! Daddy! Daddy!" I woke to Remi shaking the bars of her crib and hollering for me. She smiled her big grin at me when I opened one eye and looked up at her. Her little arm was stretched through the bars toward my head, with her fingers wiggling like it would make them longer to reach me. Smiling back at her, I reached up and took her fingers in mine.

"Hi princess. Daddy's here." I groaned as I sat up. Shit, my body couldn't take all the abuse I had been handing it lately. Once upon a time, I would have crashed on a pile of rocks in the mountains or out on the sand in the desert and slept when and where I could. Damn, not any more. I picked up the quilt I had wrapped around me and tossed it over the end of the crib.

Reaching down into her crib, I swooped her up and into the air, then plastering kisses all over her giggling face. Between this little precious girl and her momma, my heart was gone. They fucking owned it. And now... shit. Hugging Remi to me, I thought about what the doctor had told me. Remi was going to be a big sister. Part of me wondered if it was mine. I didn't know all the details of her life before we found each other again. I was going through each time in my mind, and I was pretty sure we had used protection every time. No, I wasn't fucking stupid and I knew they weren't infallible, but...

I closed my eyes, hugging Remi to me tightly until she began to squirm. I set her down and she ran off toward the living room and kitchen in search of her grandparents and food. I went to brush my teeth and get ready to go see Stephanie. If she would see me....

Chapter
FORTY-EIGHT

Stephanie

IT HAD BEEN ALMOST TWO WEEKS SINCE MY ADMISSION, AND I WAS finally being discharged. My deepest wound had developed an infection, prolonging my stay unfortunately, but after several days of IV antibiotics, the doctors had finally deemed me able to go home for the rest of my recovery. My mom had brought me a set of clothes to wear home when she visited yesterday. So here I was dressed in my yoga pants and a baggy T-shirt to prevent too much pressure or constriction on my healing wounds. The swelling was gone from my face and the bruising was fading to an awful greenish-yellow blend. All I was waiting on was the nurse to go over my discharge instructions and for my mom to get here.

Reaper had tried to see me every day, multiple times a day, and

I had turned him away and left instructions with the staff not to let him in. I didn't know what exactly had happened to me, and until I did, I couldn't stand the thought of him feeling sorry for me. I didn't want his affection if it was strictly the result of guilt. Not to mention, I felt dirty. Soiled. Ruined. Not good enough for him. The doctors told me I may never recover my memories of the incident.

The pregnancy needed to be discussed, but I was terrified it may not be his, despite what the doctor said. Just because they didn't have evidence suggesting Michael had raped me, did not mean he didn't. What if the tests were wrong and baby was his? How exact was that crap, anyway? How could I possibly expect Reaper to want anything to do with me or this baby without knowing if it was his or not? I hadn't had sex with anyone but him that I was aware of, but that was the problem. I didn't remember. If by some crazy chance it turned out this baby wasn't his, I needed to let him go and he needed to move on. Right? The doctor had tried her best to reassure me that the time frame completely precluded Michael from being the father, but fear and lack of my own memories made me distrustful.

The nurse came in and went over all my paperwork. My dad had headed back to the house late last night so I could sleep and my mom was picking me up but still wasn't here. Maybe traffic was bad. I decided to lie down and rest until she got here.

The feeling of being watched jolted me awake. I guess I dozed off. I raised myself carefully so I didn't pull anything too badly and looked over to find Reaper standing in the doorway with his hands in his pockets. His expression was unreadable, and I couldn't stop my eyes from running over his body. God, the man was still the sexiest man I had ever seen, and just looking at him made my heart ache. Jesus.

He smirked, and I felt my face heat because I knew he had noticed my perusal of his gorgeous body. Asshole. Why did he have to be so damn good looking? And why was he here? My mom was supposed to come and get me. Damn it. I wanted to run my tongue across the coarse hairs of his beard and into his dimples. *Argh! Stop it, Steph! Get control of yourself for God's sake!*

"Your mom and dad headed back home with Remi. We loaded up all of your stuff this morning in your brother's and your dad's trucks. Your brother, Sam, rode my bike back for me so I could drive you in your SUV. Stephanie, we need to talk, and I thought this would be a good chance for that." He suddenly looked tired and uncertain. Vulnerable. This was not the self-assured, hard-ass Reaper I knew.

"Maybe we don't have anything to talk about right now." I looked away from the mesmerizing quality of his blue eyes and out the hospital window. How did life go on and people in their cars just keep driving down the road when my life had been so interrupted? Didn't it affect anyone else? I felt a deep depression settling in at the thought of the empty chasm in my memories. It wasn't fair.

"Then I guess we'll spend a few hours in companionable silence. Come on, Stephanie, you can't stay here. The nurse told me you had been discharged and were ready to go. Please let me help you down to the car." He stepped back out of the room and wheeled in a wheelchair, stopping by my bedside, placing the brakes on, and flipping up the footrests.

"You know your way around a wheelchair." Oh wow. That was intelligent. Of course he did. Smooth. "Reaper, why do you call me Stephanie all the time? Everyone else calls me Steph, but not you." I couldn't help being curious, and it seemed a better topic than bringing up his wheelchair experience from his past injuries.

"Well, first, yeah, I spent more than a little bit of time in one." He gave a self-depreciated smile. "And second question, because you are so much more than Steph to me. I like to think you are more special to me than to anyone else. You're elegant, beautiful, and special. You are *my* Stephanie." His eyes took on an intense shimmer as he held out a hand to me in an offer to help me to the chair.

I looked at his hand as a peace offering, and I wasn't sure if I was ready to accept that he wanted something to do with me because he still wanted me. Pity and guilt seemed a more likely driving force. My desire to touch him won out, and I extended my hand to his. As he clasped my hand in his, I felt tingles and a jolt that flickered through my body all the way to my toes. My eyes met his in stunned astonishment. Did he feel that? His eyes widened only slightly and, had I not been looking for it, I would have missed it. Oh yeah, he felt it.

My nipples puckered under my thin lace bra in response. Of course, they drew his attention. God, did the man have radar for sexual desire? Shit. I saw him try to hide his smile, and I tried to look stern in reproof, but I couldn't stop a small chuckle from escaping. Shaking my head, I gently sat down in the chair. Shit, that hurt my stomach. Now I was wishing I would have taken the nurse up on her offer of a pain pill before she discharged me as a small groan escaped from my lips.

"Are you okay?" He was quickly down on one knee in front of me, holding my hands in one of his big, calloused palms while the other gently stroked my hair from my face. The concern on his face was genuine and touching. When I wordlessly nodded, he stretched up to kiss first the cheek his fingers had caressed and then, ever so softly, my lips. He took his time ending the tender kiss and ran the very tip of his tongue across my bottom lip as he pulled slightly away.

"Jesus fucking Christ, Stephanie. You're hurt but your body calls to mine like a siren, and I want to taste you even now." His forehead rested against mine as he gathered control of his ragged breaths. "We need to get out of here and on the road. I'm such a stupid, selfish prick."

Standing and gently placing my small overnight bag over the wheelchair handle, he surrendered me to my nurse who came in and pushed me out of the room and hospital entrance. I was disappointed I wouldn't get to say goodbye to Kristina. She had been my nurse for the majority of my stay, and I would actually miss her kindness, humor, and wit.

Reaper tucked me carefully into the car and buckled my seat

belt, ensuring it didn't place undue pressure on any of my worst injuries. God, his consideration was going to be the death of me. He left me feeling so conflicted. On one hand, I craved his touch and his love, but on the other, I didn't feel good enough for him anymore.

After getting me settled, he waved to my nurse, who repeated my instructions to stop and walk around every hour or so, and jogged around my SUV. Of course, I couldn't help but watch the muscles in his arms flex and bulge as he climbed in the driver side. Fuck me. He was sexy as shit. Yeah, I wanted to taste him too. So much so, my mouth felt like it was literally watering.

He looked at me briefly, flashing those dimples like a weapon as we pulled out and into traffic headed home to my parents. Yikes, it was going to be a long three hours.

Reaper

I could fucking smell her. She must have showered before I got there because her golden hair was shimmering down her back, ending in thick, looping curls. Her hair smelled like strawberries or some fruity shit, and her skin smelled intoxicating. My fucking cock was straining against the denim of my jeans, and I felt like a first-class asswipe for being horny when I knew she was still hurting. I just couldn't seem to control my body's desire for her when I was this close to her. It was fucking crazy. I needed to distract myself and quick.

"So the doctor's said you made an amazing recovery, all things considered." Fucking smooth, Romeo. Why couldn't I think of anything intelligent to fucking say to her? I knew she didn't want to talk about her injuries.

"Yeah, I guess so." She continued to look out the window. We had been driving for over an hour, and we had hardly spoken two words up until now. Her next words were so soft I was afraid I imagined she had spoken. "They told you, didn't they? About the baby." She chewed on her bottom lip nervously.

Oh fuck. We were going there first.

"Yeah."

Silence.

"Reaper, I—"

"Stephanie—"

We both started to speak and then silence ensued as we each waited for the other to continue. I finally broke the silence.

"Look, baby, I know condoms aren't always 100 percent. I get that. I don't blame you at all. Shit happens and sometimes it's just meant to be. So Remi will be a big sister. There are worse things in the world, right? Just promise me we'll get through this together. I want us to at least try to be a family, Stephanie. I want that so bad, you have no idea." I tried to get everything out in one breath before I lost my courage. When I saw a tear escape her eye nearest to me, I felt myself crumble. I fucking hated to see her cry. It ripped at my soul. Shit, please don't let her tell me no. Not now. Not ever.

"Reaper, what if the doctors were wrong and the baby isn't yours?" A sob escaped her as she tried not to cry. "I don't remember what happened. My days have all run together. I can't even remember how long he had me. I have to go by what everyone is telling me because I *can't remember!* What if this baby is *his*? How can I expect you to love this baby if that's the case? I just can't do that to you, don't you understand?"

"Stephanie, stop it. Was there anyone in the weeks before we found each other again?" She shook her head no. "Then I absolutely believe this baby is mine. Regardless of what may or may not have happened, this baby is a part of you, and I love you, so I'll love this baby. I believe the doctors. They know their shit. Okay? You are *mine*. Remi is *mine*. This baby is *mine*. Period."

She turned to me slowly, like she was in a trance, her hand

frozen in midair as she had reached to wipe away another tear. It dawned on me what I had just said. Oh shit. I briefly closed my eyes before returning them to the road. Gripping the steering wheel until my knuckles were white, I quickly glanced over to her again. She still hadn't moved. That was not exactly how I planned to tell her. Fuck. I was such an idiot.

"Do you mean it, Reaper? Or was that a slip of the tongue?" she whispered.

"Look, baby, I don't expect you to feel the same about me. I just needed you to know how I feel about you. I know I said it before, but I didn't want you to think I only said it because sex was involved. This wasn't exactly how I planned to make sure you knew I had really meant it, but hey, like I said, shit happens. But yeah, I fucking love your stubborn ass. I'm fucking crazy about you, and I cannot imagine my life without you and Remi as a part of it. When I thought I had lost you, I wanted to die with you. I couldn't fathom going on in life without you." I looked at her, pleading without words for her to give us a chance. Silence enveloped us for several miles while she sat with her head resting back on the seat and her eyes closed.

"Reaper, stop the car." She reached her hand over, grasping my arm in a death grip. I didn't know if she was hurting or wanting to get away from me. "Reaper! *Stop the fucking car!*" she screamed at me, and I quickly swerved over to the shoulder and hit the brakes as easy as I could without hurting her.

"Baby, what? What? Please, baby, don't hate me for having shit for romance or delicacy when telling you how I feel just now. Don't push me away. Please, baby…" I had never begged like a fucking child in my life, but for this girl? Yeah, I would fucking beg. The thought of her walking away after I had bared my soul to her, straight-up eviscerated me.

Tears ran in a steady stream down her face. She was gasping for breath and panting like a wild thing. Her eyes were staring off into space, and I thought she might hyperventilate. Jesus. Her door flew open, and she started to vomit out the door. Leaning over quickly, I grasped her hair, keeping it pulled back. When she was finished, she chugged some of her drink and spit it out. Finally, her head turned to me and she covered her mouth with a delicate hand and the other cradled her healing abdomen.

"Oh hell... I'm sorry. Reaper, I remember. Jesus, God, I just remembered. I remember some of what happened. What he did to me. I remember lying there praying for you and thinking I was going to die without you knowing I love you. He was crazy. He was going to kill me. You saved me, baby. You killed him and saved me." Ghost white, she had the look of someone who was in shock, and she was scaring me.

"I should have found you sooner, baby, and for that I'm sorry. I'm so sorry I let you down. If I only would have found you before he hurt you..." My voice trailed off, and I was at a loss.

"But you found me. Reaper, baby, you found me. This is your baby. It has to be." Her face was still white, and she struggled with her next words. "He did... things... to me, but I don't think he did anything to get me pregnant. He threatened to, but I think you got there in time. God, it can't be anyone's baby but yours."

My heart was racing, and I wanted to smile at the thought of being here for this baby as it grew in her belly. Then I felt a moment's guilt. Should I be happy and smiling when she just remembered some of the shit that fucking freak did to her? Leaning over to her so she didn't have to twist in her seat and hurt her healing abdomen, I held her face in the palm of my hands so she was looking at me. My thumbs brushed away the tears streaming down her pale cheeks, and then I ran the pad of one thumb across her lips. The kiss we shared was slow, tender, and loving. It was full of amazing fucking things. This girl sitting by me, the mother of my children, was mine. All mine. Amazingly mine.

"I love you, baby. Heart and soul. You are my angel, and I'm never letting you go." I followed my declaration with kisses and nips along the side of her neck, running my tongue along the outer shell of her ear and capturing the lobe between my lips and teeth.

"Oh, God, Reaper... yes. Please." She sat there panting, eyes closed with her lashes fanned over her cheeks and her luscious lips parted. What the fuck was I doing? She just got out of the hospital, and here I was acting like some horny bastard teenage kid. Shit, I was a douche. I groaned and kissed her lightly once more.

"We can't, baby. It's too soon. You're still hurting. I'm so sorry. That was a dick move on my part." My head fell back to the headrest, and I closed my eyes, trying like hell to regroup. Fuck.

"Well, I was just as guilty because I wanted you too. Wow!" The nervous laughter and smile in her voice told me she wasn't angry, and I looked at her in question. Laughter danced in her eyes, her cheeks were now covered in a rosy blush, and a smile flirted with her lush lips. "Reaper, baby, take me home. No, wait. Feed me first, then take me home." She took a shaky deep breath before smiling sweetly at me, and I couldn't hold in my happiness. This girl was fucking amazing. And she belonged to me. Fuck yeah.

Chapter
FORTY-NINE

Stephanie

REAPER WAS SO AMAZING AND LOVING IN HIS CARE OF ME WHILE I finished my recovery. It had been two months since I got home. I was pretty much healed up, though my scars were still pretty dark and angry looking and the scar on my abdomen still hurt if I moved wrong sometimes. Not too often, but it still happened. My doctor said that would be normal as I healed on the inside and the scar tissue within healed and stretched or pulled loose. Adhesions he called it.

Reaper refused to have sex with me for fear of hurting me. He was also afraid of traumatizing me after what Michael had done to me. What this all amounted to was me being undeniably, incredibly, sexually frustrated. I had been seeing a counselor as well, and though it was painful emotionally, she was helping me let go of the trauma I carried in my mind. Reaper stayed with me often at my parents' house, and he would hold me when I woke up in a panic after my nightmares. He would kiss me, hug me, and stroke me gently, but all that did was whip my emotions and sexual tension into a frenzy. I'd been given the okay by my doctor to resume sexual activities and had decided I was going to have to take drastic measures.

Remi and I were moving in with Reaper this weekend. He had brought me by his house, and I instantly fell in love. I could see the changes I wanted to make in decorating and painting, and I couldn't wait to get started. When he admitted to me that he had bought the house with me and Remi in mind, I couldn't help but to throw my arms around him and kiss him. The gruff, biker bad-ass was a secret softy, and I loved him.

My dad, brothers, and Reaper had been working every free moment to make the changes I wanted to implement down at the Oasis. My plan was to change the look of the interior to resemble an old time pub, complete with green glass lights and brass rails on the bar. I had been working on a unique bar and grill menu as well. I was so excited for the "Grand Re-Opening of The Oasis Pub" scheduled for about a month and a half from now. I had decided to leave the name mostly intact for posterity and continuity.

I had arranged for my parents to watch Remi tonight, and I convinced Reaper to drive up to Fairmont, Minnesota to have dinner. I ordered some sexy lingerie complete with a garter belt and sheer stockings to wear under a figure-hugging black dress that dipped down low over my back with three rope-like strings that held the two sides from falling down. As I looked at my reflection in the full-length mirror on the back of my childhood bedroom door, I smoothed my hands over my belly. It was still fairly flat, but I was early in my pregnancy. Thankfully, my morning sickness had been minimal this time.

I slipped on my new black heels and cautiously descended the stairs. Sheesh, I should have waited to put them on until I got downstairs. I could hear Remi chattering in the kitchen with my mom. Reaper would be here any minute. My heart skipped a beat at the thought of seeing him. Would the thought of him ever stop affecting me this way?

"Momma pwetty!" Remi clapped her hands with joy and displayed her devastatingly precious, dimpled smile as she saw me enter the kitchen.

"Yes, she certainly is, my princess." The low voice behind me startled me, and I jumped, placing my hand to my heart as if I could actually slow its racing pace with a touch. Reaper stood there with his hands behind his back and a sly grin on his face, torturing me with his sexy dimples. He had shaved, bringing them to their full glory. Evil, evil man. He wasn't playing fair with my heart and body. When he pulled a bouquet of deep red roses tied with a burgundy satin ribbon from behind his back and presented them to me, I almost cried. Oh yes, he was pulling out all the stops. Hmmmm, what did *he* want? I knew what *I* wanted, but were we on the same page? I raised an eyebrow as I grinned from ear to ear.

"Well, well, look at this handsome man. I don't know if my boyfriend will appreciate you bringing me flowers like this. He's a big bad biker, you know," I teased him as I buried my nose in the velvety petals, breathing the rich scent in deep. He was dressed in a dark pair of jeans and a dark blue, long-sleeve button-up shirt that made his eyes look like midnight blue. Even the button-up shirt couldn't disguise his ripped body. Yum. Just then, Remi raced to her daddy, plowing into his legs with a squeal. Playfully growling, he scooped her up and she kissed him then leaned over to kiss me. God, I loved our little family.

"I'll have to kick his ass if he shows up then." The dimples flashed again.

"Kick his ass!" Remi hooted. My mouth dropped open in horror, and Reaper had the nerve to laugh as he covered Remi's mouth with two fingers, telling her little princesses didn't say that. Oh Lord, help me.

Reaper

When Stephanie asked if we could have dinner and the evening alone, she played right into my hands and had no idea. I had been planning a night like this for about a week now. Lying next to her each night and holding her close to me was sweet torture, but I was not going to push myself on her until she was ready. I was fucking greedy, but I wasn't a total bastard. We needed this night together, just us. We had a lot to talk about, and I had a surprise at the house I wanted to show her.

Dinner was good at the little family steakhouse, and I was so damn amazed at how easy conversation flowed between this woman and me. We never had uncomfortable pauses in our conversation anymore, and when silence did enter the picture, it was comfortable and enjoyable. We fit together like a perfect fucking puzzle. This past month had been the best of my life. Granted, my cock felt like I was punishing it, and I went through a shit-ton of soap in the shower, but I wasn't going to fuck up the healing Stephanie was working on both emotionally and physically. There was no time limit. I would wait for as long as it took for this beautiful woman. I fucking loved her. Completely and totally.

We pulled up to the house as the sunset and the sky was a brilliant watercolor blend. My girl's smile when she looked at her house—'cause yeah, it was totally her fucking house even if she didn't know it yet—made my heart swell with happiness. Who would have ever thought this would be my life? Hollywood still gave me shit about being all "domesticated," but I knew he was happy as fuck for me. I loved him. He had saved me when I was at my lowest, and if it weren't for him, I wouldn't be here enjoying this amazing view in the cab of my truck.

"I have something to show you, baby." I got out of the truck and went around to open her door and help her out. I fucking loved watching her sexy-ass long legs step down from the truck to the ground. I had a fucking hard-on just looking at her legs, for Christ's sake. She was gonna be the fucking death of me.

I held her hand and led her into the dark house, flipping on lights as we walked through. When I reached the master bedroom door, I turned and wrapped my arms around her waist, pulling her close. The feel of her body against mine sent damn shockwaves up my body. After all this time, she still affected me. "Close your eyes, baby."

"What are you up to?" She looked at me with a suspicious smirk.

"You'll see." I waited for her to close her eyes before opening the door and leading her in, watching her closely as I told her to open her eyes. Her pleasure and surprise were worth all the skipped lunches this week. I had finished the bedroom and master bath with her in mind.

The walls were a soft tan with a dark chocolate accent wall. The bed was a king-size four poster with thick carved posts in a light oak. The floors were a darker oak with plush throw rugs in brown, tan, and aqua, which accented the damask comforter. Okay, I fucking cheated and her mom helped me pick it out. I was no fucking Martha Stewart here, but the results were worth all the secrecy and trouble. The master bath had a deep soaking tub, a separate double shower, and his and her sinks. Candles flickered around the room and in the bathroom. No, I didn't try to burn my fucking house down, give me some credit. Her mom came over and lit them when I sent the text we were almost home. I laughed when we passed her on the road and Stephanie didn't even notice.

"You did this for me?" She was stunned, and I grinned like the Cheshire Cat. Fuck yeah, I did this, and everything in my life, for her.

"Do you like it?" Redundant question. Her expression told me everything I needed to know.

"Oh my God, Reaper, this is amazing! I absolutely *love* it!" She slipped off her heels and ran like a little girl to check out the bathroom. I heard her squeal and knew she found the tub. She ran back out and threw her arms around me. "I love you, Reaper. You are amazing. This is amazing. I just love you."

"I have one more thing for you. Look in the top drawer of the bedside table." Her curious expression had me trying not to laugh. My fucking stomach started to flip. Fuck, I hoped I did the right thing. She opened the drawer and pulled out the single folded sheet of paper. She looked up at me, and I saw her eyes get shiny with unshed tears.

"Do you mean it? You want your name on Remi's birth certificate?" Her breathless whisper was sexy as fuck.

"Yes, I do, but I want it to be a little more than that." I cleared my throat, suddenly nervous as fuck. I reached in my pocket and pulled out the little velvet box as I got down on my knee and looked up at her, taking her hands in mine. I placed the box in her shaking hand as I opened it. She pulled her lips between her teeth and tears streamed down her cheeks as she watched me.

"Stephanie, baby, I fucking love you. You are my world, you and Remi and now this new little precious gift." I touched her still flat belly reverently. "You have made me into one happy sonofabitch, but I want us to be a real family. I need you *all* to be mine forever. Please marry me, baby?" I held my breath, waiting for her answer. Oh God, don't let her break my heart. I was afraid it was too soon and she wouldn't be ready for this step.

She dropped to her knees, with a choked out sob, and kissed me, framing my face with her soft hands. "Yes. Yes, yes, yes. Oh, my God, yes! I love you so much!"

Chapter FIFTY

Stephanie

COLTON LOVED ME AND ASKED ME TO MARRY HIM. I COULD honestly say I did not see that one coming. This was so much more than what I had planned for tonight, but I wasn't going to let this be it for tonight either. This was my man, and I was going to have him. Tonight. In this gorgeous room, on this beautiful big bed that he bought for me.

Standing up and wiping my tears away after he slid the huge diamond on my finger, I slipped my dress off. I wanted to be wearing nothing but this diamond. And, Lordy, I didn't even want to guess at how much this ring had cost. It was flipping gorgeous, and I loved it. We were going to leave it at that. Wow.

"Stephanie, what are you doing? That's not why I did this. I wasn't trying to seduce you, baby. I'll wait until you're ready." His voice was hoarse and his expression looked almost pained. Oh, yes, he was in for it, and he had no idea.

"Well, that is why *I* did this. I had no idea this was what you had planned, but I planned to seduce my boyfriend tonight—correction, my fiancé." I smiled deviously and wiggled my eyebrows at him as I stepped out of the dress, leaving me in only the garter belt and stockings. He swallowed hard and tried to keep his hands from reaching out to me as I stalked toward him with specific intent. He walked backward as I closed in on him until his legs were against the bed, and I pushed him back on the bed, crawling up on top of him to straddle his waist. He closed his eyes and groaned as I rubbed my core and ass along the ridge in his jeans. He could deny it all he wanted, but I knew he was turned on and he wanted me just as bad.

"You. Are. Fucking. Killing. Me." He ground the words out between gritted teeth, and I smiled and leaned over him, brushing my breasts along the front of his shirt before I nipped his jaw and licked his neck before biting it. My fingers deftly unbuttoned his shirt as I licked and kissed along his chest after every button came loose. When it got to the last three, I pulled the shirt open, scattering buttons across the room. I heard them bounce and roll across the floor but didn't give a rat's ass where they landed.

"Jesus, Stephanie. I've tried so hard not to rush you." The flames ignited in his eyes and he flipped me over to my back before I even saw it coming. "But if you want to play with fire, we can play." His grin included those sexy fucking dimples, and I may have come a little in my barely there panties. Fucking Hell. He wrapped his lips around first one nipple then the other before grabbing it in his teeth and flicking his tongue across the sensitive tip. I felt the shockwaves of pleasure ripple through my body. Our eyes were locked together, and I panted wildly as I watched him worship my body. He kissed every scar, bringing bittersweet tears to my eyes.

"Don't cry, baby. I plan on making you come so many times you won't remember anything but me and my touch on your satiny skin and inside your wet, silky pussy. I'm going to fuck you so hard, any thoughts of anyone else will be washed from your mind. You. Are. Mine." He growled and I loved his alpha-male side that snuck out. He made me feel safe and worshipped, not owned.

"You, sir, have a dirty mouth. But, yes, Colton, I want you. Please. Now. I can't wait much longer."

"Oh, yes, you can. You're going to come for me first, because I won't last long the first time. There's no way. And you love my dirty mouth and what it does to you." He licked and nibbled down my body until he reached the junction of my thighs. Nips along the sensitive skin of my inner thighs before burying his face in my wet folds like a starving man, had me gasping. That magic tongue laved from my clit to my bottom, running the tip of his tongue lightly around that terribly forbidden area and sending surging vibrations of pleasure through my body. I moaned and sighed, gripping his longer hair in both hands, holding him closer to me.

"Yes, pull me into you. Guide me to where you want me, baby. Fucking come on my face, and I'll lick up every drop." Oh shit. His filthy mouth should be embarrassing but it wasn't. It was fucking hot as hell, and I felt the heat and desire building with every heated breath he exhaled on me and every stroke of his tongue over my clit. Jesus, when he pulled my engorged clit between his teeth then, flicking it rapidly with his tongue as he slid two fingers deep into my core, I felt my eyes roll in my head.

My back arched in ecstasy as his fingers worked their magic. Feeling the crescendo building in my body, I closed my eyes and screamed his name as white lights flashed in my eyelids and the pulses of ecstasy exploded through my body, centered between my legs, and ending in the aftershock spasms that continued to clench on his fingers. He thrashed his tongue through my explosion of wetness, drinking it like it was the nectar of the gods, as he continued to milk more from my orgasm with his fingers stroking my G-spot.

I lay gasping and panting as he slid up my body, his hands following in a light touch up my body. His lips captured mine in a deep, emotional kiss, and I tasted myself on him. He continued to caress my breasts and kiss my face, neck, and arms, making me feel revered and adored.

His one hand tweaked my nipple slightly as the other found its way back down to circle my clit and slip his fingers back in the slick, lubricated moisture from my cum. The heel of his hand then placed a circling pressure on my clit, and I became frantic in my pleasure again. I was so overly sensitive after my orgasm, it was driving me crazy. My body clamored for release even as it fought the profound sexual onslaught of his fingers and hand. I thrashed and tried to squeeze my legs together instinctively, and he placed his knee between my legs to keep them open, allowing him access to drive me wild.

"No, baby, don't shut me out. I want you to come again. I want you to keep your eyes open so I can watch you come apart in my hands. I want to see your beautiful face and the look in those blue eyes as you lose control." He kissed me briefly as he continued to play my body like a violin. The music he created in my body was heavenly. My next climactic explosion arose rapidly, engulfing me in wave after wave of pleasure. I felt replete and my bones felt like they no longer had substance. The love visible in his eyes and the look of satisfaction on his face as he watched me come had my heart nearly bursting.

I reached up to caress his cheek and pull him in for another kiss. The kiss ended with a breathless sigh and my hand fell back to the bed to rest on my splayed, tangled hair.

"That was amazing," I exhaled in a breathless whisper. "You are amazing. I love you."

"We have only just started. Are you ready for me? I need you, Stephanie. Now. Do you want me to use a condom? I'm clean. I had myself tested even though I always used a condom because I didn't want you to ever worry. And I haven't been with anyone but you since the birthday party." His words were rushed and strained. He had moved to place both his legs between mine with his engorged shaft resting at my drenched opening. He rubbed the end of his cock through the slippery wetness and slowly pushed the tip in and out, waiting for my response.

"Yes, please. Oh God, please, Colton. And no, no condom. I need to feel you. I had my doctor test me as well… just in case… and I obviously can't get more pregnant than I already am." I smiled and tried to laugh, but it came out as a breathless sob.

"I'm so sorry, baby. I didn't mean to make you think of all that again." He rested his forehead to mine as he held his weight off me with his bent arms. The remorse on his face had no place there. This was a time for happiness and enjoyment. I wanted him. I needed him.

I raised my hips, pressing his cock a little deeper inside me, urging him to enter further by wrapping my legs around his and pulling him toward me. My teeth grasped his shoulder and my nails dug into his firm ass. Moans escaped me as I felt my walls grasp at his cock, desperate to have him gliding against them.

"Please, baby. I need you," were the only words I could get out. My heart began to race in anticipation and our coupling became almost essential to my existence.

He blew out the breath he was holding as he swiftly entered me, buried to the hilt. "Jesus fucking Christ, you are so fucking tight. Don't move, baby. Just don't fucking move yet." His head dropped to my shoulder momentarily as he fought to catch his breath and gain control. My hands stroked his back slowly as his lips hovered over my skin. When his eyes met mine again, they were brimming with carnal desire.

The first stroke sent my nerves zinging with waves of erotic desire, and I tightened my legs around him. His expression became one of determination as he began a timeless, natural rhythm of stroking in and out of me. We both became slick with sweat, and I bit and licked the salty sheen on his bicep. This set off a climatic chain of events. He groaned as he increased his speed, and triggered the escalation of the sensations centered deep within me. I could never get over how sensitive I was to this man. Dear God, the sex was incredible. He was incredible.

When he placed his hands under my ass and lifted me so he could drive deeper, I came undone. My body exploded with sensation and flashes of ecstasy, and I felt my sheath clench him tightly. He roared as he threw back his head, and I felt the pulsing surge of his cock as he filled me.

Reaper

Mine.

Coming in her tight, hot, wet pussy was the closest I would ever get to heaven. I felt like I branded her from the inside with my cum. My control was completely and totaling fucking gone in the moment I roared in completion. My cock felt like it would never quit pulsing out my seed into her as her walls continued to clamp tighter around my cock, milking every last drop from me. Slowly, I continued to glide in and out a few times, feeling our combined fluids run out each time I thrust in. Heaven knew I didn't want to crush her, but I was fucking spent, so I turned over to my back, pulling her with me so she sprawled across my chest and her legs tangled with mine.

She lay cradled in one arm with my hand resting on her ass and the other played with the silky strands of her hair. Her delicate breath drifted across my chest as she held her ear to my racing heart. One of her slender hands traced over the tats on my chest and side. I swore I could lay like this with her forever.

"Would you take me to get a tattoo when I'm able?" Her words shocked me, and I raised my head from the pillow to look her in the eye. She raised her head slightly to look at me, and I noticed the pink tinge to her cheeks. Fucking gorgeous woman. Her smile was nervous as she said, "Will you?"

"Fuck yeah, I will. But are you sure you want to do that? I'm not trying to treat you like a child, but you do know that shit is permanent, right? I don't want you to do anything you may regret later, baby." I couldn't lie, the thought of her inked up was sexy as fuck. I would love to see my name in a property tat too, but I didn't know how she would feel about that. I would have to talk to her about it, because I wanted to mark her so every motherfucker out there knew she was *mine*. Forever.

Mine. I fucking loved the sound of that.

"Yes, I'm sure. I want to cover my scars with something beautiful so I don't see a reminder of that horrendous experience every time I look at myself. I want to build new positive images in my mind and on my body. I also don't want you to have to look at the scars on my body and be repulsed." She said the last in an almost inaudible tone.

I hugged her body tight to mine, kissing her head as I stroked her back from shoulder to her ass cheek.

"Baby, you could never repulse me. Don't ever fucking say that shit again, yeah? You're the most fucking beautiful woman I have ever seen. Inside and out. I can't be within 100 feet of you without busting out in a raging goddamn hard-on for fuck's sake. But it's more than that. You do something to me, baby. You turn me inside out. I have never felt like this about any other woman. Ever. I love you, Stephanie. I love you exactly the way you are. I'll help get the tats done for you, but you don't need to do it for me." I kissed her again, and she turned her head to kiss my chest right over my traitorous heart. That fucking organ was hers too. It beat for her and my babies and only for them. I couldn't live without her now. I knew it as sure as I fucking breathed her scent in right at that moment.

Tears dropped to my chest, and I reached up to make her look at me again. What the fuck? I hated my baby crying. She smiled through her tears and stretched up to kiss my lips in a sweet chaste kiss.

"I love you so much, Colton. Thank you for being as crazy about me as I am about you. Thank you for being an awesome dad to Remi. Thank you for accepting this baby without guarantee it was even yours. Thank you for saving me. You are an amazing man and my hero, Colton Alcott." She grinned and kissed me again.

"Woman, I am no fucking hero, I can tell you that. What I am is fucking insane for you, and I would do anything to make you happy and keep you safe. One thing I'm not compromising on though is we are getting married AS-fucking-AP. I'm not waiting for you to be mine any longer than I absolutely have to. Fuck no. ASAP. I mean it. So get with your mom and your friends and get shit together. I'll be happy with a trip to the courthouse or a flight to Vegas, but I want it to be what you want. Just soon. You got it?" I tried to look stern with her, but she just smiled and laughed at me before nipping my chest with her pretty, white teeth.

"Vegas actually sounds amazing to me. Will you be able to get time away from the MC for it?" she asked uncertainly.

"Fuck, an excuse to party it up in Vegas? The guys will all want to be there. I'll just talk to Snow to see when the soonest we can arrange it." I laughed and squeezed her tight again before swatting her ass playfully. Hell yeah, this woman was going to officially be my wife soon. I was one happy, lucky motherfucker. At one time, I couldn't see myself even living. Now, I had this gorgeous ray of sunshine, a beautiful little princess, and another precious gift on the way. And they fucking completed me. My angel had saved me more times than I could count, and now she would be mine forever.

Life was sometimes complicated, and sometimes it seemed like you would never make it through. But life was also beautiful, and perhaps we had to go through some shit to be able to appreciate how amazing it really was. This little family of mine? They were my salvation.

Epilogue

THE WEDDING CEREMONY WAS HELD IN VEGAS ON A BRIGHT SUNNY, day in early October. Colton and Stephanie were married by a preacher-man who looked like Elvis with the groom in black jeans, a white button-up shirt, and his MC cut while the bride was radiant in a strapless, antique white, lace-covered gown that was fitted to under her breasts and then softly flowed to a handkerchief hem that hit mid-calf. They both had said they wanted to remember the day with laughter and smiles, and that was their reason for choosing the little chapel with "Elvis" presiding over the ceremony. Their flower girl had laughing blue eyes, dimples that knocked you off your feet, and ebony ringlets that bounced with each step up the aisle. Hollywood stood as Colton's best man, and Becca was Stephanie's maid of honor. No one commented on the tension that was palpable between the best man and the maid of honor, but everyone noticed with a subtle curiosity. The MC all had their bikes lined up, forming a gauntlet of Harley's for them to rush through after the ceremony, laughing and holding hands as they were showered with rice and the rev of Harley engines.

The next few months were not always picture perfect as they learned to live as a family, but it was still a beautiful life because they *were* a family. They made a promise on their wedding night to never go to bed mad, regardless of the situation. They kissed each other before falling asleep each night, and if they had been arguing, well, the make-up sex was explosive and cathartic. Some days Colton felt like PTSD was a creeping shadow waiting to suck him under. Other days, his family kept him grounded and sane. It was a work in progress, and he knew he would never be free of it, but prayed that there would be more days he stayed grounded than lost. Remi was so happy and excited to be a big sister, and she spoke to her little brother or sister every day while her momma and daddy listened on with happy smiles.

The Oasis Pub became a popular hangout, not just for the MC and the citizens of the town, but for people passing through and tourists staying at the lakes. Colton was constantly working on fixing up the house, and it was a few-and-far-between weekend that everyone from the MC wasn't there for a barbeque. The MC worked to become self-sufficient with legit business, but it was an ongoing process.

Colton was a basket case the day Stephanie went into labor and ran around like a lunatic trying to get everything gathered up and ready until Stephanie gently placed her hand on his arm and granted him the smile that always calmed his heart, telling him everything was in the car, they just needed to call her parents to meet them at the hospital for Remi and actually get their butts there.

Colton held her hand through the labor and swore they would never have sex again because he wasn't going to have her go through this again. The nurses all tried to prevent him from seeing their smiles and rolling eyes because they had heard that one before. Stephanie laughed between contractions and assured him she was fine and they would indeed be having sex again or she would die of neglect, to which Colton glared at her as he held the cool rag to her head.

When the doctor announced Colton and Stephanie were the proud parents of an 8 lb. 2 oz. baby boy, he smiled so big he felt his face would crack. He had a son. He had family. As he kissed his son's inky, fluffy head of hair while Stephanie held him to her breast, he felt he would burst from the pride and love he felt for his family. Yes, life was indeed beautiful.

The End

Enjoy a preview of Mason and Becca's story...

Becca

I stood at the door of my best friend's home and tried to work up the courage to knock.

Shit, how was I going to explain why I was there with all my meager belongings packed in my car? A frustrated breath expelled from between my lips.

I just didn't know where else to go. I really didn't know if it was the best place to go, considering I knew *he,* who ridiculously preoccupied my thoughts, was there in the same town, but Steph was my best, and it felt like *only,* friend at that point in my life. Telling myself I would just have to ignore him if I saw him seemed easier said than done.

Shit.

Sighing I reached up and knocked on the door.

Seven Months Earlier

I had always wanted to go to Vegas. So when Stephanie called me and told me she was getting married and she wanted me to be her maid of honor, heck yeah baby, I was there. I had been a wild child in college, but being an elementary school teacher kind of put a damper on being a party girl unless I went waaaay out of town. I don't care who you are, everyone likes to let their hair down every so often.

So there I was in Sin City, ready to party it up for Steph's bachelorette party. Of course, Reaper and the guys would be in the background the whole time since he didn't want her out of his sight after she had been attacked and tortured by her ex-boyfriend. Yeah, that really happened. I cannot make this shit up. And who could blame him? What a nightmare that was. God, I was angry she hadn't called me after it happened and I chewed her ass out for it. She had said she was embarrassed by the situation and didn't want to burden me with it, but dammit, we were supposed to be best friends. It was our job as best friends to be there for each other.

Anyway, I was dressed to kill for the party that night because if I could, I was getting fucking shit faced and laid. My relationship with Trevor had been a dismal failure and had been the most miserable, boring, shitty year and a half of my life. I had tried to live a "respectable life"—yes, air quotes and all—and keep the image of a proper school teacher, but it wasn't *me*. Now let me clarify. I'm not saying I wanted to run around and be a slut or a drunk, but I wanted to be able to go out and have a good time, occasionally.

Not Trevor. Trevor was stable, responsible, reliable, had a great job on the Air Force Base in Omaha, blah, blah, blah, blah, blah... and he was boring. God, he was soooooo boring. His idea of a night out was to go to the movies and home again. Eating out would be a waste of money when we had a pantry full of food at home. Popcorn with your movie? Forget that shit. That was "over-priced and wasteful." So? Movies and popcorn go together like peanut butter and chocolate. It should be illegal to have one without the other. Sorry, I digress. He sucked in bed. Like really sucked monkey balls bad. He insisted on the lights being out and only ever being in the missionary position. Really? Ugh. And an orgasm? What the fuck was that? I hadn't achieved one without the help of my hand or BOB since the day Trevor and I moved in together. He hated me getting dressed up, doing my hair, wearing makeup – all things he considered 'pretentious.' What he wanted was some librarian-type or better yet, an Amish woman. Yeah, that's what he should have found, an Amish chick. So breaking things off with him before I came to Vegas was the plan. The reality was he begged me to work on things when I got back. He wanted me to "go have a good time with the girls," and then we would discuss things when I returned. He said... wait for it... he could *try to change*. Sheeeit. Okay. Sure.

Yeah, discuss things? No. I was so done, but I didn't want to keep arguing with him, so I decided to let it lie until I got back.

So there I was in my tight, short red dress with my boobs flashing ample cleavage, and matte black, six-inch heels. My dark auburn hair was tamed with a shit ton of hair product, but the curls were still on the riotous side and fit my mood. I topped the look with some "fuck-me" deep red lipstick and looked at my reflection in the hotel mirror with satisfaction. I had gotten a light tan and was fit from hours spent at the gym in an effort to be away from Trevor. Man, I was so stupid for thinking I could make my parents happy and conform to society's expectations of the good little school teacher by hooking up with a dud. My parents never thought I would curb my wild ways and settle down so I tried my damnedest to show them they were wrong.

Unfortunately, maybe they had been right after all. I was a free spirit. I loved life and believed it should be lived to the fullest, every second of every day. It was amazing, but short, and we should enjoy it while it was ours.

We all met up in the lobby. It was me, Steph, Kristina, her nurse from the hospital who she had ended up keeping in touch with and becoming great friends with—yeah, I was a little jealous—Pam, her married friend from Des Moines who also used to babysit Remi for her, and her high school friend, Letty. We giggled and shouted as we headed out to the first stop—a male revue at the Hard Rock Hotel and Casino. Steph had laughed and said she didn't need a male revue because she had her own personal male revue at home, to which I gagged in mock disgust and, truth be told, more than just a little bit of jealousy, because let's be honest, Reaper was freaking hot and she was a damn lucky girl. My foot went down on this one though, and the rest of the girls backed me up. This was her bachelorette party, and much to Reaper's displeasure, we were going to drool over some sexy ass abs and butts. *Whooooo-Hooooooo!* Hey, not all of us were getting married, and even for the ones who were, they were married, not dead, sheesh.

We were preparing to load up in the limo that would be followed by Steph's new SUV with the guys in it. That was when I saw him. Fucking hello hotness. Steph told me his name was Mason, but they called him Hollywood. Naturally, I had to know. So I had asked, in an oh-so-nonchalant way, who all the guys were. He was tall, had a freaking kick-ass toned body, dark blond just-been-fucked messy hair, and light hazel eyes. Yum. Oh, and did I mention he was hot? Oh yeah, totally hot. I'm talking lick-every-muscle-on-that-gorgeous-body-head-to-toe hot. Of course, he was chatting up Kristina, which only fueled that little shit-stirring green-eyed monster and made me a little more jealous of her, which really sucked because she was a sweetheart. I felt like such a bitch. A really jealous bitch.

He laughed at something she said, and when I shouted, "Let's go, girls!" he looked at me for the first time. When our eyes met, I felt my girly parts tingle and my breath caught for a second.

Wow. Did I really just feel that shit?

I saw his eyebrow raise and his eyes slide leisurely up and down my body. *Like what you see, sexy?* I winked and headed out to the limo, adding a little extra sway to my ass. I had no intention of hooking up with one of Reaper's friends, but Hollywood was panty melting hot and if he was going to look then, hey… so I strutted as I approached the limo, sat on the seat just inside the door, and slid my legs in slowly, one at a time. I knew he was watching, and it gave me a sense of empowerment I hadn't felt in a long while.

Tonight was going to be fun. I planned to find some sexy hunk of anonymous man to scratch my itch, so to speak, and call it a good night. As they say, what happens in Vegas, stays in Vegas. With each sip of my champagne, I felt myself breaking out of the stifling shell I had built around myself over the last few years.

Yes, it was going to be a good night. I could feel it in my bones.

Hollywood

I was so fucking happy for my buddy, Reaper, and his girl, Steph. After all the hell he had been through, he deserved someone like her. It was crazy that she was the same girl he had carried around on that old useless cell phone through our last deployment together. Who would have thought they would find each other, again? Some crazy shit. They were fucking insane about each other and had the cutest little girl I had seen in a long time. Shit, they were gonna be in trouble with that little one someday. I laughed to myself at the thought. Better them than me.

Vegas was a well-deserved and much needed vacation for all the brothers and me. Things had gone well with the drop-off a few months ago, despite shit going down with Reaper's old lady and him having to miss it all. Thankfully, we hadn't needed him, but I had taken over just in case. I was a pretty good fucking shot, too, even if I had been his spotter and he was the sniper back in our Army Ranger days.

We had been a really tight pair when we were together in the Army. Shit as a sniper team, you had to be. Then, we lost touch for a while after we both got out. Before I left for home, I'd begged him to come back to Iowa with me, but he said he needed to get his head straight first. I figured he would contact me when he was ready, but I never hear from him and his number had been disconnected. So I had followed my plan by beginning the prospect phase with the Demented Sons MC and found him again, thanks to Hacker's mad skills on the computer. When I went down to Texas to pick up a bike for a customer, I stopped by his place. Fuck, I was glad I got him to come back with me, because honestly, I don't think that poor bastard would be alive today if I hadn't. He was a fucking mess. We both had been, but luckily I had my family and the MC, whereas he'd had no one. I loved him like a blood brother, probably even deeper than my love for the rest of the brothers in the MC. Reaper and I'd been through a lot of shit together, though, like life and death shit overseas. That tended to bring people pretty fucking close.

It was good to see Kristina again. She was witty and funny, and she always made me laugh. She was also fucking smoking, and at one time, I would have loved to have gotten a piece of her gorgeous little ass. Lord knew I chased it for an entire week while Steph was in the hospital and she was Steph's nurse. Of course, she just laughed at me and brushed me off. Every fucking time. It really was a blow to my ego, I'm telling you. When she finally told me she was dating someone though, I backed off, keeping it to harmless flirting. Maybe most guys would have gone after her anyway, but not me. My sister's husband had fucked around on her, and I watched her fall apart and sink into a deep depression before finally dragging herself back out of it. It took her forever to move on after divorcing his stupid ass. I vowed to her that I would never fuck around with a married woman or wreck a relationship. Not just because of the hurt it caused, but because it went against the grain. My own personal experience with getting shafted was one I would never put on anyone. Fuck that shit. Another reason I shied away from relationships. Too much bullshit.

When I heard Becca, the maid of honor, round the girls up to leave, I looked over and *holy shit*. What a fucking beauty. She looked straight at me, and I felt my heart jump and send a current straight to my dick. I grinned at her and gave her "the look" that had never failed me in the past.

She was a straight fucking knock-out. I always had a thing for redheads, and she had a deep, rich auburn head of curls that begged to have a man's hands buried in it. Twisted in it. The thought of those plump, red lips wrapped around my dick made my grin even bigger. As my gaze wandered down over the red dress she'd poured her sexy ass into, I wondered if her tits would pop out if she took too deep of a breath, 'cause I would sure as shit like to be around to see that. She had nice curvy hips that were perfect for grabbing onto when… yeah, sorry, my mind went there. All the time. It's just one of those things I've never been able to help. Beautiful women were my addiction and I made sure they were well satisfied when they were with me. She also had toned and tanned legs that I knew would wrap around me perfectly, and could I please have her leave the heels on while she did it? *Damn.*

She winked at me and I knew she saw me checking her fine ass out. I didn't give a fuck. As she shook that ass and climbed into the limo, the last thing I saw were her long legs sliding in. Jesus. She was stunning and I thought if it was my lucky night, she would be mine. I felt a "challenge accepted" smirk spread across my face. If I played my cards right, she would be screaming my name by the end of the night. After all, this was Vegas right?

Acknowledgements

First, thank you to my husband who has supported me through every decision I have made over the years. When I told him I was writing a book, he not only encouraged me, but suffered through reading the first few chapters, even though this is definitely not his type of book! Thank you for your unfailing belief in my ability to fulfill what seems like a life-long dream of becoming an author. Thank you for loving me and for your patience during the late nights of my bedside light being on and my fingers pounding the keys while I sat in bed typing because I couldn't go to sleep without getting my thoughts down.

Next, thank you to my fellow author, Sybil Bartel, an amazingly talented author who answered question after question, motivated and guided me through this insane journey. She led me to Clarise Tan of CT Cover Creations who worked diligently with me to create the perfect cover which portrayed Colton exactly as I imagined him, and to all the awesome ladies at Hot Tree Editing - Virginia and Barbara you did a great job of catching my oopsies and ensuring I wasn't being ridiculously repetitive.

Also, a *huge* thank you to my good friends Penny, Larisa and Sherry - who were my proofreaders and motivators through this entire journey. I really don't know if I could have finished this book without you! And thank you to the "M.P.P. Group" who diligently read each section as I released it to offer me their encouragement, thoughts, and criticisms, which helped this book be better for their efforts.

Last but never least, a massive thank you to America's servicemen and women who protect our freedom on a daily basis. They do their duty, leaving their families for weeks, months, and years at a time, without asking for praise or thanks. I would also like to remind the readers that not all combat injuries are visible nor do they heal easily. These silent, wicked injuries wreak havoc on their minds and hearts while we go about our days completely oblivious.

About the Author

Kristine Allen lives in beautiful Central Texas with her adoring husband. They have four brilliant, wacky and wonderful children. She is surrounded by twenty six acres, where her seven horses, six dogs and three cats run the place. Kristine realized her dream of becoming a contemporary romance author after years of reading books like they were going out of style and having her own stories running rampant through her head. She works as a nurse, but in stolen moments, taps out ideas and storylines until they culminate in characters and plots that pull her readers in and keep them entranced for hours.

If you enjoyed this story, please consider leaving a review on Amazon or Goodreads, to share your experience with other interested readers. Thank you!

Twitter @KAllenAuthor
Facebook @kristineallenauthor

Made in the USA
San Bernardino, CA
25 June 2017